The ROMANCE LOOP

MARY SHOTWELL

The ROMANCE LOOP

MARY SHOTWELL

CITY OWL
PRESS

THE ROMANCE LOOP

CITY OWL PRESS
www.cityowlpress.com

Cover Design by Jihun Art. All stock photos licensed appropriately.

Edited by Tee Tate.

For information on subsidiary rights, please contact the publisher at info@cityowlpress.com.

Print Edition ISBN: 978-1-64898-562-1

Digital Edition ISBN: 978-1-64898-563-8

Printed in the United States of America

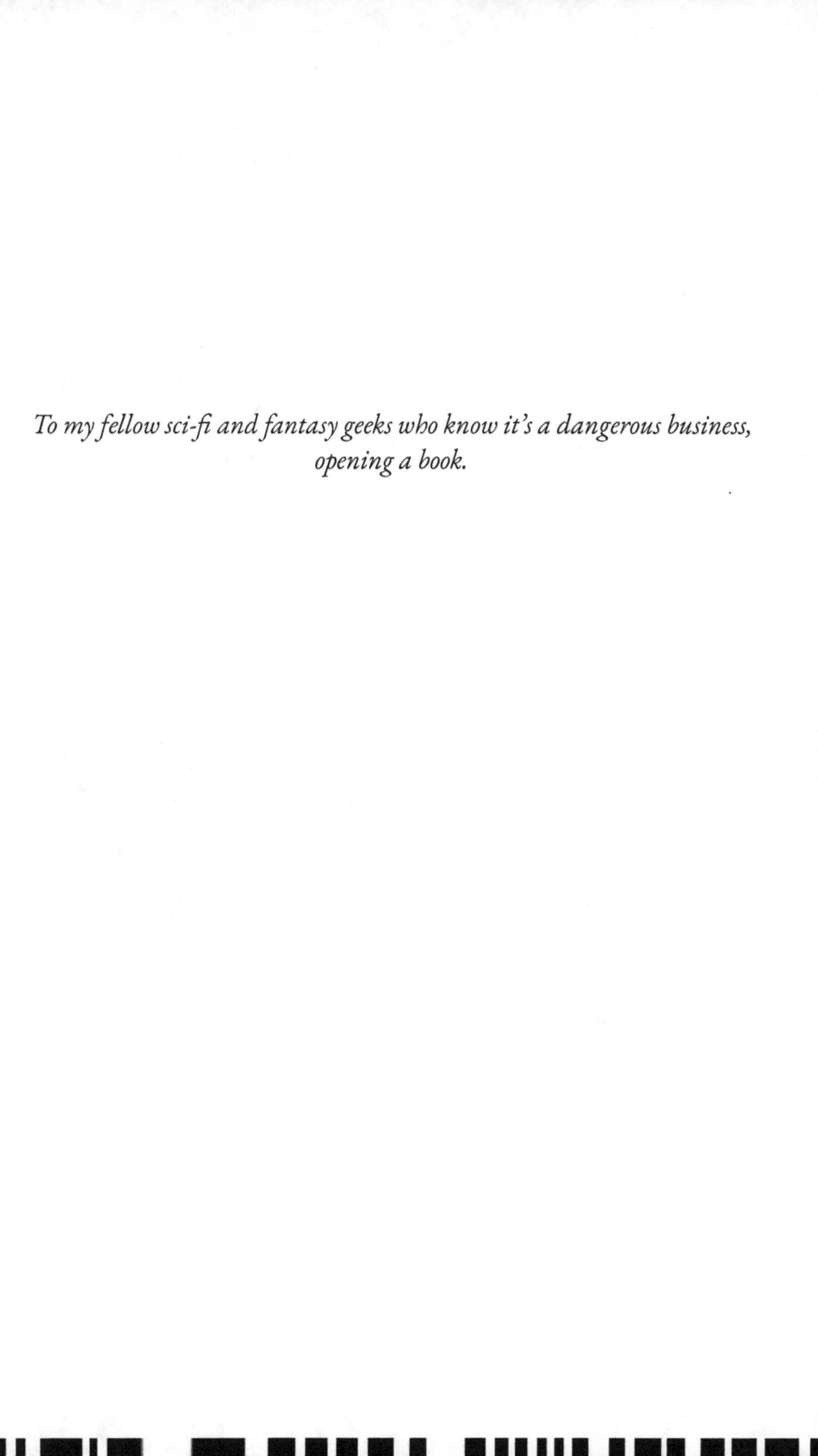

To my fellow sci-fi and fantasy geeks who know it's a dangerous business, opening a book.

Chapter One

Lacy Travers blinked at the two-star average rating on the phone the young woman held over the table.

"That's the book you're signing, right?" the forty-something woman asked.

Lacy sat at the table in the broad center aisle of Books & Bean, her gaze switching between the sad pair of yellow stars on the screen and the pathetic line of three, no, two people, led by the phone holder. The third person asked what the line was for and decided it wasn't for her.

But hey, at least enough people trickled into the suburban Boston indie bookstore to keep her from having huge gaps of staring off at the *Halloween Sale! Spooky Savings!* poster.

"Yes. Would you like me to sign a copy?" *Please.* She'd already been warned that if she didn't start selling out at signings, the tour may be a farewell one. Lacy signed the book with the two tennis players on the cover, their tennis rackets in the shapes of hearts. *Thirty Love*. Her thirteenth romance—the number not proving so lucky.

May you find your perfect love match.

"There you go." *Take it.*

"Is it like *Heartbeats of a Drum*? That one wrecked me."

"Same author," Lacy said. "Less wreckage, more kissing."

"*Just be.*" The woman sighed, clutching the new book to her chest. "The best."

Lacy took a breath. It wasn't that she was unappreciative of her fans. On the contrary, she wouldn't be in such a position with her publisher, in the middle of a three-book deal over the next two years, were it not for the very people still putting forth the effort to meet her and read her work. Granted, she originally pitched a five-book series, but the publisher wanted to see 'how things panned out.'

But creeping into hour two, she found her cheeks sore from having to smile, trying to lure other customers over to her signing during periodic lulls. The store announced it every ten minutes or so, as if no one could see her table smack in the middle of the store, in plain view of everyone walking in.

The next woman up completed the end of the sorry line. She had curly blonde hair and wore a bright orange sweater.

Lacy's eyes watered from tiredness. It didn't help that her bangs were getting long enough to meet her eyelashes, tickling with every blink. *Sell another one, buy another coffee.* She grabbed a fresh copy of the book off the embarrassingly large stack—a monument of expectations versus reality—and flipped it open to the title page to sign.

"I just adored *Prognosis Love.* What Doctor Luke did for Maya. And the ending at the aquarium with the pearls and the sandwich." The lady sighed deeply, cradling the newest crime thriller hardback by the author who need not be named—the one who could slap his moniker on a plain notebook and people would buy it—at her chest.

So, you're the one fan, she almost said. It wasn't that extreme. Not yet.

She caught the unmistakable feeling of being watched and glanced to her ten o'clock , and a head ducked behind a shelf in the nonfiction section. It happened so fast; she questioned whether she was seeing things.

She handed the fan the signed copy. "I'm glad you enjoyed it. Thank you for coming out today."

The woman nodded with glee and stepped away from the table.

Lacy glanced at the bookshelf again, this time catching the coffee brown hair of the spy before another vanishing act. Or was she so caffeine-deprived she was seeing coffee everywhere?

Another woman emerged from behind the fan.

Funny. She could've sworn the line was over. Lacy held up a hand. "Sorry, can you hold on just one moment?"

Lacy stood, the blood rushing to her head creating a second of dizziness before focusing again. Someday her body would pay her back for her early twenties, but she didn't expect it at thirty.

"Elliott?"

The man popped his head around the side of the bookshelf. He looked around as if Lacy had meant some other random person named Elliott in the store, before he left the security of his hiding spot.

"Lacy?" Elliott stood taller than she remembered. Then again, she hadn't seen her ex in...had it been six years? He wore dark jeans and a gray sweater and held a book upside down in his hand.

"I didn't realize—you're here signing books?" He stepped over to the table, grabbing a copy of *Thirty Love* with his free hand, glancing at the cover then back cover copy, flipping it around a few times. "That's great." He put it down on the stack haphazardly, correcting it to sit exactly on top of the one beneath it. As he stepped away, his foot kicked the table leg. The stack of books wobbled. He fumbled to catch them but knocked over the next stack in the process.

"I'm so sorry." He bent down, picking up the books.

"Don't worry about it." She joined him, helping to stack them back on the table. "They were a little heavy on the book ordering." She cleared her throat. "Lots of books on the table." Her voice faded off with the creeping embarrassment.

"Oh, they knew the famous Lacy Travers was coming." He met her gaze, green eyes lighter, corners of his eyes a little wrinklier. Six years had served him well. Damn men and their aging. "People will snatch these up. I mean, heart-shaped rackets? I bet they serve aces."

Her face flushed with boiling heat. She bit her lip, the sight of him triggering a mix of nostalgia and heart-wrenching memories from their shattered relationship. She stood and tugged her red plaid dress; the waistline having crept up from the crouching.

Elliott winced as he rose, using the table for support.

"How's the knee you swore didn't need a brace?" She recalled he used to have pain in one of his knees, something to do with an injury in high school.

"It's funny. Instead of healing itself as I've aged, it's gotten worse." He smirked, his way of downplaying the subject.

"Well, thanks for helping with the books."

"No problem. I'm the one who knocked them over in the first place."

"What brings you out here? Are you visiting from New York?" She straightened her bangs out of habit, wishing her hair was down instead of in a ponytail to hide her reddening ears.

Elliott relaxed a bit, loosely holding his selected book. "I actually moved back a few months ago. Fenway area."

"No kidding? That's where I'm at."

"Yeah, I'm teaching now at Northeastern, so it just made sense."

"Teaching. Wow. Good for you." She meant it in a genuine way, hoping it didn't sound patronizing. The career in publishing must not have gone to plan. Sure, at first, she had hoped it wouldn't. For selfish reasons. But that was years ago, and she had moved on from that phase of her life.

"Thanks." The ensuing seconds of silence rolled along painfully. "Anyway, I stopped by here on my way to my niece's birthday. You remember Sasha? She's turning thirteen."

"Oh, that's right. Your brother..." She clicked her fingers.

"James."

"Yes, James. I guess he still lives out this way." She shook her head. "I can't believe little Sasha is thirteen."

"It's crazy. She's already past my shoulders."

"What did you pick out for her? Maybe I can help."

"Nah, that's okay."

"I'd like to think I'm in the know. Got my favorites, of course, from when I was a teen."

"It's nothing. I'll probably get something else."

"Come on. What is it?"

"Well, I um—" He reluctantly lifted the book in the air, showing the title.

"*Putting the Me in Menopause*," she read. "Interesting." She covered her smirk.

He stared at it. "Yeah...That's exactly...What better way to empower women than with knowledge? Even if it's decades away."

"You picked the closest book on the shelf when I saw you, didn't you?"

He broke into a chuckle. "I may have panicked, a little bit." He hadn't lost his honesty. Or the lock of hair that stubbornly stuck slightly out of place over his forehead in defiance.

"So, are you not writing science fiction anymore?" Writing had been their common ground. He poked fun of her writing romance when they started dating, which led to back and forth jibes about the genres. Over the years, she'd scan the new sci-fi and fantasy releases, expecting to one day see the name Elliott Stephens on the cover.

"You know, I try to keep at it. Hard with the classes and—"

"Sorry to interrupt, but I've been waiting, and I don't know how much time I have." The woman shoved her copy of *Bakery on Sweet Street* into Lacy's hands. The silhouette of the heroine and hero faced each other, the heroine in an apron, the hero in a business suit. "This is drivel."

Her hair was pulled back into a loose bun, gray hairs sprouting from the frame of her face as if she had rubbed a balloon through it before leaving the house. "I'm familiar with all your books, from *Heartbeats of a Drum* to *Range of Attraction*. And they've gotten worse. They set unrealistic expectations for single people trying to find love out in the real world. Everything you write is too perfect."

Lacy swallowed, the lump in her throat almost not going down.

"I'm sorry you feel that way. I write these books as fun reads. A way to help people escape reality, give them hope."

"You don't understand," her voice escalated. "There's only so much time, or else—"

"Hey, now." Elliott stepped to the woman, the menopause book still in hand. "Calm down."

The lady leaned away from him, her long skirt and beaded shirt with a cat pin on the chest rattling like a shade on a scooted lamp. She broke a slight smile, yet her eyes read sadness. There was an awful familiarity to her face. "You'll help her, right?"

"How about I help you find something else to read? Perhaps you'd like the newest from Janet Rostren? It's a great work of nonfiction that really resonates." He eyed Lacy, his mouth wincing in uncertainty.

She had to hand it to him for trying.

"Fine." She pointed at *Bakery on Sweet Street*, still locked in Lacy's hands. "You can have that back." She reluctantly followed Elliott. He turned around with a look of victory.

"Thank you," Lacy mouthed.

Elliott quickstepped from the woman back to the desk. "She's terrifying. Is every book signing like this?"

Lacy shook her head.

"I don't know what you're doing after this, but if you could use a beer, you should stop by James's house. I'm sure the family would love to see you."

Her instinct was to say no. She didn't have the bandwidth for seeing her ex and his extended family in the same day. But he did help her out, and a cold drink didn't sound so bad after the day she was having. "We'll see."

"It was good to see you, either way."

He jumped back next to the lady, guiding her towards the front of the store, away from the signing table.

Already she had encountered her ex-boyfriend and the rudest reader she'd ever met, and there was still time left on the signing clock.

"Can't wait to see what's next."

Chapter Two

Elliott Stephens crept his shoulders up to his ears as he traversed the parking lot. The wind made for a chillier afternoon than anticipated, the Boston autumn air as unpredictable as the outcome of his bookstore visit.

"I'm coming, Ripley."

He patted the golden retriever, her head sticking out of the lowered window of Artax, his 1999 Ford Tempo. Ever since the once-white boxy sedan had conked out going up Heartbreak Hill like Artax in The Swamp of Sadness, the name stuck. The chipped paint and door that fought him when opening were exterior manifestations of its inner workings.

After finagling with the key and lock, Elliott scooted into the driver's seat. Ripley greeted him with kisses with her wet nose and floppy tongue. "All right, all right." He stroked her head and behind her ears. "Go on, in the back."

She stared at him, panting, her canine butt at ease in the front passenger seat.

"I keep asking in the hopes that one of these days you'll listen." He threw the latest Atlas Bradley bestseller for Sasha in the back seat. Most likely unimaginative drivel that rivaled the average sixth grader's writing. It was frustrating, knowing people like Bradley were successful writers, while several of his manuscripts in various stages of development either sat deep in the recesses of a USB drive or drifted through the ethers of a storage cloud. Then again, Bradley had made it to *The End*. More than the zero times he had.

At least Lacy continued to publish. Good for her.

The thought of Lacy brought back the humiliation as he drove west through the suburbs.

"*Putting the Me in Menopause*." He shook his head. "Of course. Couldn't have been *The Art of War* or *Cosmos*, huh, Universe? *Captain Underpants* would've been better, for cryin' out loud."

It had made her smile, though. Lacy had always been a looker, but when she smiled...he'd forgotten how good it made him feel. The satisfaction, a warmth in his heart—

A honking horn jolted Elliott back to the present, the traffic signal on green. He waved a hand in apology, refusing to look back at the driver behind him, who probably waved an offensive finger back.

Maybe going to her signing had been a bad idea. Who was he kidding? Of course it was a bad idea. He reached out for Ripley, scratching her back while she reveled in the sunshine. "You're the only girl I need." Ripley refused to turn around until he stopped petting, then stared at him. He resumed petting, and she stuck her nose out the window again. "That's about right."

He pulled onto Templebrook Avenue, sidewalks lining the neat row of houses with their one tree in the front yards. Blue and purple balloons waved in the wind off a mailbox halfway down the street. He half-expected a bouncy house in the fenced backyard, but then remembered Sasha was turning thirteen, not six. Several cars filled the driveway, so he parked along the curb.

He retrieved the book and held the driver's side door open. "Let's go." Ripley looked at him, not budging an inch. He shook his head, licking his bottom lip. "Such a diva." He walked to the passenger side and opened the door, Ripley happy to exit Artax.

He knocked on the door to James's house before opening it. "Hello?" Music blared inside, the living room decorated with streamers and balloons. A flock of teenage girls giggled in the corner, playing some sort of group game on a phone.

"Uncle Elliott!" Sasha smiled amidst the gaggle of friends. "Dad's out back." Indeed, James stood outside on the other side of the sliding glass doors.

Elliott nodded. "Happy Birthday." He considered giving the gift to her but didn't want to interrupt the game.

Ripley opted to stay inside, lapping up the affection from the tweens and teens. Elliott walked outside, sliding the glass door shut behind him.

"Elliott." James gave him a stiff hug. They shared the same green eyes, but that was the extent of their similarities. James was eight years older with the frame of a left tackle, while Elliott's was more of a left-handed golfer. "Want a beer?"

"Sure."

James grabbed a bottle from the cooler and popped off the cap.

"Nice to see you." James's wife, Jules—the nickname James had given her from Julie—hugged him. "I can get used to this, Uncle Elliott living nearby."

"If you're cooking, I'm here."

She introduced him to a group of neighbor friends before they walked over to the snack table.

"How's it going? Long time no see." Elliott gave a friendly shake to Dex and his wife Norah. Dex, James, and Elliott were part of a high school group of friends that didn't quit after graduation. At least, not all together.

"We heard you moved back." Dex's grin indicated he still pictured the three of them getting into trouble.

"Yep, in time to start the fall semester."

James handed Elliott the opened beer and they all clinked bottles.

"It's the best season here," Jules said. "I was so happy it didn't rain today so we could set it up for the girls out here."

Elliott scanned the backyard, two decorated tables with drinks and streamers along the fences.

"But the girls complained about it being too cold. So now it's the only quiet place for adults." Jules glanced at the bag under his arm. "Is that for Sasha?"

"Yeah. Picked it up on the way in."

"You can set it on the gift table." She pointed to one of the tables filled with gift bags and wrapped presents.

"You went to Books & Bean?" Norah asked.

"I knew Sasha was a fan of Bradley."

"Yes, but..."

"What's the big deal?" James asked.

"Maybe I have my days wrong but, wasn't Lacy doing a signing there today?"

"Lacy..." Elliott drew the name out, squinting to the sky. "Nope. Name not ringing a bell."

"His ex, Lacy?" James asked.

"Oh, *that* Lacy?" The crack in his voice betrayed him.

Jules pointed at him. "You saw her, didn't you?"

"It's a pretty big store, lots of people go in and out." Elliott shrugged. "I...I really don't...I may have bumped into her."

"I loved Lacy." Jules gave a sorry pout. "How is she doing?"

"She's good." He hadn't really obtained a whole lot of information from her. He'd been the one updating her on his life.

"Is she married? Single?" Norah asked.

James tsked. "Jump right to it, don't you?"

"I actually don't know the answer to that." Why didn't he think to look for a ring on her finger? Maybe because he was too panicked to think coherently. That last thing on his mind was her dating status. Okay, maybe not the last thing. Alright, it was probably at the bottom of his top five, or three things, who was tallying. He was curious how she'd been the last several years. Being settled now in Boston, maybe there was a chance at striking up a friendship. His heart fluttered at the thought.

"I did sort of..." He scratched the back of his head. "I might've mentioned Sasha's birthday party, and casually, you know. Said something about stopping by. If she wanted to."

Norah gasped and slapped him on the arm. "Get out! You did?"

"Alright, Elaine," he joked. "Settle down."

"I hope she comes. You two were so good together."

"Well, if that were true, it wouldn't have ended now, would it?"

"Liked her better than Nicole," James said. "Remember her? Always bringing her own meal to parties. Who does that?"

"Or Morgan," Dex said. "She'd go three or four days without answering his texts or calls."

"Yeah, she was shady," Norah said.

"There was that other one," Jules said. "Oh, what was her name? Nitpicking at him over every little thing. Stephanie!"

"Stuffy Stephy!" they all said in unison.

"This is a fun time." Elliott tugged on the neckband of his sweater. What were those teenage girls thinking, too cold out here? If anything, it was too hot.

"All we're saying is that we would support you if you got back together with Lacy," Norah said.

"That's quite a leap you're making. Who knows if she even remembers how to get here." *Shoot*. What if she didn't? It didn't stop him from having an ounce of hope that she would. And what then? Did he really think there was a chance to rekindle things with her? He had a failing writing career, a mediocre-paying job, and slightly thinner hair and more wrinkles than years ago. How was he better for her now than back then? That wasn't accounting for the way it had ended, either.

No sense in thinking about it. But his friends and family made it hard not to. His other girlfriends since then hadn't quite lived up to the kind of connection he'd felt with Lacy. Would he ever find that again? Or had he peaked with Lacy?

"James, it's time." Norah nodded to the house.

"Time?" he asked.

"For the food. We said we'd wait for Elliott to get here."

"All right." He shrugged. "You heard the lady." He paused, hand on the glass door handle. "You may want to cover your ears."

Elliott chuckled while James slid the door open, the cacophony of laughs escaping the living area. He almost asked the girls if a woman had come by, on the off-chance she did come by and quickly changed her mind.

But Lacy wasn't coming. The sooner he got that out of his head, his hopes, his heart, the better.

Chapter Three

At quarter past three, the store manager officially closed the book signing, much to Lacy's delight. While it was generally lovely to meet fans, especially ones that had stuck with her writing through it all, it wasn't so great meeting a critic. Not even a critic, really. Just loud.

She had never experienced a confrontation like that before. When it came to being an author, there was a first time for everything. First rejection, agent, fangirl, news interview. Surely there were more firsts she'd experience in the future.

She gathered the scattered bookmarks on the table, her eye catching black ink writing on one of them. James's address. Elliott must've scribbled it down when they were picking up the spilled items off the floor. She threw the bookmarks in her purse that refused to zip, and approached the store associate, who diligently tore down the table setup.

"Thank you, again, for today."

"No problem." She smiled cheerfully. "We love hosting authors. I just wanted to apologize for that rude woman. I was busy at the register but overheard some of it."

"I'm fine. I've heard worse from other authors." It was true. One author friend got caught up talking to a 'fan,' when really the fan distracted her from an accomplice who stole her purse. Lacy's interaction wasn't so terrible in comparison.

What she couldn't shake was the familiarity. If she read all her books, perhaps she'd been to other book signings. She did have some regulars, at least in the beginning of her career.

Lacy turned her gaze to the front window.

"Is there a problem?" the employee asked.

"No. I thought I saw..." Someone standing there, staring at her. But clearly, there wasn't. "Never mind." As she waved goodbye, her phone buzzed for the third time in the past ten minutes. She knew it was Miles, her publicist. He was great at his job, which currently meant she had seven more of these events in the next two months across the country. This time, she accepted the call.

"Hey, Miles."

"Just checking to see how the big-time author did with the book signing."

"Hm, then I guess you dialed the wrong number."

"You're too funny. Maybe you should incorporate that humor into your writing."

"I'll think about it for the next book."

She left the store and walked across the parking lot, spotting her white Honda Civic in the employee parking at the far end, with its *Follow too closely, you'll end up in my novel* bumper sticker, two rows over.

"Speaking of the next one, it's going to be about a gay publicist with a penchant for sarcasm."

"Sounds amazing."

They shared a chuckle.

"For real though, everything go smoothly? Wanted to check before..."

"Before what?" Lacy stopped. Miles may have been great at his job, but he was horrible at delivering bad news. Then again, would she want someone who delivered bad news with a smile? "Just come out with it."

"I didn't want to kill your high so soon after the signing."

How she felt was anything but a high. "While I appreciate your respect for my feelings, you do realize you make it worse by dragging things out, right?"

"Fine." He huffed, as if the bad news pained him as much as it would her. "The publisher canceled two more dates on the tour."

Not one, but two. *Ouch*. "Which ones?"

"Los Angeles and Denver."

"The two out west." The most expensive to get to.

"Sorry, Lacy. Let's focus on the ones you do have, and the one you completed today. Tell me all about it."

She set aside fully processing the bad news for later, when she'd uncork wine and stream *The Princess Bride* or *Bridget Jones* to feel better. "It was...what it was. The store was prepared, table ready, all that stuff." *And a woman who caused drama*. "There was one thing that happened. Not a big deal."

"What was it?"

"It's nothing. Probably didn't even need to say anything."

"Well now I'm curious."

Lacy sighed. "There was this woman. I swear, she appeared out of nowhere. When she approached the table, she kind of went off on my writing."

"Oh dear. Don't people have better things to do with their time?"

"I told you, not a big deal. It was awkward for a minute, but—"

She glimpsed movement to her right, someone else in the lot near the island of oak trees stretching up the aisle.

It was her, the woman who had caused a scene, standing next to a beat-up station wagon. Her long skirt billowed in the wind as she held a stack of books in one hand, gray-streaked hair messy as if she'd just walked out of a windstorm she hadn't finished arguing with.

"I gotta go."

"Lacy—"

"I'll call you later." Lacy hung up but kept the phone in her hand.

The woman's stare followed Lacy's deliberate steps as she passed. Lacy gripped the phone tighter. Should she confront her again? Go back inside the store until she was on her merry way?

The woman simply stood there, the only movement was the turn of her head.

That wasn't true. The woman's lips moved, whispering something in the air. A fluttering of her mouth, while her eyes stayed focused on Lacy.

Unnerved, Lacy picked up her pace, keeping an eye on the inhospitable woman while fumbling for her keys. She sat inside, hitting the locks as soon as she shut the door.

The woman still stared, but her lips had stopped.

Lacy started the car, and the woman finally retreated into hers, disappearing from view.

Lacy pulled out of the parking lot and made her way onto Boylston Street, checking her mirrors. What did she think was going to happen?

Somewhere around a quarter mile down the road, she checked again, the usual traffic to be expected during leaf-peeping season. And a beat-up station wagon pulling out of the bookstore lot.

"It's nothing. You're being paranoid. Disgruntled ex-fan's gotta get home, too." She signaled with her blinker, getting off at the first exit and heading south. She sighed with relief at the sight of a white SUV behind her, until she noticed the wagon behind it.

"What the hell?" The eerie feeling danced up her spine. Should she find a police station? A busy parking lot? She made a right turn, her purse tipping over, spilling the bookmarks on the seat.

She looked around at the shops, office buildings, plazas around her. Unfortunately, not an area of town she knew. What if she got cornered somehow, branching down a one-way street?

She glanced down at the mess of bookmarks, one at the top having the address. He did invite her... It was somewhere to go, somewhere that wasn't her address but familiar. She'd been there a handful of times with Elliott years ago, on the occasions when James and his wife would leave Sasha with the grandparents, and the four of them would drink and chat late into the night.

The painful price of loving a boyfriend's family. A breakup meant severing ties with them, too.

She typed the address in the map app on her phone.

With each turn onto a new road, the station wagon followed. This couldn't be coincidence. As she neared James's house, she opted for a spot along the end of the street. She didn't exactly want to put anyone else in danger, either.

She hurried out of the car, locking it then quickstepping along the sidewalk. She heard the wagon and dared to turn around. The woman—definitely the same wiry-haired woman from the bookstore—glanced over and nodded before putting more weight on the gas, driving off.

Lacy shivered, pulling her jacket closed. She hurried up the street, not even caring that she was about to see people she hadn't seen in six years. Until she stopped at the front door of James's house.

She knocked, the sounds of voices singing "Happy Birthday" behind the door.

She took a few breaths to calm herself, straightening out her bangs and tucking the loose strands of hair behind her ears. She pressed her lips together. *Could probably use some lip gloss.* The thought was discarded. That woman could appear any second again on the street, and Lacy wanted to be inside, safe, before she did.

Was it rude to walk in? James and Jules had said their door was always open. But that was when she'd been dating Elliott. And when did that saying ever mean literally?

Not wanting to risk being out in the open any longer, she tried the handle, the door unlocked. She tightened the grip on her purse straps over her shoulder, took a deep breath, and opened the door. The singing halted, as if the air sucked out of the room.

Then the world turned black.

Chapter Four

Darkness engulfed Lacy. She held her breath, shocked by the starkness. There was no noise, no smell, no wind. Nothing to touch.

The din of the room hit her ears before her eyes focused. A machine beeping. A faint smell, like burning hair. Bright light shining on her gloved hands.

"*There we go. Suction.*" Words clearing through the fog. A masculine voice. "Prepare the bone flap."

A patient on the table. Someone standing next to her. Two people facing her, another one standing by a monitor. Her gaze shot to the right, down to the other end of the table. Thick yellow socks on feet. Her eyes wandered up the body to the portion right in front of her, suction slurping up fluids around the squishy tissue.

"Oh my God, that's his brain!" She backed away, nearly knocking over the assistant next to her.

"Hey, hey." The surgeon, in full gown, mask, and cap, handed the suction to his left. He stepped away from the patient on the operating table and worked his way to her.

She pointed at the square of exposed wet pink blob on the table. "Where's the rest—put him back together!"

The doctor grasped her arms, gently holding them down. "It's okay." He directed it towards the three other souls—awake ones—in the room, around the patient.

He leaned in, steady and calm. "You did it. You removed the tumor. They'll complete screwing and finish up with stitching."

Lacy looked at her own clothes. Full gear matching the doctor in front of her. Her heart jump-started, a lump in her throat swelling, drying up the little saliva in her mouth. The thirst hit her almost as hard as the distorted reality.

A dream. This was a dream. It had to be.

"I—" The blood rush to her head spun the room around.

"Whoa." The doctor caught her before her weak knees let her hit the floor. "I got ya. Angela, take Doctor Walsh out for some air. Benjamin, have Doctor Chadha scrub in."

One of the women escorted Lacy out of the operating room to the scrub room, where she helped Lacy take off her mask and gown and gloves. She led her through more doors and a hallway until reaching a side room of lockers and benches.

"Here we are," she said.

"Angela, is it?" Lacy asked. There were too many questions to ask, and asking for a name seemed the most normal, realistic thing to do.

"Yes, Doctor Walsh. It's Nurse Angela." She formed a worried smile. She wore her graying dark locks smoothed down into a low ponytail, while crow's feet etched into her dark skin putting her somewhere in her late fifties, early sixties. "How about I get you some water?"

Lacy simply nodded. Another realistic step.

Nurse Angela handed her a white plastic cup filled with ice and water, and Lacy took a sip. The cold water traveled down her throat. Had she ever drunk water in a dream and it felt so real?

"You just sit here and take some deep breaths. Sometimes being in the thick of it during surgery can get to the best of us."

Lacy imagined the cut-open skull, shaky hands threatening to spill the water. "What was it—what did you call me?"

"Doctor Walsh." She drew it out, the concern naked in her voice. "Should I page someone to sit with you?"

Lacy shook her head. "No, I'll be fine. Just need a minute alone." *Walsh...Doctor Walsh...*

"Alright," Nurse Angela said hesitantly. "I'll come check on you in a minute."

Lacy nodded as the nurse left, then jumped up to the nearest locker. A pair of men's sweatpants sat on the tiny bench inside, and a hoodie hung on a side peg.

She opened another one, the large men's shoes in the top bin giving away enough.

Lacy moved to the next. Nothing seemed familiar. A faded gray sweatshirt and black yoga pants. Pink sneakers. A name badge. MAYA WALSH, M.D., NEUROSURGERY. *The name rang familiar for the wrong reason.* Like an obscure actress in a film seen long ago. Or maybe a grade school acquaintance.

This was the wrong place, wrong occupation. Wrong life.

A red leather purse sat in the top bin, next to an old-school, black flip phone.

"My purse...I had my purse, walking to James's house!" She clapped her hands. It all came back, which gave her a second of joy. An anchor of reality. But how had she arrived here?

Lacy closed her eyes. "I went to James's house, knocked, opened the door. 'Happy Birthday'. That's the last thing I remember."

"Who's James?" Nurse Angela had returned, standing by the door. "And it's his birthday?"

Lacy stood straighter, retrieving the name badge. "I don't know exactly what's going on, but I'm not Maya Walsh. I've never even been to Baltimore." Although that was going to change soon, with the upcoming book tour. If that signing hadn't been canceled yet.

"May I?" Nurse Angela retrieved the driver's license out of the red purse and put it in front of Lacy's face. Lacy had been more concerned with the data than the picture of the blonde woman. There was a familiarity to the photograph—the woman in the headshot had Lacy's eyes, cheekbones, heart-shaped face. But blonde hair, with no bangs.

Lacy was certain of two things. She'd never been blonde. And this definitely wasn't her license.

"There's been some mistake. That's not me. I don't even have blonde hair. I have bangs for cryin' out loud!" Funny though, they hadn't been tickling her eyelashes. She reached up to wave the locks through her fingers, but she hit bare forehead.

"I one hundred percent believe you believe you're telling the truth."

Lacy grabbed her dangling ponytail forward. A lighter shade of brunette, and a stub of a ponytail compared to her normal hair. Without bangs. "It's not—that's not right."

"You say you've never been to Baltimore, but that's where you are right now."

Screw it being a dream. This was a full-blown nightmare. Had to be. "That's not possible. I live in Boston." She took a mouthful of what was mostly ice chips left in the plastic cup, wishing it contained whiskey or tequila or heck, moonshine. Something strong to pull her out of this. She caught the gold logo on the side.

Baltimore University Hospital.

Water from the melting ice trickled down her throat, catching her cough reflex. She tried holding it in, but her face turned red, and she needed to breathe.

"How are we doing?" A young, tall man walked into the room. "They're closing up. Doctor Chadha is overseeing."

She was clearly hallucinating. Clean-cut, dark brown hair. Glistening blue eyes. The dark blue scrubs somehow accentuated his ripped yet lean body.

Lacy spit the ice back into the cup. A trickle of ice chunks and spittle crept down her chin. *Of course it didn't come out neatly.* She wiped her mouth in the shoulder of her scrubs, then thought how terrible it was for her to do such a thing. That patient's brains could've seeped through all the layers to her skin.

The handsome man didn't manage to hold back his amusement, a killer smile greeting her, teeth white but not that overly bleached kind of white. "You okay?"

Lacy held the coughing in as long as she could. "Yeah." It came out in a wheezy breath, and she let the coughs out in restrained fashion, spreading them over what felt like ten hours.

She composed herself, wiping the tears from the corners of her eyes. "Sorry about that. I think I was seeing things."

"Oh." He approached and took out a light pen. "Let me take a look."

"No, I—"

But he was already checking her pupils, and it didn't exactly inflict pain in looking at him. *Wouldn't want to make his job harder*.

"Looks okay." He returned the pen to the chest pocket of his scrubs.

"And I'm telling you, she's not okay." Nurse Angela gave him wide eyes.

"I've never seen you panic like that during surgery before."

God, he smelled like scrub soap and latex. Aromas that shouldn't evoke a warmness and comfort to them, but nothing made sense here.

"Any headache?"

Lacy shook her head. "No."

"Now, what kind of things were you seeing?"

"It's funny. I thought the cup said Baltimore University Hospital." She chuckled. "See, I'm a writer, and that was a fictitious hospital I had come up with for one of my earlier books."

The man's face turned serious, a statuesque stone carving of a face.

"See what I mean?" Nurse Angela said.

He nodded at her in dismissal, then touched Lacy's hand, ever so gently. "You *are* at Baltimore University Hospital."

She giggled. "That's funny." She pointed at him. "I don't know what kind of..."

"I've never known you to write. Is that something you did before med school?"

Lacy stared at him. He didn't know her, nor she him. He was good at acting. Very convincing, that was for certain. But who would play an elaborate joke on her? Why would this be a prank? If it were, it would be the prank of all pranks.

Miles. It was one of his publicity stunts, wasn't it? A reality show, prank show. A way to get her name known again. And this was a set and obviously this doctor was a paid actor. It made sense now. She just had to reveal the set for what it was, and they'd all have a good laugh.

She walked to the window, pulling the chain to raise the shade. The city could've been any harbor skyline until the triangle of the National Aquarium cut through haze. The aquarium *in Baltimore*.

A green screen?

She felt where the window met the wall, cool to the touch. Wind mildly howled. They certainly got the sounds right.

She leaned in closer to the glass. A bug flew into the window, the tap scaring her back a step.

Not a green screen.

This was a real building, with a real window to the outside.

And she was Maya Walsh. The neurosurgeon from *Prognosis Love*. The character who made a rival in med school, only to find him in her new department at Baltimore University Hospital. The doctor who was...

"Doctor Devereux."

Just saying it curled her toes. His eyes softened—killer blue eyes—at her remembering his name.

"That's right. But it's weird, you calling me Doctor in private. It's Luke between us, right?" He smiled, the perfect teeth, the charm.

She knew how to write them. As she had written all of this. She was in a nightmare of her own making. And she needed to get out. To wake up.

"Yes, Luke. That's right. See, my memory, it's all coming back to me. Is it okay to go home now?" Wherever that was. Wait, Oakhaven Avenue, from the driver's license. *God, this was so many books ago.*

How was she one of her heroines? Did she hit her head in real life, and was now unable to wake from a coma? Did people experience realistic dreams during comas?

Maybe if you researched more for the book, you'd know. She about laughed at herself. This was absurd.

What was she to do? *What would happen if I somehow got back to Boston? Would I wake up?*

"How about I take you back?" Luke asked.

"Okay." She needed him to leave. "Let me get dressed."

Luke paused, as if there was something he wanted to add. He looked at her longingly, lost in thought. Or mesmerized. Whatever the reason, the silence was excruciating.

"I guess I'll change, then."

Luke snapped out of it. "Right. I'll let you...get to it." He walked out of the room but not without a final warm smile.

This was it. This was her chance to get out of here. *She* wasn't Maya. This wasn't her life.

Lacy considered staying in the scrubs, but thought they'd point her out too easily. She put on the faded gray sweatshirt and black yoga pants, the latter a little too tight around the thighs. "Of course. A neurosurgeon and a stick."

She slipped on the pink sneakers, fitting well enough if she didn't tie them too tight. Lacy opened the door slightly, enough to see down the hall. Nurse Angela was on the phone, Luke out of sight. She waited for a patient to walk by, then slowly opened the door. She peeked down the hallway, looking for an exit. There, to the right. A stairwell.

She ran for it, half expecting to hear yells and footsteps after her. But she made it to the stairwell, the door clicking behind her.

And nothing.

Nobody had followed her.

She ran down three flights of stairs and exited out the side of the hospital, the door locking behind her.

It was nearly as chilly as it had been in Boston earlier in the day, but she set this story in spring, not fall. The trees concurred, teeny tiny buds on the branches painstakingly waiting to get out.

After three blocks heading toward the aquarium, she saw a white sign with a black M. The subway. Her ticket out of the city. She rushed down the stairs and stopped after five steps, nearly falling into the black abyss below.

She slowly dipped her foot. No sixth step. She lowered it further.

Nothing.

She turned around, going back up the steps. What did that mean?

She walked further, another two blocks. Then four blocks. The buildings started to look repetitive. Coffee shop, salon, corporate offices. Coffee shop, salon, corporate offices.

Until she hit a wall.

It wasn't exactly a solid wall. It was blurry, and the further she walked away from it, the clearer the landscape looked beyond it. But there was no getting beyond it. She followed the blurry edge in an arc for several blocks until she came to terms with reality.

This was the end of the city.

Why? The answer was unsettling, but it was the only one that made sense out of the nonsensical situation.

The city ended because that was as far as she imagined for the story. All the action took place within the city. No cars or pedestrians, no buses or subway went beyond her imagination bubble.

A bubble she was somehow stuck in.

Chapter Five

"...Happy Birthday to you..."

Elliott stood at the edge of his brother's kitchen, straddling the transition from plank tile to taupe carpet in the living room. Hearing a dozen teenage girls singing "Happy Birthday" wasn't the most pleasant sound, but Sasha's grin of sheer joy made it worth it.

"Stop that." Elliott looked down at Ripley, who looked towards the front door, tail slapping his leg. Despite her affinity for royal treatment, she never sniffed people inappropriately when walking by, never so much as peeped let alone barked at them and always sat for anyone asking to pet her.

She growled, gaze fixed on the front door.

"What is it?" Elliott patted her back, but she took a step toward the front door. The kitchen roared with clapping and cheers, and the scent of candle smoke wafted through the room.

Ripley ran off, stopping short of the door and sounding off a loud bark, startling Elliott.

"What is going on with you?"

The door unclicked, slowly swinging ajar.

"Someone here?" Elliott walked over, leaving the safety of the cluster of partiers, heart pounding. His mind went to the worst-case scenario—that old-timey reverend with the hat in *Poltergeist II.*

Something nefarious to have gotten Ripley all riled up. As he took hold of the door handle, his thoughts switched to a more positive outcome, clinging to that bit of hope he desperately tried to bury.

He opened the door wide.

Nothing. No one.

He stepped outside, looking left, then right, Ripley at his heels. "Nobody's here, girl."

He had seen the door open, right? Maybe someone hadn't closed it all the way when coming or going. Or a gust of wind did it? One thing certain was that no one had opened it. Especially not Lacy Travers. He closed the door behind him, shutting out any more thoughts of his ex for the rest of the evening.

Chapter Six

"Okay. Nightmare." She walked not just the streets of Baltimore but the *imagined* streets, the ones she envisioned clearly, or not so clearly, for her book.

What she needed was a way to wake up, and the best way she could think to find one was to return to the hospital. Besides, she had left her—no, Maya's—purse in the hospital room. How had she expected to pay for transportation from here to Boston, even if it existed?

But maybe there was a drug she could be given, something that was powerful enough in the dream world to snap her back into the real world. It sounded ridiculous, but so was the fact she was here to begin with. And it beat out the alternatives she conjured, involving *Groundhog-Day*-level death scenarios. There was no guarantee a risk here wouldn't hurt her for real.

A growing fatigue had washed over her, and she longed for a hot meal, or beverage, or even just a nap. She walked around to the front entrance of Boston University Hospital and entered through the double doors. She reflexively patted down her borrowed clothes to check for objects to spill out at security, only to realize no security existed. There was nothing on her anyway, not so much as a piece of lint or fallen strand of hair.

A patient waited ahead at the triage desk, doubled over in pain, their spouse arguing with the nurse. Several sat in the waiting room to Lacy's left, a few mindlessly watching the television in the upper corner, others trying to catch shut eye in the uncomfortable seats.

She bypassed the triage desk and approached the double doors to the patient rooms.

A male nurse at the triage desk stood from his post, waving. "Afternoon, Doctor Walsh. Forget your badge again?"

"You know me." She shrugged in jest. *You know me better than I know me.* Technically, she created Doctor Maya Walsh, so she should know her better than anyone else.

The doors swung open, and she walked through them down the hallway. Now what? Go find some pill to take, some adrenaline injection? Get her keys to go to her fictitious home? Did her purse even have keys in it? It had a wallet, flip phone—

Her breath caught in her throat. A phone. She rode the elevator to the third floor, the prospect of the phone giving her a slight hint of optimism. The doors opened; the floor as mildly busy as it was when she had snuck out.

She walked past the nurse's station, one of them staring at her while holding the phone receiver. She took a stab at which direction to go to the locker room.

"There she is! She's here!" Nurse Angela stopped her in the hallway, out of breath and hand on her hip. "And just where were you off to? Doctor Devereux and I were worried, leaving us like that out of the blue."

How long had she been gone? Did time work the same in this hell hole? She wanted nothing to do with the hospital or these people, but now she craved to lie down, take up a hospital bed, and let people take care of her. Which begged the question, had she ever been fatigued in a dream before? Ever dreamt about sleeping?

"I forgot my belongings."

Nurse Angela sighed, shoulders relaxing. "Come on." She led her to the locker room, and Lacy shot to the locker, shuffling in the top bin for the phone. She flipped it open, the ancient screen and graphics almost comical. The battery icon had one bar left, but more importantly, it had service.

Who should she call? Of course her contacts wouldn't be in Maya's phone. Whose number did she know by heart? Mom and Dad. No, she couldn't call them. Mom would have half of Massachusetts looking for her and work herself up to a heart attack. The only other number that came to mind...Miles. She dialed the number, pushed the green button and hoped for the best.

It rang.

"Hello?" A female voice, high-pitched and laughing, answered.

"Hi, is Miles there?"

"What? You have the wrong number." The clarity of her voice diminished. "Allen, don't touch that—"

The call ended.

Of course it was the wrong number. Nothing here was right.

"Angela? What's today's date?"

"March twentieth."

Lacy nodded, knowing the next question would only confirm Nurse Angela's right to be worried about her. "And the year?"

"That's it. I'm getting—"

She stuck out a hand to stop her. "Please. Just tell me the year."

Nurse Angela remained in the room. "Two thousand four."

Of course. The year her book was set.

She pressed her finger on the bridge of her nose. It was all she could do to not break down and cry.

"Oh, thank goodness." Luke arrived and flashed a smile of relief. He leaned a hand on the doorway, his forearm muscles taut, bicep peeking out of the short-sleeve scrubs.

"She's all yours." Nurse Angela rolled her eyes, happy to hand Lacy off. "Wandering out of the hospital, not knowing what year it is." She brushed by Luke and vanished around the corner.

"You know Angela. She gets a little salty by the end of her shift, but she's one of the good ones." He smiled again. No wonder Maya had a crush on him. Look at him. It was almost sickening how handsome he was, still with the slight hint of scrub soap wafting from him like a pheromone specifically compatible with her DNA, and the way he looked at her? It was as if the longer he looked, the deeper he fell.

He sat down on the bench, urging her to do the same. "I think I know what this is about." He nodded, face serious. "I was offered the position in San Francisco, the one I had applied months ago, back when we first started here. Back when we didn't..." He huffed, fidgeting on the bench.

Of course! She knew this part of *Prognosis Love*. Now that she had returned to the hospital, back where Maya was supposed to be in the story, it continued as she had written it.

"I know you found out, and you're right, I should've told you. And I know you're scared. Scared of what this is, because I feel it too. I want you to know that maybe at the beginning, I'd wanted to run from it. But I won't do that now. I won't run away before giving us a chance." Luke took her hand in his. How had she described his hands in the book? Strong and agile, and dammit if they weren't that. He stared at her for a second too long, his eyes practically glistening blue glitter.

Lacy bit her lip, mesmerized by his gaze. *Get a grip. He's not talking about you; he's talking about Maya.*

If this was a dream, eventually she'd wake up. If this was something else, some alternate universe, how was she going to get out of it, get back home? Was she supposed to play along with the plot?

Even though Luke wasn't real in her world, he was real in this one. She didn't want to lead him on if it didn't help her get back home. She didn't want to lead him on if it did, either. Was it really that bad to indulge herself, though? To have a good time?

Yes, Lacy. This is not reality!

Then why would it matter? There'd be no ramifications of any actions, right? Have fun.

Get out of here!

Live a little.

Run!

"Shut up." Lacy pressed her lips together, too late. She shook her head. "I'm so sorry. I didn't mean to say that." *This is why you can't date nice guys in any reality.*

The story flooded back to her, the crush Maya had on him in med school, the flirting disguised as fighting between them during their rivalry, the surprise and rush of feelings seeing him again years later.

Strange how they felt like real memories.

Regardless of how she felt, this was real for Luke. She didn't have the heart to tell him otherwise. "I meant that...I just don't know what to say, myself."

He caressed her hand and grinned, as if in pure joy that she sat with him this very second.

She felt sorry and happy for him, and confused and worried about what was happening, and nauseous from the lingering surgery images.

"You don't have to say anything." He moved closer. Lacy knew what this was, but it did nothing to dampen the shock it was happening in front of her. *To* her.

He brushed his hand along her cheek, tucking her loose strands that had snuck out of her ponytail behind her ear. His hand reached further back, caressing her face until he cradled her head in his hand. He leaned in, and she caught his gaze.

She was too astonished. Frozen.

It was fast and slow, sensual and sexy, innocent and lustful. His lips met hers in a soft touch, his tongue ever so slightly feeling her lips, then her tongue, in a moment's touch, before he pulled away. He kissed like he did everything in the OR, delicate, calculated, fueled by passion.

He sat back, a boyish grin on his face. "I couldn't live with myself if I hadn't kissed you once."

Lacy worked at a smile, probably a frightening one. She sat in a made-up hospital sitting across from a man she created for a story. A man who was in love with her—in love with who he thought she was—and just kissed her.

"That was nice." *This strong, brilliant, emotionally reserved man opened up, kissed you, and the best you can say is nice?* "Can you excuse me for a second?"

He nodded. "I hope I wasn't too forward."

"No, you're fine. It's fine." *It'll all be fine.* She stood and made for the door, either going to pass out or vomit. She wanted to scream at the conflicting voices in her head. Either way, she needed time. Solitude. Something, some*where*, other than this. She stepped through the doorway, the background noise of the hospital cutting to silence, the voices in her head ceasing.

Then everything turned black.

Chapter Seven

Elliott refilled his travel mug with coffee in the Humanities faculty lounge at Northeastern University. He glimpsed at himself in the framed mirror hanging above the couch, a few wrinkles around the corners of his eyes, hints of silver streaking his hairline at the temples. After bumping into Lacy, he couldn't help but wonder how different he must've looked to her. Thirty-two wasn't *that* old. Right?

Elliott fidgeted with straightening his hair, a lock on the top of his head not complying with the others. At least he still had his hair. For now. Dad had a hearty head of hair, and he was in his sixties. But his dad, Grandpa Jack, was another story. Elliott couldn't remember a time Grandpa Jack didn't have a bald crown. If that was one of those genetic traits that skipped a generation, he was screwed. His future meant baseball hats or comb overs. No, never the latter. He'd shave off whatever hair remained before succumbing to the comb over. With his luck, instead of rocking baldness like Jason Statham or Vin Diesel, he'd end up more like Dr. Evil.

He put on his flannel-lined jacket over his blue long-sleeve shirt and grabbed his mug and bag before heading out.

The lecture hall lay across the quad, a walk he enjoyed. Lecturing, not so much. But it afforded him his own place, one in a good neighborhood close by, and it was more than writing had provided him. Even though he had some writing credits with articles and short stories in *Beyond the Milky Way* and *Vertices* and the like, the goal was to publish a novel. Lately his inspiration lay dormant, his childhood dream a flight as fanciful as a journey across the country in a Trimaxion Drone Ship.

But seeing Lacy yesterday had ignited a voice that implored him to give it another go. To get words on the page again.

First, he had to make it through Fantasy Literature.

He swiped his badge on the door lock, propping it open as students filed in. He opened his lecture slides on the computer and lowered the screen for the projector, starting promptly at 10:00.

"I hope you all had a great weekend. And a chance to read the assigned materials, because today we are going to start exploring how authors creating their own words and even languages impact the genre. When do new words enhance a work? Do they ever hinder a work? Let's begin with the very famous poem "Jabberwocky," from Carroll's *Through the Looking-Glass*."

He split the class into groups, analyzing stanzas. The discussion grew so hearty that he startled when, fifteen minutes in, someone pounded on the door.

"Someone's late," one student said.

Elliott checked the time. "Very late."

The pounding sounded again, this time harder.

And something else.

Yelling.

"Guess they really want in," another student said. The other had a laugh.

Elliott stepped down the long steps to the door. What appeared in the narrow window shocked him. He cracked open the door and stepped into the hallway. "Lacy?" Her eyes were wide and wild with fear.

She folded her jacket closed. "This is, um—I'm sorry to interrupt you like this." Was she wearing the same dress as yesterday? She scanned up and down the hallway, then gave off a nervous giggle. "You know what? I should go."

"No." He held out a hand. "Is something the matter?"

She put her hand over her mouth, eyes watering. "I just didn't know where to go or what to do. Who to turn to." She choked back the last words.

"Hey, it's okay." He turned back to his class, peeking in the doorway. All eyes were on him. He was going to ask her to wait in his office, but the dark circles under her eyes, the nervous movement, it wasn't like her. At least not the *her* he knew. Something had shaken her. She came here, of all places. To *him*.

"You know what? Let me wrap this up here. Just wait right there. Okay?"

She nodded, backing up to the wall.

He retreated back into class. "My apologies, something has come up. I'll post today's prompt online and be sure to submit by midnight tonight."

Some students grumbled while others softly cheered getting out of class early. He waited until the last filed out, only to fill alone with Lacy in the hallway.

"I'm sorry to spring this on you," she said.

"Whatever it is, I'll try to help."

A glimpse of relief fell over her eyes. "Thanks."

He led her back to his office across the quad. He unlocked the door and pointed her to the seat students occupied during office hours. The glass frame of the *Doctor Who* poster reflected the light from the lamp on his desk beneath it, a miniature of the iconic blue TARDIS. In moving back to Boston over the summer, he'd saved some of his memorabilia for his office. Not the expensive stuff, though.

He shut the door and took his seat at his desk.

"This office." She scanned the tiny room. "Very you."

"Thanks." He wasn't sure how to take it.

Her hands clenched the armrests as her eyes stayed busy. "What's that?" She pointed to a stack of pages on the desk.

"Oh, that's nothing." He gathered up the manuscript he'd printed out, one of his earlier pieces he'd thought to revamp, and threw them in the top drawer. "So...what's going on?"

"There's no way I can say this *and* sound sane." Although her lips were curled in a smile, her eyes looked again as if they'd drop tears any second. "I don't even know where to start." She bit her nail, hands shaking.

"Just take a breath. You're here, where it's safe. Would you like some water?"

"You're not gonna hand it over in a cup that says Northeastern University, Faculty of 2065, are you?"

He looked at her blankly.

"Never mind." She closed her eyes and shook her head. "I'll just come out with it. Yesterday, I knocked on your brother's door and blacked out. I woke up in an operating room, in Baltimore, in the year 2004. Then I came back, right on his porch, this morning. And drove here."

"You blacked out?" Elliott's throat was dry. "Did you suffer a concussion? Get hurt?"

She chuckled slightly, half maniacal. "Hurt or traumatized?" She rubbed her temples.

Elliott frowned, disconcerted. "You came to James's house—did anyone see you?"

"I don't think so." She sat up, slightly more alert. "A dog barked just before it happened."

Elliott sat back, taking a moment. Ripley had barked at the door. She never barked at anything. He opened the bottom drawer of his desk and pulled out a bottle of whiskey, waving it above the desk. "Forget the water."

"You keep that at work?"

He shrugged. "Sometimes students can be assholes." He took out his glass and poured two fingers' worth. "Down the hall is Professor Hopkins. He's like a hundred and seventeen years old. Like, Gandalf old. Practically has his own bar in a big cabinet. No secret to any of us."

She downed the drink and offered the glass for more.

"Okay. A little thirsty." Elliott refilled her glass, then took a swig himself. "So, go back to the beginning. Tell me everything."

"All right." She shifted in the chair, sitting straighter. "After the book signing yesterday, I saw the address you left on the bookmark, and stopped by your brother's house."

"Whoa, wait. I didn't write anything on a bookmark yesterday."

"You didn't? Then—" Her face turned pale, eyes staring off to nothing.

He was losing her. "So you made it to James's house." She didn't hate him after all this time. Then again, she had moved on quickly after him.

"I knocked on the door, but no one answered. You were all singing 'Happy Birthday' so probably didn't hear. I turned the knob to come in, but before I could understand what was happening, I went somewhere else. It's like I blacked out, but without the passing out part."

He leaned over the desk. "And you woke up in an OR."

"Performing a craniotomy."

He took another gulp from the whiskey bottle.

"I know how crazy I sound. But it happened. And I came to you now because—" She pressed the bridge of her nose again. "I don't know. Maybe it has something to do with your brother's house, because I came back to that same spot this morning. Like I blacked out and was suddenly on your brother's front porch.

"When I returned, I was so scared of it happening again, right there, that I ran back to my car. I started driving and didn't know where to go, and you had said you worked here, and I thought...I called the department, found out about your class, and... I shouldn't have come and dumped this on you." She rose out of her chair.

Elliott did the same, reaching over the desk. "I'm used to being dumped on." He paused in the ensuing silence. "Not like, literally. I don't have a fetish or anything." He sighed. "What I mean is, students come to me with problems all the time."

"Not like this." She opened the door.

"Lacy." He circled around his desk. "Whatever this is, I'll—"

She flickered.

The doorway was empty.

Elliott reached the threshold and stared at the quiet hall.

One second, she had been standing there, and the next, gone.

He had watched her disappear.

Chapter Eight

The lights went out. The ground broke beneath her feet before coming together again.

She blinked off the confusion, eyes adjusting to the light. The blurriness cleared.

She sat in a cold, metal folding chair, a plate of petit fours and cut strawberries and cheese on her lap. She examined the clothes beneath it, her shoes. A pink floral dress, white flats.

Laughter in the room.

"Savannah?" A young Black woman in a purple dress smiled from the seat to her right.

Lacy looked to her left. A slightly older White woman bounced a baby on her knee.

A circle of seated women filled the room, all dressed nicely in summer dresses. An assortment of gift bags and presents wrapped in baby blues and greens sat in a pile in the corner. Hors d'oeuvres dotted a table covered in white linen around a cake in the shape of a onesie with camo-colored icing. The table banner read *Landing January 2018.*

"What?" she asked, in response to the woman or to the confusion of what was happening.

"We were asking if you could see yourself with Holton." The woman had a kind face, the silver butterfly earrings dangling from her ears matching the belt sitting high at the waist of her purple dress. "We know how nosy we can be."

"And how we need this kind of excitement in our lives," said the woman with the baby.

The other handful of women chuckled.

"I, um..." Her body sweltered, the running air conditioning doing little to stop the nervous, panicky sweat beading on her.

"You don't look so great," the woman said. "Someone grab a glass of water?"

A figure popped up out of a chair by the kitchen, blurring away.

Lacy closed her eyes tight, breathing heavily. *Not again.* She turned around, the blinds of the window open. The whooping of helicopter blades reverberated off the window, civilians in uniform running across asphalt. A flight tower loomed in the distance, along with a scattering of gray cargo planes, tail fins poking in the sky like sharks in a distant ocean. A taupe building near the chopper had a familiar symbol, wings with a star and circle in the middle, painted in blue.

Bucksworth Air Force Base.

And she was Savannah. What was her story? What name did she say...Holton. Her mind cleared through the fog.

"Here you go."

Ice clinked in the glass of water, condensation already forming on the outside. Lacy took a sip, swallowing it slowly. Better.

She opened her eyes. The women stared at her, waiting.

"Oh, shit." She remembered. *Not this story.*

The ladies giggled.

The woman in purple—Irene...Iris! Damn, she needed to better remember character names—tapped Lacy's knee gently. "You don't need to answer that. They can mind their own business about you and Holton. Right ladies?" She gave them wide eyes, and the women nodded.

The plot came together. This was a baby shower for the pregnant woman in yellow, Billy, across the room. At the hall on base.

Her main character's full name was Savannah Berrington. And if memory served correctly in timing, as her ringless left hand indicated, tonight she'd be engaged to Holton Walker.

Chapter Nine

Elliott set the bottle of whiskey down on his desk. Drinking the last of it did little to quell his nerves. He had witnessed Lacy vanish. Completely gone.

Poof.

What was he to do? Report it to someone? They'd think he was as crazy as he had thought Lacy.

At least at first. He had wanted to believe her. He certainly believed she was scared about something. He could smack himself. She came to him, and he blew it.

Nothing new there, Elliott.

But now what? Now that he believed her words more by the second, what should he do?

He considered locking his office door, mainly to avoid getting caught drinking at work. Sure, Professor Hopkins did it, but just because the school turned a blind eye to perhaps their most senior member—heaven help the faculty member longer in the tooth—didn't mean they'd do it for him. But then he remembered something Lacy had said—that when she disappeared at James's front door, she reappeared in the same spot. What if closing the door somehow prevented her from coming back here, or coming back at all?

He giggled nervously to himself. This was downright silly.

He checked the window, as if she'd be running across the quad right now. Nope, only a few stragglers roaming campus while classes were in. Maybe he could check the security camera footage. "For what?" he said. Did he really need further confirmation than what he'd witnessed?

He had to come to terms with what he had seen, and what he'd seen doesn't happen. People don't evaporate into nothingness. They don't stand in a doorway one second and cease to exist the next.

Still, he couldn't fight what his gut felt. Lacy was in some sort of trouble, and she came to him.

Whether or not he believed she would suddenly reappear in the doorway didn't matter. She knew to find him *here*.

Elliott entered his username and password into his desktop. If he had to stay put, then he needed to find answers.

Chapter Ten

Lacy stared at the empty plate she set down next to the sink, mind wandering over the clinking of glasses and silverware. Iris and the youngest of the crowd, Gigi, washed and dried dishes.

Despite the whiskey, she was aware she was in *Her Dog Tag Hero*.

What was it that triggered her to transport here? Why had her gut led her to seek help from Elliott? Maybe it had to do with seeing him yesterday, being the last person she knew that she'd spoken with. Maybe the excuse she'd given him rang true. Or maybe it was that first loves were hard to let go.

But she regretted it. There was a reason—reasons—why they had broken up. He'd made the choice to pursue the opportunity in New York. Made the choice not to be with her. She hadn't been what he wanted. They'd gone their separate ways for six years, and then she pulled this on him. How crazy she must've sounded, interrupting his class for it. She had realized her mistake, after embarrassing herself, left his office and—

She'd been walking through the doorway when it happened. Just like at James's house.

"Savannah." The pregnant woman, Billy, nudged Lacy with her elbow.

Lacy blinked back to reality.

"I keep seeing your focus traveling somewhere else. I think I know what's going on."

"You do?" *Heaven knows I don't.*

She smiled softly, grasping Lacy's hand. "It's your first deployment knowing Holton, isn't it?"

It's because this world doesn't exist. Shouldn't exist. But she wasn't about to tell that to a fictional character appearing quite realistically in front of her face.

What was she to do? Trying to escape didn't work out last time. Why would it this time?

Maybe instead of wondering what brought her here, she should focus on what had brought her back. The hospital in Baltimore... Doctor Luke kissing her...excusing herself from the room.

She'd been walking through another doorway when it happened. That has to be it—thresholds. But she had walked through several, so why then? Why *that* doorway?

"Like right now, perfect example." Billy chuckled, waving a hand in front of Lacy's face.

"I'm sorry." Lacy put a pin in her transport-solving. She needed time aside to think.

"I know how hard it can be to see our loved ones off, knowing they're headed toward danger, not away from it. Trust me." Billy rubbed her swollen belly. "I'd tell you it gets easier over time, but I'm not much of a liar."

Lacy warmed up, giving her a smile. It was after playing along with *Prognosis Love*'s story last time, giving in to Doctor Luke Devereux, that she had transported home. Maybe that was what she had to do. Play along.

"I can't imagine having to go through it pregnant." Lacy took both of Billy's hands in hers. Billy's story was the focus of the previous book in the three-book *Fly, Fight, and Love* series. As bad as Lacy's situation was, it could've been worse—she could've taken Billy's shoes and found herself nearly eight months pregnant with twins.

Focus on the positive. You're not pregnant in this alternate universe of horrors.

Shouts broke out in the party room. Lacy stood in the doorway, half-hoping luck would transport her back by doing so. Two airmen had arrived, exchanging banter with the partying women. Goodbye hugs were had as the women trickled out of the party to start their evenings doing whatever imaginary people did when off the page.

Lacy shook her head. Did they still exist outside of the scene? Of course she didn't account for every character's whereabouts throughout the entire book. How did that translate here? Everyone at Baltimore University Hospital had still existed when she returned, even though her actions had veered away from the plot for a short while. There were even extras in the waiting room. Had she described those in any scene in the manuscript?

The front door opened, and Lacy's heart stammered, a flush of fear keeping her movements slow. She knew this man—this character—as she had written him more recently than Doctor Luke. Holton was tough on the outside and a softie once he let his armor down. His passion for Savannah was visceral, almost beastly in his hunger to be near her, protect her.

Lacy closed her eyes and focused on her breathing. *Follow the plot and get home.* She opened her eyes. No more avoiding.

Holton Walker stood in the middle of the room wearing a sharp white shirt under a navy-blue suit, his physique almost too ripped to be contained in it. His hair was kept shaven, and his skin ran a deep brown, stark against the white collar. Short stubble outlined the shadow of a beard, green eyes outshining the stems of the bouquet of daffodils in his hand.

Lacy was speechless.

"Are you okay?"

"Hm?" Lacy snapped out of her trance on him.

"It looked like you might faint."

"No, I'm great." She waved her hand and cleared her throat. "You look nice."

"Thanks." He unbuttoned the suit jacket. "Borrowed it from Becks." His voice was a smooth, low bass that reverberated through the room, through Lacy's veins. "I know it's a little small."

"Looks perfect." Gigi appeared next to Lacy, smiling with giddiness.

"Gigi, get back over here," Iris whisper-shouted from the kitchen.

Lacy chuckled out of nervousness. Gigi nudged her enough to make her take a step forward, closer to the source of heat firing through her muscles. Gigi winked and disappeared back in the kitchen.

"I know how much daffodils mean to you, with your dad and all." He extended them out to her.

She accepted them in what felt like slow motion, recalling her character's background—close with her dad, he'd buy her daffodils on her birthday and take her to dinner, died when she was...early teens, somewhere in there.

"Thank you." She stood in awe of the man before her—the man she had created on paper. Other authors had commented on what it was like to see their books come to life on movie or television screens, but to see the character manifest before her eyes, in person—was this how she imagined him? This perfect?

Perfect. The word caught her thoughts, reminded her of something...

"I know you said you wanted a quiet night inside together before tomorrow morning, but there's somewhere I wanted to take you, if that's okay."

Lacy nodded. Who was she to argue? If she were able to snap out of the impossibly-handsome-man-before-her trance, she'd recall the details of the evening. Instead, her thoughts flew away with the helicopter outside.

"Iris," he shouted, "would you mind taking care of these flowers for the evening?"

Gigi ran out of the kitchen. "I'll take them." She sniffed them, eyeing Holton. "They're gorgeous. Not as gorgeous as the giver."

"Gigi!" Iris stood in the doorway, hand on hip.

"Thanks, ladies," Lacy said.

Holton took her hand in his, a thick, strong hand, the kind she wouldn't mind being enveloped by. *Focus, Lacy!* Playing along to get through the plot was one thing. Being enamored by her own characters...

She needed a pause button. A timeout.

Holton led her out of the building to a motorcycle parked outside, a Harley Superglide gleaming black and red. She gasped, holding her hand over her mouth. "The *Top Gun* moment."

"What?" Holton handed her a shiny black helmet.

"Nothing." She put on the helmet, squishing her hair. It was a rich strawberry blonde this time, long and wavy. From what she could tell by the reflection in a spoon during the party, her bangs were growing out, angled around her face. She had never ridden a motorcycle but always had that fantasy of having to hold on, arms wrapped around the driver tight. Sun setting in the background. The thrill of speed increasing the sexual tension and excitement.

She straddled the bike behind him, an awkward spreading of her legs. She pressed the dress beneath her thighs, like tucking in corners of a bedsheet. Holton started it up, revving the engine.

The regret was immediate. What the hell was she doing on the back of a Harley with a stranger? She wouldn't die though, right? *That* wasn't in the story. No proper romance novel had the heroine dying.

They took off, her stomach taking a second to catch up with the rest of her body. The engine noise battled the howling of the wind. She nearly screamed as a bug splattered on her visor, and her head grew hot in the helmet. The dress threatened to rip off with the wind, along with her skin, and her arms grew weary of holding the man in front of her.

This was not what Berlin meant with "Take My Breath Away."

Thankfully, they approached their destination, a wooden dock leading out to a lake. Holton signaled for her to get off first.

Her legs wobbled, butt numb from the vibrating seat. She took off her helmet and ruffled her fingers through her hair, but it was already back in its place. No bug splatter on the helmet visor. And her dress draped perfectly wrinkle-free on her body.

She stepped away from the bike, wobbliness and numbness gone. It was as if she had never ridden the damn thing in the first place.

Holton placed his helmet on the bike and threw his jacket over the seat. The white shirt beneath lay crisp and sharp on his body. He took her hand. "Come on out here."

They traipsed through a patch of grass to the dock, stepping up onto the wooden planks and walking to the end of it.

He let go of her hand and slipped off his shoes.

"Wait, you're not jumping in there, are you?"

He chuckled. "No. I wouldn't do that to you. I know how you can't swim." He slipped off his socks and rolled up the pant legs up to his knees. "Sit with me." He sat at the edge of the dock, feet dangling into the water.

Better than jumping in. Although Lacy could swim, so did that mean Savannah could too, or would Lacy not be able to? A brief flash of drowning splashed in her head, cold body, mouthful of water. She quickly joined him sitting, content not testing out the answer.

The water was refreshingly cool, the sun hanging so low it reflected across the entire lake, a golden surface where the summer insects flew in flighty swarms and the grass beyond the shoreline billowed in the slight breeze.

"It's beautiful here."

"I thought you would like it. Despite your fear of the water."

Lacy didn't know where to guide the conversation. She let the evening buzzes and soft lapping waves take up the air. Who knew when she would see a place like this ever again. Or maybe she'd be stuck here forever. Were both equally likely?

The thought caught in her throat. Paradise ceased being paradise when it meant forever.

"I hope that doesn't scare you." He grabbed her hand again, interlacing his fingers with hers and resting them on his thigh. "I wanted to bring you here because I knew being this close to water would be a leap for you. A step towards facing your fear."

She stared at their hands, her breathing picking up speed and heaviness.

"I wanted us both to push up against our fears at the same time. Maybe seeing you do this would help me with mine."

"Which is?"

"Commitment." He said it so confidently. "Joining the Air Force was my first real trial. And I got my feet wet and realized that commitment is something powerful, something sacred." He leaned back, taking his feet out of the water. "Would you mind standing, Savannah?"

Damnit. She shook her head. She couldn't play along with a proposal. Too many levels of wrong. "I'm okay here."

He took to his feet, and she pulled on his hand. "Come back down here with me. Really, I think I might not be so afraid of the water anymore." She scooted more off the edge. A picture ran like a movie through her mind, her underneath water, struggling. Gasping for air, reaching hands up. Sinking. "Shit." Savannah's childhood memory, drowning in the town's watering hole. Her father had plucked her out, resuscitated her. The memory was real enough to send panic through Lacy's body.

"Come on, Savannah. You don't need to do that for me." He pulled her up, helping her to her feet. With his strength he could've thrown her in the air. There was something sexy about a strong man who knew how to be gentle.

Gah! It was like being under a spell. Stop this!

Holton took a knee at her feet, staring up at her. He opened the small box he had fished out of his pocket, though how it fit in those snug pants was beyond her.

Sloppy writing, girl. So many things wrong.

The ring glistened in the dying sun.

Her emotions battled amongst themselves. She hurt for this man, thinking he found his soulmate, pouring out his feelings despite how hard it was for him to open up. Contrasted with the fact this place, the ring, they were all made up. *He* was made up.

"To be honest, I didn't know if I'd do this tonight. I know I haven't said the words yet. But being here, in this moment, with you by my side, I know, one thousand percent that I love you."

The sun died, Holton vanished, the lake dropped away. It was sudden yet slow this time, as if the world erased piece by piece in front of her, until nothing was left but black.

Chapter Eleven

The haze in her eyes cleared with her blinking, her body pushing against the ajar door. She looked out in the hallway, a handful of people with backpacks, some chitchatting, others off in a hurry. She turned back into the office.

Elliott sat in his chair, feet propped on the trash can by his desk, head tipped back. His mouth sat open, soft snoring escaping. It would've been endearing, if not for the fact she appeared here after living through another one of her novels. Never mind he wasn't supposed to be endearing, not after he'd ended things with her all those years ago.

She closed the door behind her most of the way, then leaned over the desk. "Elliott," she whispered. Not even a twitch. She put more force behind her voice. "Elliott."

"Huh?" His feet fell into the trash can, and he fumbled with it, shoes clinging to the oversized, thin plastic bag knotted up inside. The bin hit his metallic desk and floor with the frenzied battle, creating a din of thuds and clangs. He set the can down in victory, then looked up at her. "You're here."

"So are you." She glanced at the empty bottle of whiskey on his desk. "So much for sharing another drink." She chuckled, nervousness laced in it.

"You, um—" He stood, straightening his pants and shirt. His gaze went right to her eyes with an underlying connection in their focus. An understanding. "You disappeared."

She bit her lip and nodded. Thank God someone had seen it.

"What you said, about my brother's house." He rubbed the back of his neck. "I figured there was a chance you'd show up here again."

"You stayed here? For me?"

"Lacy, what happens? Where do you go? And what's in your hair?"

She pulled a strand in front of her face, a streak of strawberry blonde through it. "Shit." What else of Savannah had transferred with her into the real world? Would she be scared to swim from now on?

"You're really scaring me."

"Tell me about it." Fatigue hit her, the weight of having traveled out and back again, not having rested for who knew how long. "What day is it?"

"Still Monday." He checked his phone. "One-thirty."

"I've gotta get home. Get some rest."

"Let me drive you." He grabbed his jacket.

"No, that's okay." She eyed the empty bottle.

"There was hardly anything left, and that was nearly three hours ago," he said. "What if you disappear in the middle of driving?"

He had a point, even though the whole doorway thing wouldn't fit in line. But what about driving under overpasses? Would that act as a portal to this nightmare of hers?

"I'll drive, and you can tell me what happened this time." He grabbed his laptop bag and held open the door. "I mean, *everything*."

She sighed, too tired to argue. She made him walk with her through the doorway and out the building, following him to the faculty lot. The familiar white Ford Tempo looked like a desperate student's in a sea of reliable, mid-range sedans and SUVs.

"You still have Atreyu?" she asked. "I can't believe it still runs."

He cleared his throat. "Artax."

She put up her hands in apology. A mistake she'd made years ago, getting the boy character and his horse mixed up, and apparently still didn't get them straight. A lesson in why not to have two important character names in a story starting with the same letter.

"Of course she still runs." He patted her on the hood. "All it takes is some oil about every two weeks and she's good to go."

"So eco-friendly, is what you're saying." She grinned, a sliver of satisfaction poking fun at him. As if she had room to do so with the happenings of the past twenty-four hours.

She got in the passenger seat and buckled. "Remember that time she conked out on us on the way back from Newport? And we had to walk forever to get gasoline?"

"I kept singing that song from The Proclaimers." He nodded his head back and forth. "You know, the one about walking hundreds of miles."

"Please, don't sing it. I still can't listen to that song."

Elliott raised a finger. "That wasn't Artax's fault." He petted the steering wheel. "I pushed her too close to empty. Besides, it turned out okay."

Lacy scoffed, shaking her head.

"What?"

"You didn't want to leave the car to find gas." They'd argued on the side of the road. He was convinced leaving was the wrong choice, while she couldn't sit there waiting for help to magically appear. "If it weren't for me, you would still be waiting on the side of the road."

The incident about summed up their relationship. Elliott had never been the risk-taker. Always chose the safer option, even if it meant it was the worse one in the long run. A behavior that he stuck with so wholeheartedly that it had ended them.

"If it weren't for me coming with you," he said, "who knows what would've happened to you with those guys."

She turned, loosening the seat belt enough to face him. "Are you serious right now? You mean Gus and Vincent? Two elderly Vietnam veterans who supplied us with a gas can and fuel?" She shivered in mockery. "I thank God every day you were there with me."

He frowned. "Well, it could've been other guys."

"But it wasn't." She leaned her head on her hand, elbow on the door.

"I didn't know you remembered their names," he said, almost inaudibly.

Frankly, she didn't either until thinking about them right now. She could barely remember her own characters' names. But that day, that argument, was ingrained in her memory. Retrieved as easily as if she'd searched for a file on her laptop.

She looked out the side window, not wanting to rehash their past, or her present. As they approached the first overpass, Lacy tightened her fist around the door handle, closed her eyes, and hoped to God the darkness wouldn't swallow her again.

Chapter Twelve

Rehashing old fights was the last thing Elliott wanted. Six years apart, and somehow it felt like no time with her in the passenger seat.

He nudged her as they got closer. "Mind if I grab Ripley?" He couldn't just drop Lacy off at her place in this state. "I don't like leaving her alone when I don't have to. She paws at the door sometimes when I'm away." And he needed to hear Lacy's full story.

"No, go ahead."

He parallel parked a block from his place, hurrying along the sidewalk and crossing the street, laptop bag bouncing with each step. Although the apartment complex was said to be pet friendly, the landlord meant cats and any animal that could be kept in glass. Elliott assured him Ripley was the nicest dog he'd come across, but doubling the deposit was what changed his mind.

He ran up to his apartment on the third floor, winded and frazzled, which only exacerbated Ripley's excitement in seeing him. "Want to go on a little trip? Come meet someone?" He set down his bag, grabbed her collar, and glanced out the window. Having a unit facing the road came with the perk of morning sun and the downside of traffic noise. Artax sat along the curb a block away, but he couldn't see if Lacy still sat in it.

"Let's go." He guided Ripley out of the unit.

"Oh, Elliott!" It was Mrs. Winters, his neighbor from across the hall, who enjoyed long-winded accounts of her past he'd heard more than a time or two. But she'd graciously watched Ripley a handful of times when he'd been held up at work. She even took Ripley on walks now and then, a win-win for the both of them, he suspected. "I got a new bag of treats for Ripley."

Ripley's ears perked up, and her tongue hung out of her grin.

"That's so nice of you. I'm kind of in a hurry right now, but I'll come by later."

"I should be home all evening, God willing."

He nodded in goodbye, walking Ripley down the stairs and out the building, back to the car. Lacy's eyes were closed, head back on the seat rest.

He opened the door, and Lacy shot to attention.

"This is Ripley." The golden retriever jumped into the driver's seat and sniffed Lacy.

"Nice to meet you, Ripley. I'm Lacy." She patted Ripley on the head, then scratched her chin.

"In the back," Elliott said.

Ripley glanced at him, then hobbled over the center console to the back seat.

"Wow. I'm impressed," Lacy said.

"Oh, you know." Elliott took his seat and shut the door. "Takes patience, but you just have to let them know you're in charge."

Ripley shoved her nose between them and barked, startling them.

"Okay, you made your point. I'm not in charge." He shook his head, smiling despite himself. "Now, where to?"

"Actually, we're not too far from my place, if you're up for walking."

"Oh, all right." He got out of the car, Ripley following Lacy onto the sidewalk. She grabbed the leash, but Ripley made no moves to run off.

"How long have you had her?" Lacy handed him the leash as they started walking.

"Two months now. One month after I moved into my place."

"I'm surprised you took on such a responsibility." She stopped, holding her hand up. "Not that you couldn't handle it. Just, moving and a new job are big changes themselves."

"You remember my mom?"

"Of course."

"And how she can be a bit flighty and go-with-the-flow."

Lacy winced. "You're saying it, not me."

"You know that's an understatement. That time she invited us out to the middle of Vermont for a retreat, only to have left hours before we got there?"

Lacy shrugged. "She's...unique."

"Anyway, Ripley here was a shelter find from Mom, who passed the responsibility onto me. One of her *it'll be good for you* presents that requires time and energy and money to maintain."

"If it's any consolation, she does seem good for you." Lacy smiled, sending that thrill of hope again through his limbs.

The hope that, try as he might, refused to fade.

Chapter Thirteen

Lacy shuffled down the street, feeling like a zombie as they walked two blocks north, then west for another two blocks. “Right here.” The black metal *42* hung above the door, years of rust overtaking it.

“Of course,” he said. “The answer to everything.”

She didn’t have the bandwidth to pinpoint his reference. Standing at the front door, shuffling for her keys, she realized how the building itself didn’t fare much better than the address numbers. The five-story establishment sat in a strictly residential block of similar-style apartments in various shapes of wear and tear.

She wondered if it caught Elliott by surprise. That famous writer Lacy Travers should’ve been living in a decked-out penthouse downtown, or some flashy city across the country. Rent here was manageable—for the time being—and she had no impetus to move to another city. In Boston she had a city with tons of activities, a coastline, and family not far away mid-state. She had everything she needed.

“Mind if we take the stairs?” She glanced quickly at his knee. “The elevator’s moody.” The last thing she wanted was to be stuck. They walked through the foyer, past the mail slots and up the stairs, four flights to Lacy’s floor. Paisley red carpeting lined the narrow hallway, more decorative than cushioning at this point, the middle portion faded from the years of trampling residents. Never did she expect to welcome the faint musty smell of the hallway, or the violin music seeping through the door of *402*. But those were signs she was home. Signs of normalcy.

She led him down to the end unit, *406*, making sure they walked through together. Exhaustion hit as she closed the door and leaned up against it, as if someone had chased her for miles. Her knees buckled but she managed to stay on her feet. Her body craved sleep. Her mind craved reason. Most of all, she wanted warmth, to cleanse herself, a shower to wash away the past hours of her life.

She threw her jacket and keys on one of the gray couches in the living room, another matching one facing it. In between, on the far wall, sat a small television stand holding up a modest flat screen that wobbled on its base if she accidentally hit it when opening or closing the curtains along the windows behind it.

She mindlessly grabbed the clicker and turned on the television. A daytime talk show played on the station, the host and celebrity guest laughing at an old high school picture. The quiet had been too jarring, especially with Elliott awkwardly standing still shy of the doorway.

"Feel free to grab a drink or snack." She pointed across the living area to the kitchen, white flat-panel cabinetry dating the building worse than the worn carpeting out in the hallway. Their thin metallic handles looked like they belonged on a 1950s Chevy. Unlike more modern places, there was no island. She wasn't much of a cook, so extra counter space wasn't needed. Her stove and oven were rarely used, except on the occasion of boiling ramen, or heating up a frozen lasagna she bought on sale.

"If you don't mind, I'd really like to take a shower, get some clean clothes on."

"Go ahead." Elliott walked toward one of the couches and lowered to sit, Ripley happily taking a seat on a cushion.

She took a step towards the bathroom, in the back corner to the right of her one bedroom, then backtracked. There was no easy way to ask Elliott, but staring at him, pink-faced, probably wasn't the best alternative.

"What?" He looked up from the seat. "What's the matter?"

"I—" She sighed. "This is going to sound kind of crazy. As will most of what will come out of my mouth from here on out. Would you mind coming with me?"

Elliott swallowed. "To the shower?"

"Just in the room. Not actually in the shower." She bit her lip. "I don't want to be alone right now. Please."

He thought it over and gave a slight nod. "Okay. Yeah, sure." He followed her towards the bathroom. She grabbed his wrist again as they walked through the doorway until she was in the room far enough to feel safe from any doorway magic.

She pulled back the shower curtain, careful not to catch the metallic hooks on the middle partition of the rod, as they annoyingly tended to do. The shower knob squeaked as she turned it all the way to the left. The older building, and being one floor shy of the top floor, meant it took a minute or three for the hot water to reach the pipes. She took off her boots and socks, and the glimpse of herself in the mirror caught her off guard. Dark circles underscored her tired, bloodshot eyes. But her hair...

"Oh my God. I didn't realize it was so much." She ran her fingers through her hair behind her bangs, strawberry blonde streaking through the brunette. Would shampoo get it out? Last time she'd been thankful her bangs came back. Did this time mark her permanently? At least until her hair grew out, or she colored it.

She grasped the skirt of her dress and paused. "Do you mind?"

"Oh, right." He turned around, the mirror giving him just as good a view. "Hold on." He sat on top of the commode, facing the wall opposite the shower. "There. I'll stay this way, promise."

Lacy smiled as she stared at Elliott's back. If someone told her two years ago that she'd be stripping in her bathroom to take a shower, with Elliott Stephens sitting on her toilet...Heck, if someone told her two days ago, it would've sounded outlandish.

What did he think about this? If the roles were reversed, she surely would've thought him crazy. Certainly wouldn't have stuck around. Despite the awkwardness, his presence comforted her.

She showered in silence, asking halfway through if he still sat out there, getting confirmation. It felt heavenly to wash her face, her hair. Wash away the ickiness of fake Baltimore and Bucksworth Air Force Base. She reached out for her towel and dried herself off, wrapping it around her body before pulling the curtain back and stepping out.

"Okay, we can move to the bedroom."

Elliott slowly turned around, standing after seeing things were covered.

She grabbed his wrist again as they neared the doorway.

"Hey." He stopped her, taking her hand off his wrist, then holding it in his. "I got ya."

She wanted to cry. How crazy he must think the whole situation was. But he stuck with her anyway. More than she could say six years ago. She threw aside the creeping thoughts of the past as they cleared the bathroom doorway, then the bedroom. He sat on the bed, facing the bookshelf along the wall while Lacy dressed in yoga pants and a UMass sweatshirt around the other side of the bed. Ripley invited herself in, lying next to the bed.

"Okay." Lacy sat on the bed, propping herself up with a pillow at the headboard.

Elliott turned around. They sat staring at one another. Elliott broke first. "Okay. Start with the first time. You said a hospital?"

"Right." Lacy nodded. She folded her legs, one over the other, and leaned forward off the headboard. "It's going to sound ridiculous. But you're a sci-fi writer."

"Thanks." He smirked.

"I only mean that you delve into the weird and unusual in your stories, right?"

"I guess. I like to think it's more a stretching of the truth, what could happen, but okay."

Lacy licked her lips. Why was this hard to say out loud? Because it was nonsense. If he came to her acting the way she did, telling her these things, she'd get as far away as possible from him. "I need a drink; you need a drink?"

He rested a hand on her knee. "Hey, it's okay. We've both had enough." He quickly moved it away, like he was alarmed at his casualness. "I mean, I know we've lived our separate lives for a while, but I'd like to think we know each other more than strangers. We've made it past the stick-around-in-the-bathroom-while-showering stage, at least."

She chuckled, cheeks a little flushed with embarrassment. "No, you're right. I just don't think that explaining myself would make sense to anyone, no matter how well they knew me." She closed her eyes, taking a deep breath. She *had* to tell someone, and Elliott was here, willing to listen. And who better to tell than a fellow writer?

He folded his arms over his chest. "Try me."

Lacy explained, from arriving at James's house, up through the return to Elliott's office. He listened for ten, twenty, a thousand minutes—her concept of time was ruined—and not once did he move to run out.

He sat there, eyes off to anything but her. He nodded. Breathed. Nodded.

"You think I'm crazy."

He cleared his throat. "I mean, who am I to diagnose anyone?"

"I know what it sounds like, trust me."

"Let me see if I'm understanding this." He turned toward her more, bent knee up on the bed. "You were teleported *into* one of your romance stories. The setting, the characters—you filled the shoes of a character—"

"The heroine."

"The heroine, not once, but two times now."

"Two different books."

"Two different books."

"You're just repeating what I'm saying."

His arms raised in the air. "Maybe saying it over again won't make it sound so bad. I don't think it's working, though."

"I'm not making this up. Both times I'm walking through doorways—which you've witnessed for yourself, might I add—and it's like I black out. I'm not out of it, like unconscious. I'm awake but there's nothing—nothing to be seen or heard. Then, light and sounds reappear, and I'm in a different world."

"Okay." He rubbed his mouth, his jaw, probably contemplating handing her over to the police or calling a mental health provider. Two options that seemed better by the minute.

"Let's say all of that is true." He waved a hand in the air. "Not saying it is. Not saying it's not, because, as you say, I did see the unexplainable. So...just to delve further. Why is it happening, and why now? What do you think started this?"

There was something she hadn't considered until the second time around, in seeing Holton Walker. Getting off the motorcycle. Sitting on the dock at the lake. It was all perfect. *Too perfect*. The same held for Doctor Luke. His looks, his words.

"That woman from the bookstore."

His eyebrows rose. "You mean the blunt critic? The one who convinced me I may never want to have a signing? That one?"

"She confronted me in the parking lot when I was leaving, then followed me, all the way to your brother's street."

"Jesus, Lacy. Should we be calling the police?"

"Well, not exactly a confrontation." As if that justified not calling the police. "We didn't speak two words to each other. But she had waited for me out there. Staring at me. Her eyes...they followed me all the way to my car, and she said something under her breath. I couldn't hear it, but her lips were definitely moving. I got spooked and tried to lose her. Then I saw the bookmark, remembered what you said about the birthday party, and I wanted to be somewhere safe."

"What do you think she was saying? Why follow you?"

She feared saying it, as though the very act of expelling the words would finalize it. "I think she cursed me. And she wrote James's address and chased me there to somehow start it all."

He tilted his head side-to-side. "I'd put that more in the realm of fantasy than sci-fi."

"I'm serious, Elliott." Her lips shook, tears welling in her eyes. She hadn't believed in curses, not until two seconds ago. It most certainly had to be a curse. And curses were out of her control, out of her realm of reality. This could last forever. "I don't know what else to do. Who to turn to."

"Hey, it's okay." He patted her shoulder. "I know fantasy, too."

She chuckled, half wanting to smack him, half thankful for his levity.

"We'll figure this out. If a curse is what we're dealing with, at least we know now, right?"

She dabbed the corners of her eyes. "I don't see how it makes things better."

"Knowing what you're up against is the first step in solving a problem." He clapped his hands, rubbing them together like he was about to dive into a hearty meal. "Let's think this through. You think it's walking through doorways, when you're sent away? Like they're portals."

"Yes. I'm almost certain of it."

"Okay. What about coming back? Same thing?"

"Initially, I thought so. The first time it happened, I was walking out of the staff locker room."

"And the second?"

"That's how I know it's not doorways to get back. We were outside at a dock on a lake. No rooms or doors. Holton was proposing, even though I was trying to delay it."

"Like, *proposing* proposing?"

"Hence the trying to delay it part."

"Geez. What about the first guy? What was he doing when you left?"

"Just sitting on the bench, waiting for me to come back."

"How about right before that?"

"We were chatting. It was this speech where he reveals he knows that Maya—who was me—knew he got offered a position somewhere else. That even though he was scared too, he would stay to give them a chance. Now that I think about it, it was pretty awkward to be on the receiving end of that." People didn't really talk that openly, candidly, as Doctor Luke had, do they?

"I didn't even think about that." Elliott's green eyes lit up. "Living through your stories, you can see what works, what doesn't work. I mean, what if it's a gift, not a curse? You can edit your manuscript based on what you experience." He stared off into the room. "It could be a cure to writer's block. I might be able to finish a manuscript with that ability."

"Hey." Lacy snapped her fingers. "Take it from me. It's not a gift."

"Sorry." His enthusiasm quieted. "So he gave a speech. Did he propose also?"

Lacy shook her head. "No." She sat up straighter. "But...hold up." She shuffled over Elliott, trying to get off the bed from his side.

"Okay, yeah." He held back his hands in confusion. "Go that way. Makes sense."

She held up a hand to shush him, then rifled through the bookshelf along the wall. She slipped out *Prognosis Love* from the shelf and flipped through the pages.

"That's it."

"What is?"

"That scene. It followed what I wrote." For the most part. Maya was a bit more prolific in response to Luke than she had been. "Doctor Luke kissed Maya. And then 'it struck him, as sure as the sun was setting and would come up again from the east in the morning, that his heart belonged to Maya Walsh.' Ugh. Not my best writing." She shook it off. "Anyway, that's when he realized he was in love with Maya."

"So, you're saying, he kissed you—her—when you were there? When *you* were *her*. Kind of left that part out initially..."

Lacy waved her hand, shushing him. This meant something. It had to. "And Holton. He felt pressured to propose since he was being deployed, but when he did it, said the words, he knew for certain, and admitted it to himself, that he was in love with Savannah."

"Was there, uh, kissing involved in that too?"

"What? No." She waved the book in the air. "This has to be it. Doorways pull me in, and I come back when the hero knows—really knows—he loves the heroine." She practically jumped in excitement.

Elliott smiled either with her, or out of politeness while thinking she officially lost her senses.

She sat back down at the foot of the bed, heart racing.

Elliott scooted over next to her. "Okay. So you solved when you get back."

She nodded. At least now she knew, if it happened again, at what point she'd return. What point she needed to get to in the story.

"Oh God." Her excitement faded into horror.

"What?"

"The first story, I got there right before Doctor Luke realized his love for Maya. And same with the second. I got there shortly before Holton realized he loved Savannah. What if I get thrown in the beginning of a story? Or one of my slow-burn stories?" She stood again, a wave of panic hitting her. "What if I'm stuck in a second-chance romance, and it's only the first chance? Can that happen? Will I have to stay for years to get to the end of the second chance?"

She shook her hands in the air, as if the bad thoughts crawled over her fingers like ants.

Elliott stood and gently grabbed her wrists. "How about we not jump to conclusions yet, okay? Let's calm down." He guided her back to the bed, sitting next to her. "You didn't have to go to the end of *Her Dog Tag Hero*, remember? He gets deployed and returns wounded, and you have the whole aftermath of that—he rediscovers his love for Savannah. If it's the moment the hero knows he's in love, there's a first chance that happens for there to be a second, and you lived through that first chance, right? You came back."

She stared at him, her heart calming, breathing returning to normal.

"You're going to make fun of me for knowing what a second-chance romance is, aren't you?" He shook his head and threw his hands up. "Go ahead."

"You read *Her Dog Tag Hero*? Have you read others?"

He backed away. "Oh, you know, Jules is a fan and may have had one or two laying around the house whenever I visited. I mean, you see them frequently enough around, you end up picking one up here and there while in front of the TV, or you know, in the bathroom."

Red crept up his neck, to his ears, and he rubbed his hands on his thighs. "I thought it wouldn't hurt to know what you wrote in case I'd see you around. Good to know for extra fodder. You know how we would do. You'd make fun of cyborgs; I'd make fun of sex with cyborgs."

Lacy tried not to smile. He had revealed a secret, a piece of himself he probably had no intention in revealing. He had read her early work when they were both trying to break out in publishing, giving each other notes as if they were experts. Who would've thought he'd keep up with her books—even one—when she thought he wanted nothing to do with her?

As shocking as it was, she didn't want him to feel bad about it. She was the one telling him she was transported inside her books, after all.

He swooped down, grabbing Ripley's leash off the floor next to her. Ripley looked half-asleep, head on her paws. "Well, I think you've given me a lot to think about, and you probably should get some rest."

"What? You're leaving? Now?" The thought of being alone tightened her throat.

"I should probably bring Ripley back."

"It's okay, she can stay." She reached for his hand. "Please. Just for a little longer. At least until I can fall asleep?" What did he want her to do? She wasn't one to beg someone to do something they didn't want to do, but she was scared to sleep. Scared to walk around. Unfortunately, now he was the only one who knew what had happened to her.

He stared down at Ripley, then back at Lacy.

Yes, I'm sure I look pathetic, and I don't care.

He breathed deeply, the waiting agonizing. Finally, he opened his jacket, slipping it off.

Lacy nearly cried. "Yeah?"

Ripley moved to the bedroom doorway and settled there, as if Elliott had commanded her to sit and stay.

He groaned but nodded. “Yeah.”

Chapter Fourteen

It didn't take long for Lacy to fall asleep, which was a good thing, because Elliott wasn't sure what to do.

What was he to think about it all? Call a psychiatrist? Some sort of help line? Take her to the hospital? What good would any of those do? No one would believe the words coming out of her mouth more than he did.

One thing was for certain—Lacy wholeheartedly believed what she said. The woman was terrified, the fear in her eyes, worry in her voice. Whether her story was reality or not, she was scared, exhausted, and alone.

The only thing he knew how to do was to be present, so that's what he did.

After she fell asleep, he snuck off to the living area and posted the prompt for his class on his phone, then doom-scrolled for anything that explained this situation. Nothing did.

If her story wasn't true, though, how *did* she disappear in his office doorway? *I checked the hallway.* He hadn't seen her return, not exactly, since he'd dozed off. But why would she come back at all if she had left the building? It wasn't like she'd been hiding in some secret annex out of *House of Leaves*, for what, to watch him fall asleep?

As the early afternoon stretched into late afternoon, his stomach grumbled louder and more frequent. He could've gone out for takeout or picked up groceries, but best not to leave her alone if she were to wake. Ordering delivery was a crapshoot, at least in his experience in the area, never knowing if it'd take twenty minutes or one hundred twenty.

He perused the fridge and her cabinets, scrambling ingredients together to make stir-fry. Enough for the two of them. She'd likely wake up hungry, and it wouldn't hurt to have something she could warm up easily. A meal she loved. At least, she had six years ago.

He picked out the largest pan she owned and sizzled frozen veggies in oil on the stove. Rarely did he cook a proper meal for himself. Usually, it was a sandwich thrown together, or takeout. He didn't want to think about the extra sugar and salt he'd consumed the last few years from Chinese, Italian, and bar food.

Luckily, she had a few packages of ramen, along with a substantial collection of takeout packet sauces, chopsticks, and plasticware stuffed in a drawer. It was amazing their paths hadn't crossed until yesterday, and that had been on purpose.

Was it obvious he came to her book signing on purpose? Did she think it weird? Most likely what happened to her was more alarming than his behavior.

And how embarrassing it was to reveal he had read *Her Dog Tag Hero*. At least she didn't press him too hard about it. Wouldn't want to admit to reading four or five of her books. They weren't his usual genre of reading. Romances tended to be too predictable for his taste. Usually, the guy did something stupid three-quarters of the way through to almost ruin things—which tracked with his dating history—then they'd make up—which didn't track with his history.

Even so, there was something special about Lacy's writing. *Heartbeats of a Drum* had reeled him in. Her descriptions, the chemistry between characters. He could see why it catapulted her career. *Her Dog Tag Hero* hadn't held the same grip over him, but why admit that? No author wanted to hear that kind of criticism, especially from someone who had yet to publish a manuscript. Especially from an ex-boyfriend.

"That smells amazing."

He snapped to attention, Lacy standing just outside the bedroom doorway. She looked more refreshed, her face not as pale, yet faded blonde still streaked through a lock of hair.

He caught himself staring too long and returned his attention to the pan. "I hope it's okay. I figured you'd be hungry, and Ripley here was whining."

Ripley betrayed the last bit, her head lying lazily on her front paws on the floor at his feet.

He cleared his throat. "Have a good sleep?"

"Definitely needed it."

He poured several packets of sauce in the pan and stirred the sizzling concoction. "How are you feeling otherwise?"

She sat in a chair at the kitchen table, elbows propped, hands wiping her face awake. "That depends. Is it still Monday?"

He nodded. "All day. You do realize you walked through..." He nodded toward the bedroom doorway.

"Gosh. I'd nearly forgotten."

"You're still here, though." He smiled at her before turning back to plate the cooked food.

"Maybe that's how I beat this thing. Just stay groggy all the time to forget about it. Or run out of energy to care."

He set a plate down in front of her and the other across from her.

She gasped. "Stir fry?" She picked a piece of broccoli off her plate for a taste. "Where'd you order from? That's a good idea to reheat it in the pan. Just isn't the same out of the microwave."

Elliott couldn't wipe the smirk off his face as he handed her a glass of water and sat down with his drink.

"What? Do I have sauce on me or something?"

"No." He looked down at his meal. "I made it."

Her right eyebrow arched up. "What do you mean?"

He shook his head.

"A frozen packet?"

"Are you for real right now?" He waved toward the stove. Exhibit A.

"Are you telling me *you* cooked this? Did I have this in my kitchen?"

"Used what I could find."

"I can't believe it." She shook her head, mouth ajar.

"That you had this in your kitchen, or that I cooked it?"

She chuckled. "I guess a bit of both. When did you learn to cook?"

He shrugged. "I picked it up here and there." The reality was that eating out alone, picking up takeout for one, became depressing. Sure, he'd dated on and off after Lacy, but more off than on. After taking a free cooking class, he did his own research and worked his way through basic culinary skills. He had a flare for it, and it was a fun way to take up his evenings. Ripley didn't mind taking care of the mess-ups, either.

"Think of all the money we could've saved in grad school, not eating out at Mac's." It had been where they met, well, first spoke to one another. They were in the same MFA program, but it wasn't until one night at Mac's Tavern that he bought her a drink and after a few more for the both of them, dove deep into which book on writing was better, *Save the Cat!* or *On Writing*.

"Then we would've never met Charles and Samantha." He put the seasoned noodles and carrot in his mouth, his stomach groaning even more now that he had a taste.

"Oh, my goodness." Lacy covered her mouth. "I forgot about Charles and Samantha."

They were a couple who had just returned from a year in Europe, who delighted in teaching Lacy and him about 'proper' fondue, late dinners, and water 'with gas.' The price was that they had to put up with the constant criticism of how everything was better overseas.

"Whatever happened to them?"

"Last I heard they got married and moved to Quebec, but that was years ago." The sentence lingered in the air, as if he'd said, *Yes, Lacy. They lasted, and we didn't.*

"So, you cook now." He was happy she moved on. "Very well, I might add. What other secrets are you keeping from me?"

Elliott choked, the sauce erupting in his nose, his eyes tearing up. He coughed in his hand and put up a finger for her to wait. He took a sip—a gulp—of water.

"You alright?"

"Sorry," he said, throat tight. "Went down wrong." *If she knew his deepest secret, he probably wouldn't be sitting here.* Then again, it had been years. Who knew if it would even be of any consequence to her now?

Lacy took another bite, eyes closed, savoring it. "This is so good. If you ever start a takeout service, let me know."

I'd gladly do it again, is what he wanted to say. There was just the minor issue of her teleporting into her books. Twice.

"Thank you, for this." She held her chopsticks and looked directly at him. "For staying."

"Of course." He didn't want this comforting, content feeling to end, yet eventually he wouldn't be able to avoid the stuff she had told him. Now didn't seem like the right time. Was there a right time to bring it up again? Her mind was set—that she was cursed. And he obviously witnessed *something* outside of the realm of reality. What could be done?

Ripley stood abruptly at attention, sniffing the air.

"Oh, now you want some food?" *Way to have my back ten minutes ago, girl.*

She trotted to the front door and barked.

"Ripley, what are you doing?" he asked. "Cut that out."

Lacy rose from the table and made her way to the door.

"Don't worry about her," he said.

"It's okay. We're just not normally allowed pets inside. My neighbors aren't always the most relaxed people when it comes to rules." Lacy put her hand on Ripley's back. "Hey, it's okay."

Ripley continued barking, ignoring Lacy.

"Hey, girl." Elliott got up from his seat and made his way over. "What's your problem?"

Ripley's bark turned into a whimper, her muzzle by the door handle. She hadn't acted like this before, except for the party...

"Something out there?" Lacy reached for the handle, and Ripley reluctantly moved to her side.

"No!" Elliott yelled.

Lacy opened the door and quickly turned around, panic in her eyes, reaching out for his arm. Instinctively he grabbed her hand, as if she were falling over a cliff.

And then darkness.

Chapter Fifteen

Running water. A faucet.

Weight in her hands. She blinked. A tray of lasagna in her arms.

No, no, no…

"I'll take that." The young woman smiled, taking the heavy tray from Lacy.

Lacy found herself in a cyan blouse, short sleeves light and frilly over her shoulders, and white capri pants.

The kitchen was large with an island and adjoined a small living room with a television and sofas. Drawings in crayon and marker were tacked to the bulletin board alongside a calendar set to the month of June on the wall leading to a hallway.

It could've been any of several books, many of them spanning more than one season. And did shelved manuscripts count? What if she got stuck in an unfinished manuscript? Would there be no way out?

Don't panic.

The windows along the long wall revealed an enormous garage on the other side, yellow hoses attached to wide pipes stretching across the high ceiling. Which meant she was at the fire station, which meant this was one of the books in the *Burn Index* series, following two brothers and a sister who were firefighters. But which in the series was this one?

The woman set the lasagna on the counter next to a large bowl of salad. She had beautiful sharp amber eyes, brought out by her dark hair and copper skin.

"Carmen?" Lacy asked.

She looked up. "Yeah? You okay?"

Just confirmation..."No. I mean, yeah, I just need to step out, use the restroom." Lacy glanced at Carmen's hands, a wedding band and engagement diamond on her left hand. That made this either book two or three. The first book followed Carmen's love story. But which subsequent book was she engaged?

"All right. You don't need permission from me." She smiled.

Lacy panicked for a second, not remembering how to get to the bathroom until she stepped near the bulletin board and glanced down the hallway. She walked down it, her sandals rubbing between her big toe and second toe, hitting the bathroom at the first door on the left. She shut the door behind her and dared to look in the mirror over the sink.

She gasped. It wasn't the hair color this time that threw her off, which was only slightly lighter than her own, but rather the thick curls that coiled like springs from their roots. She couldn't so much as get a curl to stay with a curling iron on the hellfire setting.

Curly hair...

Book two, then. Because book three followed the sister, Sadie, who had short straight hair. She was Rhonda...? Rita? She sighed. The name didn't matter. At least she placed where she was and when. And how—her front door this time.

Oh, god. What about Elliott?

She washed her hands, as if Carmen were listening in the hallway and would be onto her ruse. The water felt good on her hands and wrists, cooling her off and fighting off the panic.

She walked back to the kitchen; Carmen was still the only other body in the room. She poured dressing over the garden salad and mixed it in with tongs.

"By any chance, did a man show up here a few minutes ago?"

"What?" Carmen shook her head. "Are you expecting someone?"

"Oh, no, I—"

Carmen laughed. "Derrick and the others will be back here any minute. Jeremy messaged me they're on their way."

"Right. Derrick."

Carmen tapped Lacy's shoulder. "You don't have to pretend with me. In fact, we all know what's going on."

Lacy relaxed a little, shoulders not so close to her ears. "And what exactly do you think is going on?" Of course Lacy knew what was going on, but didn't know how far along in the goings on they were.

"I mean, it's pretty obvious. You never showed interest in volunteering here before you met Derrick. What is this, your third, fourth time you're rattling the pans?" She winked.

"No. You're right," she said on autopilot. She hadn't thought about it last time, but was there a way for Elliott to get to her if he was at the transport site? Or better yet, retrieve her?

"Here they are." Carmen's attention moved to the window, the bulk of red machinery pulling into the station.

A handful of bodies moved about, their chatter loud as they took off their coats and helmets, disappearing from view. Her beating heart quickened, the anticipation of meeting yet another hero nerve-wracking.

"It never gets old," Carmen said. "The excitement of them returning from a call. Knowing they helped and they're safe. Being able to hug them again."

A man led the way into the living room, a handsomely built dirty blond wiping his brow. Carmen ran to him, and he easily lifted her up in his arms in the hug as if she were made of air.

"Hey, baby," he said. Carmen kissed him on his cheeks, his forehead. "Let me shower first, will ya?"

She let go as another man entered behind them.

He was scrawny compared to Carmen's Jeremy, the suspenders and pants nearly falling off his frame. His wide-eyed stare made him look buggish and jumpy. There was a familiarity there, his face covered in dark soot, hair flattened and sweaty from the hat, except for a few locks that stood up around his crown.

Her breath escaped. "Elliott?"

He moved toward her, skeptical and cautious. "Do I know you?"

Lacy guided him toward the corner of the living area as the rest of the team made their way into the kitchen.

Elliott's eyes grew bigger, a surprising feat considering the level of shock he was in to begin with. "Jesus Christ, is that you, Lacy?" He touched her shoulders, nearly pulling her into a hug.

She'd forgotten how different she looked with the curly hair. "It's me. I'm so glad to see you." She wanted to cry. She wasn't alone anymore.

"You have no idea." He looked suspiciously around the room.

As the shock and relief of seeing him wore off, Lacy registered his shaking hands. "Are you okay?"

"No, Lacy, I'm not okay."

Another firefighter walked in, turning his head at the sound of her name, raising an eyebrow as if confused.

Elliott eyed him until the man cleared well away.

"Here, I'm not Lacy."

"I don't care if you're half-man-half-dog. Do *you* know how to fight fires? Because today I learned—scratch that, confirmed—that I do not."

"Oh my gosh, Elliott." She had appeared here holding a lasagna. Never had it crossed her mind Elliott would transport into a character as well, let alone one that was out on call for a fire.

"They literally yelled at me the entire time. I've never felt dumber or more scared in my life. And by the way, are the hoses really as heavy as Artax, or did you write them that way? Because, if you did, not cool."

"I'm so sorry." The urge to hug him overwhelmed her, to help his shaking and honestly—selfishly—because she was so happy to have him here with her.

"Needless to say, I believe you now." Elliott traced the room with his eyes. "So what do we do now? You're the heroine, right? You said you go back when the hero realizes his true feelings."

"That's the theory." She sensed a tone in him but bypassed addressing it. It was his first time experiencing this. She had to cut him some slack.

"Which one is he? I'm assuming one of these is *the* guy?"

As if the question signaled his entrance, another firefighter walked through the doorway. His chest, arms, abs, even through the shirt, were chiseled, the soot on his perfectly shaped face as if it were strategically placed to enhance his cheekbones, dark eyebrows above gray eyes, straight nose.

Derrick Harrison.

He held a fluffy white kitten in his thick arms. The other firefighters clapped and cheered as Derrick held up the cat *Lion King* style.

Her voice came out weak. "That's him."

"Of course it is. I mean, why wouldn't it be Fireman Wolverine?"

Derrick caught sight of Lacy and flexed a smile. He stepped over to their corner, overshadowing Elliott.

Elliott slowly looked up at him.

"Hey, Rory."

Rory! I knew it started with an R. "Hi, Derrick."

"Aaron bothering you?" He nudged Elliott, who took two steps to not fall over.

She ran the question in her head three times before interpreting it. "Right, Aaron!" She patted Elliott on the shoulder. "No, Aaron just..." She looked at Elliott, something like desperation or absolute confusion in his eyes. "He wanted to know what I brought for dinner."

Derrick shot him a look for affirmation. Elliott nodded yes, like Ralphie when Santa suggested a football, too in shock to ask for the Red Ryder BB Gun.

"We found this little guy hiding in the crawl space." He petted the kitten.

"No thanks to Aaron," another firefighter shouted from across the kitchen, downing a bottle of water. "Wouldn't go in there. Kept whining about his knee."

Elliott looked at Lacy, leaning in for a whisper. "Your hair changes, yet I look entirely the same? Couldn't *Quantum Leap* this, have me in some muscleman firefighter body like the rest of them?"

Lacy smiled, aware of Derrick's stare. "You think I know how it works?" she said, moving her lips as little as possible.

"I don't know about you all," Derrick spoke up, looking around the room. "But I think it's only right to hit the showers before we eat this beautiful meal provided by Carmen and Rory." He winked at Lacy.

"Who the heck winks?" Elliott asked.

"So it's not as natural in reality as it sounds on the page." She shrugged.

"Hurry up, everyone!" Carmen set down a stack of plates. "Before it gets cold."

"Yes, ma'am." Derrick smiled and handed the kitten off to Lacy. "Save me a seat." He winked before heading off down the hallway.

Elliott shook his head, lip curled up in disgust. "Could you have written him any cheesier?"

Lacy sighed. "Let's just get through this. I returned home two other times. If we came here together, who's to say we can't go back together?"

"Aaron, you coming?" Another guy stood in the hallway, arms leaning on the walls.

"Oh, God." Elliott tipped his head back.

"What?"

"Please tell me Aaron's love life is settled after yours."

Lacy bit her lip. "Don't worry, I kept the side romances to flirtation."

Elliott loosened his tight jaw. "Do you remember everything about this book?"

"I've been piecing it together."

"You've either written way more books than I thought, or you have the worst memory of any writer I know."

"Oh, I'm sorry. Do *you* remember all the details of your published books?" It was catty. A low blow in her frustration.

"Thanks for that."

"Sorry."

"No, don't be. If I were a successful writer, I'm sure I'd forget the stories that made me successful."

Lacy sighed. "I didn't mean it. I'm sorry."

Elliott shrugged.

"It's just, whenever this happens, my brain gets fogged up. It takes a while to clear my head and remember." The kitten mewed in her hand, Lacy's palm under its arcing belly as if she held her cell on speaker phone.

The first of the showered firefighters came back to the kitchen wearing fresh clothes, hair wet.

"All right, real quick," Elliott said. "What do you remember?"

Lacy took in a breath. "Small town in Illinois. Derrick's the middle child of three siblings in the series. I'm—Rory—is a town planner. Meet-cute at a development site, Rory finds excuses to visit the fire station. This is the dinner when—" Her throat seized, a fit of terror hitting her. "Shit."

"What is it?"

"The dinner leads to..."

Elliott's eyebrows raised high, his hand circling the air for her to go on.

"Rory and Derrick have sex tonight."

"Oh." He jerked back. "So...that's tonight."

"Yes."

Two other firefighters arrive, one of them Derrick, hair wet and face fresh. He wore a tight navy tee with Maconfield Fire Department on it in white lettering. He shot her a smile before fixing himself a drink.

Damn. It wouldn't be that bad, would it?

Elliott folded his arms across his chest. "You realize you're almost drooling, right?"

"What?"

"You don't actually want to sleep with him, do you?"

"No." It came out high-pitched. "Of course not." That would be reckless and wrong on several levels. No sleeping with men she just met, no matter how attractive they were. Or how nonexistent they were in reality. "But he tells her he loves her...right after."

Elliott shook his head. "Then rewrite the story." He said it so matter-of-fact.

"I don't know if it works that way. If that scene doesn't happen, he may not realize."

He leaned in. "Did you honestly write a character that only fell in love with you—with Rory—because of the sex?"

"No." It was offensive to think she would. "Of course not."

"Then you can find a way around it. If he's developed a love for Rory, something else could trigger that realization in him. It doesn't have to be the sex."

"I don't know." Veering off the plotline seemed risky. But he was right—did she want to go through with the alternative?

The next showered firefighter came through to the kitchen, the sister with the short hair, Sadie. She returned Elliott's glance with a middle finger.

"Geez, Lacy. Wrote that one a bit sassy."

Lacy shrugged. "When your brothers are Derrick and Jeremy, you've gotta be tough."

Elliott shook his head.

"She gets a redemption arc in book three."

"Good to know."

"Rory, can I grab you for a sec?" Carmen attempted scooping a slice of lasagna on a plate, the pasta slipping into a sloppy mess.

"Sure."

"I'm gonna shower and hopefully find better clothes," Elliot said. "I feel like I'm in clown pants."

"Just don't leave me here for long, okay?"

He must have sensed her fear, her desperation, because the tautness in his face loosened. "Okay. But you'd better get to rewriting. The clock is ticking."

Chapter Sixteen

Carmen pulled Lacy into the kitchen.

"Did you need help?" Lacy asked.

"No—I'm saving you from Aaron."

Lacy knew damn well it was weird for Rory to be chatting with Aaron for so long.

Carmen leaned closer. "A bit of advice? From someone married to a Harrison, those lot are awfully jealous. They would never admit it outright but trust me. A few more minutes with Aaron or anyone else like that, and you'll see a different side of Derrick."

She smiled at Jeremy who sat at the table, giving him a brief wave. She spoke through her curled-up mouth. "Look. He can't stand that I'm spending precious minutes with you and not him."

Was that how she had written Jeremy? He and Carmen made it through a bad accident, giving them perspective on life, vowing to live it to the fullest. Did that translate into a hyperfocus on spending time together? Her epilogues were too short to show anything other than a glimpse into the couple's happily ever after. Any role in the subsequent books in the series had them as side characters, just to show their love endured.

Lacy's writing gears were grinding, and she channeled her frantic energy into petting the small fur ball of a kitten in her hands. After about thirty seconds, it nipped at her fingers with its teeny teeth.

A hand touched her shoulder. Thank goodness Elliott hadn't left her for long.

She turned around, hitting a wall of muscular chest. Not Elliott. Derrick.

"Here. Let's find a place to set her down for now." Derrick's hands dwarfed Lacy's, the roughness brushing hers while he took away the kitten. He spoke in baby speak to its face before placing it in a large plastic bin, leaving the top off. "That should do for now."

He stared at her, as if he ached to hold her now that his hands were free.

The rest of the crew filled their plates and sat down at the long table, Carmen taking her place next to Jeremy

"How about I fix you a plate?" She smiled at Derrick, his fixed yet warm stare making her blush.

"Thanks." He stood opposite her across the island and leaned in, elbows on the counter holding his head up. "So what was that all about?"

"What was what?"

"With Aaron?" His questioning eyebrows punctuated his gray eyes.

"Oh, you mean just then? He was, um—" *Suggesting I not have sex with you*. "Saying something about the kitten and his knee? I didn't catch it all."

Derrick stood straight, his chuckle smooth as bourbon. "Poor guy. It's like he forgot how to do his job today."

"You all have off days like that, right?"

Derrick shrugged with one shoulder in half-agreement. "I will admit, if he hadn't been in the wrong place, he wouldn't have found Scoop."

"You mean the kitten?" She just realized she definitely hadn't written Scoop in the book. Elliott's actions—or inactions—made that change. So he was right. At some level, she had the ability to change the story.

Derrick nodded in delight. "She looked like a scoop of vanilla ice cream had fallen off a cone."

Damn, that was clever. Did Elliott come up with that?

Derrick's glance turned toward the doorway behind Lacy. His mouth curled down and eyes turned serious.

Elliott was back.

And he wasn't the only one who had been right. The distrust in Derrick's eyes confirmed what Carmen had said.

Lacy formed a plan.

"Here, Derrick. You go ahead and sit down. I'm going to fix myself a plate."

He accepted the plate but didn't move away. "You sure?" His eyes remained fixated on Aaron.

"Yeah. Save me a seat." She winked, feeling like a complete idiot with its unnaturalness.

Elliott appeared at her side. He wore sweatpants a little too long for his legs, the Maconfield Fire Department T-shirt looser on his frame. He actually looked quite cute despite the circumstances.

He took a plate and worked a slice of lasagna out of the tray. "Guess it doesn't hurt to eat, right? Unless this is fake food or something?" He dipped a finger in the sauce on his plate and tasted it. "Oh, thank God."

"I think I know how to get Derrick to confess his feelings." She spoke out of the side of her mouth, Derrick's eyes meeting her every now and then amongst his talk with the loud crowd at the table.

"His personality—I framed it in a more delicate way, that he's protective. But really it's jealousy."

"Okay..." Elliott dropped salad on his plate, not caring it landed on the lasagna.

"Are you catching my drift?"

"Did you say drift or draft? Cause I'm pretty sure I caught sight of backdraft not too long ago, something that is much cooler in a movie than experiencing in reality."

Two men turned around at his raised voice. Lacy smiled, piling salad on her plate as if nothing happened. The men's attention turned back to the table.

"I get it. You want out of here. We both do. I'm trying to tell you that I think there's a chance Derrick will find you a threat."

"Me?" He set down his plate and poured himself lemonade. "I'm like pre-serum Steve Rogers to his Captain America."

Lacy sighed. "He'll find you a threat because you're going to flirt with me."

"I am?" Elliott met her eyes, his mouth open with shock or terror or something.

"Flirt with me at the table to make him jealous."

"I don't really think that's in my wheelhouse."

"Oh really? We met because you bought me a drink and struck up a conversation."

"We argued about writing as a craft. Not exactly what I would call flirting."

She thought it over, and he was right. The fact he was genuine and wasn't flirting was probably what had won her over. "Okay, fine. What about all those nerd jokes you make?"

"That's just my personality." He sipped from the lemonade cup. "Look, I'm not a very natural actor, okay? I had to be in one school play, in third grade. I was so bad they stopped making it a requirement for the next class."

"Would you rather I flirt with one of these other guys? They'll think I'm crazy."

"I'm not sure I want to piss off the fictitiously strong man."

"And I don't want to have to screw him. Do you think any man in the real world would ever be able to live up to that experience? I mean, look at him. The sheer perfection of his body. It would take days to touch every muscle. Like a statue come to life, but with a delicate touch that would melt your bones, turn you into putty in his arms."

"Okay, that's...that's a bit of embellishment."

"He'd ruin sex for me, Elliott. That man is a sex ruiner."

"Fine." Elliott froze, looking off into space, then back to Lacy. "I'll flirt. *Jesus.*"

"Fine. When I look at you, that's your cue. Say…say how you've enjoyed my visits lately."

"Then what?"

"Just roll with it from there."

Derrick waved Lacy over to the empty seat next to him. She nodded with a smile. If he had taken in as much as the tone of their conversation, he'd never believe the two of them were interested in each other.

Derrick pulled out the chair for her, and she sat down.

"This is great, ma'am," one of the firefighters said.

"Yes, really good," said another.

"Oh, please. It's nothing." What would she have done if she had arrived before it was completed? Maybe it would've magically appeared in the oven.

Elliott took the empty seat across from Lacy. The men erupted in shouts, two of them standing from their seats.

"What the hell is the matter with you?" Jeremy asked.

Elliott looked around, then to Lacy, confused as she was.

"What's gotten into you today, Aaron? You know that's Sanchez's seat."

Shoot. Forgot about that. Elliott was right with another thing. Her memory for her story details bordered on abysmal.

"Remind me again?" she asked. "He was new?"

"He was a probie. Roof collapse during that hotel fire. Bit of a tradition, a way to honor him, to keep a seat open. At least until a new rookie comes along."

"My bad." Elliott shifted his plate to the head of the table, adjacent to Lacy. He sat in the chair, his knees grazing hers. A better seat strategically for her plan.

"They're a tough group." Carmen grabbed a hold of Jeremy's hand on the table. "But they're sweet."

"What's sweet is you bringing us this meal." Derrick reached for Lacy's hand. She about jerked it away before remembering that was supposed to happen. What she needed to happen.

She gave his hand a faint squeeze, aware that his hand could probably break some bones with its strength. But he held it as gently as he had cared for the kitten.

She met Elliott's gaze, widening her eyes. He didn't get the signal to flirt, stuffing his face with more lasagna. She kicked his ankle under the table, and he let out a groan.

He swallowed and cleared his throat in a handful of coughs before taking a sip of water. "So, Rory"—he emphasized the syllables—"been seeing a lot of you around here. What's...your deal...?"

She pursed her lips, wanting to smack him. This was his idea of flirting?

"Could you be ruder?" Ollie, the firefighter down the table, asked. His short, salt-and-pepper hair aged him as one of the oldest of the young bunch.

Derrick's grip grew tighter.

"It's okay," she said. "To be honest, I met Derrick here a while back."

He released his hand from hers, continuing eating, looking shy over the attention.

"What is it, exactly, that drew you to him?" Elliott asked.

Derrick's leg shaking from irritation nearly vibrated Lacy's chair.

Sadie turned, lip curled up, forehead wrinkled, looking at Elliott like an alien sat next to her.

"That's easy," another one said. "Look at him. Mr. Handsome over there, saving kittens."

"Runs in the family," Jeremy said.

"Let's not get too confident," Carmen sassed.

"There's something to be said, doing what we do," Ollie said. "It takes courage, heart, but also discipline."

"And don't forget a touch of insanity," Derrick's neighbor, Hal, said. "How could anyone resist?"

The guys chuckled, but Derrick placed his fork on his plate, face serious. "We joke about what we do, and how it may seem attractive, but in reality, it's a hard life. We're a family here, but it can still be lonely. Anyone we date has a lot of anxiety to take on. I don't pretend to think otherwise." He stared into Lacy's eyes. She had designed this part, but hearing the words choked her up more than writing them on the page.

A tap on her left knee veered her gaze away from Derrick to Elliott. He gave a slight shrug. As in, he didn't know what to do, or that he was waiting for her to do something? Neither one of them successfully steered dinner off course.

"I think I'll start the dishes. Anyone care to help?" She eyed Elliott, hoping he'd get the message. His track record wasn't great.

"No, you sit." Derrick stood. "You hardly touched your dinner. We can do the clean-up. Right, guys?"

Most of the others stood, taking their plates to the sink.

Derrick stared at Elliott for a second.

"Just finishing up," Elliot said. "Will be right there."

Lacy waited for Derrick to clear the table. She leaned in closer to Elliott, whispering, "What was that?"

"What do you want me to do?"

"I said flirt to make him jealous, not act like someone who's never conversed with humans before."

"Oh, okay. I'm up against Mr. Perfect over here. Does he ever say anything a real person would say? Or just what your ideal man would say?"

"He's not my ideal man, okay?" She glanced up at Derrick, who pretended not to notice Lacy caught him watching the two of them, and returned his attention to the dishes. "I create characters I think readers would want to read about."

"Really? Well maybe curse lady was onto something."

Lacy leaned away from him.

"Sorry." Elliott pinched the bridge of his nose. "This is a lot to take in."

"No." Lacy sighed. "You're right. She was right. I'm beginning to see why each book sells less than the one before it."

"No, I have no right to judge. I mean, I'm an unpublished wannabe resorting to teaching about literature instead of writing it."

"Don't be so hard on yourself." She placed her hand on his forearm. It happened so quickly. So naturally. His hand met hers, and for a second, she didn't pull back. She let the tingle travel up her arm, igniting an ache in her core. She stared at their touched hands, then at Elliott's eyes, which looked at her with an intensity not reserved for acquaintances, or friends. Or exes.

She let go of his arm.

Derrick appeared at the table in front of them, behind Sanchez's seat.

"Oh shit." Elliott said it low, but not low enough. He sat back in his chair, in an almost wince away from Derrick.

"Rory, can we talk?"

"Yeah." She cleared her throat. "Sure." She stood, glancing at Elliott, a shot of fear with a hint of hope running through her.

Derrick took her hand and guided her to the hallway entrance, near the bulletin board, her back unfortunately to Elliott. "I've really appreciated you coming out here and bringing your dinners."

Lacy bit her bottom lip, planning out the words. "It's the least I can do."

"I wondered if, uh..."

"What is it?"

He looked down at his feet, and she took the chance, gesturing to Elliott to come over. She needed him close by, within touching distance, in order to go back together. She was sure of it.

Elliott shrugged in confusion. *Did he need a billboard to spell things out?*

"Being out there today, knowing you were waiting here at the firehouse. It kept me going."

He reached for her hands, and she let him hold them.

"The fire today, or any day for that matter, could take a turn for the worse. You heard what happened with Sanchez. But it could've easily been any of us."

She gripped his hands a little tighter, an excuse to wiggle her fingers as her palms sweat.

"I don't know if it was thinking I might not make it back to see you again, or seeing the way Aaron was looking at you just now..."

She pulled out of his speech. "Wait, what do you mean, Aaron?"

"Just a second ago. He looked at you like you were the only person in his world that mattered." He shook his head bashfully. "Maybe it's all in my head."

It wasn't just in Derrick's head. She had felt it, too. But that couldn't be right. Elliott knew Derrick was watching. He played it up, and this time his acting wasn't terrible.

"I don't want anyone else to look at you like that. I want to know you're here waiting for me. It's scary not knowing if I'm going to survive another day. But knowing that I have your heart would make me that more careful that I do return."

"Derrick." She touched his chest. His hewn out of the muscle of Ares, artwork of a chest.

She openly glared at Elliott. *Over here!* she mouthed.

Realization hit him, and he brought his plate to the island, then hovered near the two of them, staring awkwardly at the fridge.

"What if I told you, you have my heart?" She tried her best to look at him lovingly.

"I'd say thank goodness, because you already have mine."

His hand slipped behind her head, too quickly for her to step to Elliott. His lips pressed against hers in a shockingly gentle, tender kiss. Her body was in conflict, lips and tongue wanting to give in, brain telling her otherwise.

The lights dimmed.

She frantically flailed her hand in the air. She couldn't go back without Elliott. It wouldn't be fair. It wouldn't be right.

The room grew darker, and then she felt it.

A touch of a hand.

Then black.

Chapter Seventeen

Elliott's surroundings flashed in a beam of light. He held up a hand and waited for his eyes to adjust.

White kitchen. Living room, two couches. Investigative crime show playing on the television.

Lacy's apartment.

Ripley jumped at his legs, pawing his thighs, tail wagging furiously. "There's a good girl."

Lacy stood next to him, rubbing her eyes, the blouse and white pants replaced with the UMass hoodie and yoga pants. She'd made it back.

They both made it back.

"Is this...now? Real time?" He hadn't understood it before, but Lacy's paranoid questioning made a lot more sense. Who knew if she had written a book with an apartment that mimicked the one she lived in? Teleporting to another story was as plausible as returning to Boston. But he knew his Ripley, so it had to be now.

Lacy clutched his arm, taking her first step, as if the floor would give way underweight. "I think so." She pointed to the TV clock. Monday, 8:15 p.m.

Outside, the sky was dark and the streetlights shone bright, neighboring apartments a speckled pattern of dark and lighted windows. Lacy pulled the curtains shut over the living room windows.

"Poor Ripley. I've gotta take her out."

"No!" Lacy reached out to him. "I just mean...do you really want to take your chances, walking through...?" She nodded at the doorway.

"It's been hours. I can't expect her to hold things in forever."

"Can't she go on some paper towels or something?"

Elliott frowned. "Lacy, I get your fear. I really do. But we can't stay in this one room forever."

He clipped the leash. "Five minutes. Promise."

She crossed her arms and bit on her thumb.

He wasn't asking for permission, but he appreciated her conceding with a nod. He slid a hand through the threshold, took a step. Exhaled in relief.

Ripley tugged on the leash with her forward momentum, and he hurried down the hallway and stairwell with her. She quickly relieved herself at the first corner, which was fine by him. At least she hadn't made a mess in Lacy's apartment.

He shoved the image of Derrick the flawless fireman kissing Lacy out of his head.

He tried not to think she'd enjoyed it. How could she? The man wasn't real. Guilt crept in, realizing how selfish it was to think about how it made him feel. What about Lacy? She had to go through kissing someone she hardly knew, and more than once.

He didn't have a plan or the answers to any of it. What he did have was a promise to keep.

He shook Ripley's leash. "Come on. Let's go back up, get you something to eat."

They walked back up to the fourth floor. The hallway was quiet minus the violinist practicing scales. Lacy's door remained open, as he had left it.

She stood by the windows, curtain closed.

"Hey." He said it more to snap her out of whatever thought hole she was digging than as an announcement.

Elliott led Ripley to the kitchen table, only to find that whatever stir fry had been left when they vanished had been consumed. He couldn't be mad at Ripley. If anything, it showed she'd survive an apocalypse. At least for a little while.

He loaded the sink with soapy water and the dirty dishes, then shuffled to the sofa. He'd have to face the shock of the situation eventually. Might as well start.

"That...was a lot."

Lacy sighed, her shoulders lowering, but she remained facing outside, as if turning around would expose her in a way she didn't want to be exposed.

"I can't do that again," he said.

She whipped around. "I can't either!" She smacked her hands on her thighs, breathing heavily. "I'm sorry." She shook her head and sat on the opposite sofa.

"You don't have to apologize."

"I kinda do. It's my fault you went through that. But now you know I haven't lost my mind. That I'm stuck in this...this back and forth. Walk through a doorway, into a book. Hero confesses his love, back to reality. Repeat."

"Just to make sure I have this right, how many times—"

"Three. First time with company." Her lips curled up a little, as if she considered it funny for a split second before facing the harsh reality.

Elliott rubbed his face. There had to be an explanation for it. For why it happened when it did. For where she'd been taken each time. For how to prevent it from happening again. "How many books are we talking, here?"

"Around two dozen, counting shelved ones."

Jesus Christ. "Twenty-four? I mean, I knew you were more prolific than me, but..."

"What if it doesn't end after that? What if it loops back through them, or goes to new story ideas in my head, or ones I hadn't even thought about?" Her hands shook as she waved them in the air with her words.

"Hey." He switched couches, hurrying to her side. "It'll be okay. We can figure this out."

"Can we? What if there's no figuring it out? What if that woman cursed me forever? I swear, if I ever see her again..."

Elliott held up a finger. "Okay, first, no curse that I know of, albeit all of them are in the realm of fiction, doesn't have a way to be broken. Even the ones they call unbreakable have some work-around."

She looked up at him with such sad, hopeless brown eyes.

He sensed skepticism in her quietness. "Don't tell me you don't remember *The Lord of the Rings* chess set."

She dabbed the corners of her eyes. "The one with a glass cover on the end table by your desk?" She chuckled. "The only chess set I'd ever seen out for display yet off limits to touch?"

"People need to see it, Lacy. See, not touch."

They shared a laugh.

"Point is, the ring could be destroyed by the fires of Mount Doom. Ariel and her voice, the prince as a Beast, Aurora and sleeping, all curses with a fix."

"You're big into Disney, too?"

He straightened. "They were all based on fairy tales long before Disney put their spin on them."

She shook her head and giggled.

It was okay that it was at his expense. It felt wonderful to make her laugh. She was beautiful enough as it was, but when he made her smile, it was impossible not to look at her.

"My point is, this curse has a way to end, too. We just need to figure out how."

She exhaled, returning to seriousness. "How do we do that?"

He thought it over. "The first thing in knowing how to end a curse is fully understanding the basic rules of the curse. From what I can tell, the curse isn't on an object. For instance, it's not your apartment because it happened to you in other places. Which leads me to think it's on you, as a person. Your dragging me into it, having a hold of me when it happened, only strengthens that theory."

"*Dragging* is a little extreme."

"Oh, really?"

"No, you're right. I'm sorry. It's not right of me to ask you to keep going with this. I don't know if I could bear it, knowing I may have passed it on to you."

He shook his head. The idea had crossed his mind, Lacy transferring the curse to anyone she touched. If that were the case, Ripley would've crossed over with them. Her nose had been at his leg when Lacy made contact with him. Unless the curse only applied to humans.

"It's all right. In a way, I kind of deserve it."

"What do you mean?" Lacy pulled down the blanket hanging off the back of the couch, lifting her feet onto the cushions and resting her head on his shoulder.

The reddish-blonde streak was still there in her hair, but now two random ringlets of curls joined in. Her shampoo smell returned, a warm and cozy scent drifting softly from her hair.

But he wasn't deserving of this, of any of her affection, even if it was platonic. It tightened his stomach, not having told her sooner. It was supposed to have gone away over time. Six years should've been long enough. But all it did was rot and fester, and he couldn't go on without confessing.

She deserved to know the truth about him. What really happened to break them up. Why he took that internship in New York. How her publicist had planted the seed in his head, showed him what her life could be. What it was going to be. She was at the doorstep of success, and being with him would only pull her away. How he convinced himself that the sooner he let her go, the sooner she could get on with her life. With her dream. That was why he'd broken it off. Why he'd cut off contact. Only to realize his mistake when it was too late.

He couldn't carry on not letting her know the truth. How could they have any kind of relationship without him mending his wrong?

He looked down at her precious face. "Lacy, I—"

Her eyes were closed, her breathing soft. How could someone's breathing be beautiful?

He didn't want to disturb her, to disrupt her sleep. He also didn't want this moment to end. The moment she was okay with him there, that she trusted him enough to fall asleep.

He'd tell her when she woke up.

He followed her lead and closed his eyes.

Chapter Eighteen

Ripley's whimper pulled Elliott awake. Lacy was asleep on his chest, his arm dead weight under her.

He savored holding her for a few more seconds, then maneuvered himself out from under her. He propped a sofa pillow beneath her head. She turned, facing the back of the couch, still asleep. He adjusted the blanket on her and tiptoed to the door.

"Come on." He fixed Ripley's leash and glanced at Lacy. Would it be okay to leave her alone? Was there a chance he'd vanish through the doorway this morning? It didn't happen immediately after they returned last night, but Lacy had said there was time between her incidents.

He rifled through two drawers before finding a pen and scribbled on the back of an envelope from the small pile of mail on the kitchen counter. For a moment, he worried about his mail, wondering if there were important bills awaiting him. But then he'd only been away from home for twenty-four hours. Felt like twenty-four hundred.

Had to take Ripley out, he wrote. *Will bring back breakfast.*

He patted his pants pockets, making sure he indeed had his wallet. Teleporting, or time travel—more like alternate-world travel, whatever the situation would be called—didn't make a whole lot of sense in terms of the specifics. Some of their physical features changed, mainly noticeable for Lacy. They manifested in her novel in different clothes, returning back in the clothes they'd worn in reality. Time didn't seem to operate in a one-to-one ratio. How long had they been in fictional Indiana, or Illinois, or wherever it was? Technically they had dinner there, but the sun hadn't set, in contrast to how late and dark it was here when they returned. And he'd been hungry there, when he'd just eaten stir-fry here.

Ripley tugged at the leash, nose aimed at the door.

"Okay," Elliott whispered. He found keys on the counter, then slowly opened the door. Ripley squeezed by, clearing into the hallway.

Elliott waved a hand through the opening. No vanishing.

Ripley looked up at him, panting.

"Had to be sure. Didn't want to leave you again."

He locked the door, making the leaving her alone part feel a little better, and led Ripley out of the building.

This time they made it to The Fens, the largest, busiest park this side of Boston. The Tuesday morning crowd of walkers and runners had died down, most people heading off to work. He didn't walk Ripley the full trail loop, though, not wanting to leave Lacy alone for too long. Plus, the lasagna dinner felt like ages ago.

On the way back, he stopped at Bagel Lox Nation, remembering how Lacy had loved their cinnamon bagels. He grabbed two coffees with it and hurried back with Ripley to Lacy's apartment. He cartoonishly juggled the drink carrier, bag, and leash while Ripley did her signature zigzagging until he swiped the key fob at the front door.

He'd have to cut out of Lacy's by midday today. Tuesday mornings meant office hours, which were easier to get away with skipping, but an afternoon of classes wouldn't be, especially as the newest faculty hire. How was he supposed to focus on teaching with this going on? A tinge of guilt hit him. This wasn't his curse. It was Lacy's. She carried a burden she didn't ask for.

He reached Lacy's hallway, quiet compared to the bustle outside.

Ripley let out a low growl.

A man dressed in a gray suit pounded on Lacy's door.

Elliott briefly considered letting Ripley take off. She wouldn't bite, and it would prevent spilling piping hot coffee all over himself.

They made it down the hallway, and Elliott placed the drink carrier on the floor. "What's going on? What are you doing?"

The man turned to Elliott, dark hair and eyes, face thin and young. "Who are you?"

A lump formed in Elliott's throat. For as quickly he was thrown into Lacy's life, he didn't know much about her, at least not currently. Was he staring at her boyfriend? *Fiancé*? Surely, not husband. How could she not mention a husband after yesterday's events?

"Who are you?" Elliott asked.

The man put his hands on his hips. "I'm Miles, Lacy's publicist. And you are...?"

Publicist. He'd rather this man be her boyfriend. "I'm a friend." The words stung, but he had walked into her life—again—two days ago. He raised the paper bag of bagels. "Brought her some breakfast."

"I see." Miles scanned Elliott head to toe. "Would you know why she hasn't called me back or answered my texts?"

"Yeah, uh...Lacy is going through something." He handed Miles the bagel bag, who held it out as if it contained Ripley's poo and retrieved the key. "I'll let her get you up to speed." He knocked.

"I've been knocking. Do you have a special knock or something?"

"Just wanted to be polite. Didn't want to barge in." He unlocked the door and opened it slowly.

Ripley marched in, rushing to the couch, sniffing where Lacy had been when they left twenty minutes ago.

"Lacy? When did she get a dog?" Miles quickly rummaged through the apartment, poking his head in the bathroom and bedroom. All the doors were open, the blanket splayed on the couch.

"She didn't." Elliott's throat tightened. He went for the note he'd left, on the slight chance she went somewhere herself. No response written on it.

Ripley barked near the bedroom, staring at the top of the doorframe.

"She was here this morning?" Miles crossed his arms over his chest.

Elliott rubbed his forehead. "Yeah. Not even an hour ago."

"Where would she go?" He eyed the coffee table, picking up Lacy's phone. "And without her phone?"

Elliott slumped his shoulders.

"You know something."

"What?" Elliott stepped back, his high-pitch voice betraying him. "You don't even know me."

"Yes, but I know people, in general. It's my job. And you said she's going through something."

He could lie. Say no. Make up a story about her leaving for a few minutes. But then this guy Miles would wait for her to come back, wouldn't he? It wouldn't take long to figure out that her door was locked, but Elliott had the key. And Miles wouldn't believe Lacy had given a copy of the key to Elliott, considering he'd never heard of him until three minutes ago.

Elliott agonized over what he was about to do. If this guy was her publicist, and the curse kept sending Lacy away, he'd eventually need to know. "How do I know I can trust you?"

"Really?" Miles shook his head, then pulled out his wallet from his pocket, handing Elliott a business card. Matte black with white font.

"Miles Astair," Elliot read. "Choreographing Publicity in Your Best Interest."

"It's a play on my last name. You know, Fred."

"No, I get it." Elliott nodded. "Clever." Or corny.

"That's me. My number's at the bottom."

"I see that." Elliott studied the man's face. His pushiness already set off alarm bells, but something about the look in his eyes told him it was more bravado. That he was genuinely concerned. "I'm going to be honest with you."

"Please do."

"I've dealt with one of Lacy's publicists before, and things didn't turn out so well."

"If you're referring to Damien, yeah—he nearly tanked her career."

It boiled Elliott's blood to hear the name. He'd only been in New York a few days before knowing he'd messed up. When he came back for Lacy, Damien had already swooped in, as her publicist, and as a shoulder to cry on. A cheating shoulder.

"Luckily, she hired me after that. I've worked with her the past five years, which she could confirm if she were here." He looked around the living area, like she'd magically appear.

Which she very well could. But Miles didn't know that.

"It's important I get a hold of her, since I have news about the future of her book tour. Now your turn. Why do you have a key to her apartment? I didn't know she was dating someone."

"She's not." He shook his head. "Actually, I don't know if that's true or not." But if she were dating someone, wouldn't her significant other have been around this weekend? Or called? Or maybe she missed calls and texts like she'd missed Miles's attempts. But if Miles thought she was single...

"I'm starting to wonder if I should call the police," Miles said.

"The thought has crossed my mind." Elliott knew he wasn't helping the situation, but how was he supposed to tell someone what has been going on? That Lacy likely walked through the doorway to her bedroom, and vanished, teleported into one of her romance novels?

"Either you tell me what's going on, or I'm making a phone call." Miles stared him down, Ripley making her way to his legs, snarling.

"And say what? That one of us has a key to her apartment, and the other is trespassing?"

Miles inhaled deeply, puffing his chest. "I told you, it's my job to know people."

Ripley continued with the growling, baring her teeth.

"It's okay, Ripley." Elliott patted her head, calming her down. He sat on the couch, Ripley jumping up next to him, her head on his lap.

Elliott looked up at Miles. For a beat, he hated he had to tell another soul. But Lacy's life was at stake. He could've died fighting that fire—and she could be thrown into something just as dangerous. Lacy was more important than any of his discomfort.

As Lacy's publicist, would Miles have known about the incident with the woman at the book signing? What if he could find her, get her to break the curse?

He looked at Ripley, who turned her nose to him. He wanted to be around if Lacy came back. No, *when* Lacy came back. He couldn't sit with the possibility of her never returning to reality.

Truth it is. Unfortunately.

"Okay, I'll tell you." He glimpsed the relief on Miles's face before he was about to erase it. "Have you ever watched *Quantum Leap*?"

Chapter Nineteen

She felt the breeze first, a brisk wisp before registering the sound of engines, tires screeching, brakes squealing. Trees in the median of the road weren't losing their leaves. Rather, young green leaves sprouted from their branches.

But she knew this place. Downtown, in Boston.

A lanyard flew against her chest with the made-up blue and red logo of Boston News Channel 6, along with her name—Anna Summers.

This was a story she had started while dating Elliott and finished after they had broken up. The one she didn't care to be reminded of because of the heartache and anger and gamut of emotions that had coursed through her veins in completing it. *The Relationship Barometer*.

"Anna, where've you been? They've been waiting for you." A young man stood at the front door of the building, propping open the glass door. He wore a button-down shirt and belted slacks, the same kind of lanyard around his neck, first name Will.

Lacy hesitated for a second, but Will waved her in. He certainly held a handsomeness, but he was too young to be the hero, instead a college intern dipping his toe in the industry.

She followed him inside, showing the man at the front desk her badge.

"Afternoon, Ms. Summers," he said. "Loved your story on the best brunch places. The wife and I have a reservation this weekend at Casser Des Oeufs."

"Thank you." Yes, it was a tad cliché, her storyline. News anchor tired of the small stories, looking for something bigger. Wondering if she should change her line of work. Her hero, the weatherman, helps her see she's right where she belongs. "I'm sure you'll love it."

She rode with the intern in the elevator up two flights and the doors opened to the newsroom offices. The room was filled with cubicles, people working at their computers. She followed Will to the right, where they entered through doors into a darker room, a lighted set in front of her.

Was she to do the news broadcast now? Her heart jumped into her throat. It was one thing to meet and mingle with fans at a signing who, in general, already liked her. It was another to read a teleprompter in front of a camera for live television, a task well surpassing her comfort zone. The digital clock hanging high on the wall read *2:23 PM*. Still some time before the five o'clock live broadcast. Relief washed over her.

"Found her, Kimberly!" Will led her to a seat in front of a bright mirror, the table in front of her filled with various makeup products and lotions.

"Good lord." Kimberly sat her down in the chair, pushing Lacy's shoulders. She clearly spent her time off in a tanning bed, her long nails painted a flashy pink, her hair streaked with blonde in a high loose bun. "Jerry's been on and on about filming these promos, acting like I'm behind with my job."

"Sorry," Lacy said. Promos...filmed snippets for commercials. *Okay, not so bad*. It wasn't live television. If she messed up, she could try again.

"Ow!" Her hand flung up to the nape of her neck, checking if a swath of hair had been ripped out.

"It's not my fault you're late, and your hair hasn't seen the bristles of a brush in who knows how long."

Lacy grimaced, clenching her jaw with the brush sweeps. Kimberly worked through Lacy's hair, a much darker shade of brunette, fussing over a random lock of curl that had not disappeared in Lacy's transition from worlds. The spray was a bit much, smelling like she had spent the afternoon bottling strawberry jam.

Her shoulder was tapped, and she met the stunning green eyes of a man with a shaved head, dressed in a suit and tie. Although paler than Kimberly, his skin looked naturally sun kissed. Of course she had made the weatherman the sexy outdoorsy type.

"Your favorite," he said. "Promo day."

She smiled, not knowing if he'd gone for sarcasm or truth. Lacy sure wasn't excited about it, but was Anna?

His smile flipped in a downward curve of concern. He leaned in, his whisper soft, an appealing freshness to his touch of cologne. "Are we okay?"

This will never be okay. "I'm fine." It was neutral enough to cover her bases. "Just a little tired." She fought the compelling urge to feel his arms under the suit jacket. Some serious biceps under there, no doubt.

He nodded. "I'll leave you two at it." He walked away, turning back for one more concerned look.

"Okay, what is going on with you two?"

Lacy looked at Kimberly via the mirror. "What do you mean?"

Kimberly came around facing Lacy, leaning gently on the makeup table. "How stupid do you think I am? You don't think cameraman Connor over there told everyone he could about seeing you and Lawrence together yesterday?"

Lacy got her bearings on the story timeline. This was Monday, after she—Anna—and Lawrence had spent most of the weekend together. But then Connor spotted them out and, worried about the future of her career, she had brushed off Lawrence, upsetting him. Then they had fought about making their relationship public—she didn't want it to be, while he wanted to come out with it.

Which meant she was near the end of the story.

She let out a long exhale. What were the chances she'd get placed so close to the ending again? Was it part of the curse, having to hear the moment of realization or the confession from the heroes? Was it to point out how cheesy and predictable each one was? Was that the disgruntled fan's intent in cursing her?

"It's complicated," Lacy said.

"That's the best you can come up with? Anna, please. Love isn't complicated. You either love someone or you don't. It's the human behavior around the emotion that mucks everything up."

Lacy chuckled. She remembered writing that line. At the time, it represented the culmination of her relationship with Elliott. She had loved him and was convinced he had loved her. But after she got her first book deal, things changed. She hired a publicist to help make her debut as successful as possible and received invites for interviews and readings. Her dream finally came true, and all she wanted was for Elliott to be with her, in the moment. But he pulled away, heck, pushed her away. When he got an internship with a publishing company in New York, she offered to move with him, but he broke it off. Stopped answering her calls. Dropped off her things at the doorstep of her old apartment. And that was it.

The simple fight in this story? That wasn't complicated, not compared to reality.

"Kimberly, you are wise beyond your years."

"Don't forget it." She smiled, then ran over Lacy's face with a powder brush that flittered a cloud of beige dust in the air. "You're all set."

"Thanks." Lacy stood, surveying the room. She didn't have an inkling of experience in broadcasting, despite her research for *The Relationship Barometer*. Knowing the tips of acting natural in front of a camera and carrying them out were two different things.

A yearning grew from the depths of her thoughts. *If only Elliott was here*. He would calm her nerves. Make her feel grounded. But he didn't want to transport here any less than she did. Heck, he had to fight a fire, and here she was, fretting over saying a few words in front of a camera.

Elliott didn't deserve to be a part of her curse, regardless of the hurt he caused in the past. But maybe she did deserve to be cursed, having perpetuated the idea of happily-ever-afters coming too perfectly. In setting the bar unrealistically high, she gave readers false hope at their own chance of happiness.

She should've never gotten up off the couch. She'd worried about Elliott, that he vanished without her. A silly thought, considering Ripley hadn't been in the apartment, either. If Ripley hadn't transported with them last time, why would she have the next time? That went for Elliott, too. They had no evidence that he could transport without her.

But she'd gotten up anyway and saw his note. Getting breakfast for her. For them.

She smiled at the idea of *them*, then quickly brushed it off. Did she really want to go down that path again? He'd gotten a dog, learned to cook, moved out on his own, started a career. He'd changed. But had he *changed* changed? All the back and forth between worlds was screwing with her thoughts.

"Anna, over here!" The film crew waved her over to a well-lit spot at the side of the news desk.

She hated having to do this. What was Elliott doing while she had to get through this? Was he waiting for her at her apartment? Or did he go back to his life, teaching and taking care of Ripley. Back to his apartment.

His apartment.

The idea hit her as an assistant positioned her at her mark, her male co-anchor standing next to her, canned smiled on his face.

"Let's get through these quickly." His voice was solid, his words deliberate. Well-suited for a news anchor. "None of those retakes like last time. I have to swing by my son's soccer match clear up in Somerville before the broadcast."

"Somerville?" she asked.

"I told you Nancy moved out that way, despite my pleading.

Wanted to be close to her parents. Of course, the irony is that if she hadn't cheated, dissolving our marriage, she wouldn't have had to move at all."

Lacy wanted to back away from the conversation but couldn't move off her mark. *Somerville.* If that existed, surely Allston was on the map.

And if the old apartment in Allston existed here, so did the people in it.

Chapter Twenty

It took a while to convince Miles what Elliott said rang true. Miles either believed it or had absolutely nothing better to do on a Tuesday—did he not have other clients?—because he stuck around Lacy's apartment. They decided to first get to know Lacy's stories inside and out. Maybe there was a pattern to where she teleported to, or what time she arrived, or who knew what other factors.

The good news was that Elliott had read a few of her books. The bad news was that Miles hadn't *technically* read any, as he put it.

"You rep Lacy and haven't read the books?" Elliott filled a bowl with water for Ripley, setting it on the kitchen floor.

"It's more about presenting her as a brand. The bigger picture."

"But her books *are* her brand."

Miles closed his eyes mid-roll. "I know it sounds like I'm one of those 'in it for the money' creep publicists." He sighed. "Okay, part of it is the money." He held up a finger. "But I'm not a creep. I've known Lacy for years, and she's a good person. I wouldn't trust anyone to present her in any other way."

Elliott had moved on to the bedroom, grabbing the few print copies Lacy had on her bookshelves, but it was when he searched online that it sunk in how prolific Lacy had been. Over a dozen published books in six or seven years.

It wasn't jealousy that built up in him. That would've been excusable. He was disappointed in himself. How had she written so many, when he couldn't finish one manuscript?

Because Lacy didn't make excuses. That was how. Despite what was going on in her personal life, the whole breakup with him, whatever else since then, she persisted. She didn't wait around for things to happen to her. She walked down the road to get help instead of sitting by the car for it to appear.

He was too chicken to take a risk, to put his work out there, so he never completed it. That about summed up his life. Risk avoidance.

Even in the bookstore, instead of telling that woman what he really thought of her—

"Miles!" Elliott's heart pounded with the idea as he walked into the living room.

"What is it?" Miles's head shot up, a copy of *Thirty Love* on his lap. "Lacy back?"

"Were you asleep?"

"I was skimming." He picked up the book, and when he couldn't find his place, set it down on the couch.

"We spent all this time looking at the source material, when maybe we should be focusing on the source of the curse."

"You mean, the lady from the bookstore?"

Elliott nodded. "Maybe they have security footage—or if she did make a purchase, they'd have a name if she used a card." He wasn't sure what all he could legally obtain, but the idea was a start. "Who better to know how to break the curse?"

Elliott's cell phone pinged with the arrival of an email, which alerted him to the time.

"Shit!"

Elliott stuffed the phone in his pocket, then grabbed Ripley's leash, attaching it to her collar. "I was so wrapped up in this I forgot about class."

"Can't you skip it? My teachers never cared."

"I *am* the teacher."

"Oh."

Elliott stared at Miles. Granted, he knew the man for a few hours, but he seemed the type to fixate on his own problems and not care about other people's obligations. He did soften his tone when talking about Lacy, as if she were a dear friend. Maybe that was what made for a good publicist, someone who cared about their client and themselves.

Elliott rolled the apartment key in his hand. "I don't know how I feel about leaving you here by yourself."

"I'll be fine. I'll contact the bookstore, see where that leads."

That wasn't Elliott's concern. He wanted to be the one she saw when she returned.

"If what you told me is true, then she'd probably feel better having at least one of us here when she gets back." Miles stood, rubbing his neck. "And if you've been spewing lies, she can tell me where to find you." He grinned.

Elliott laughed nervously, not sure of the seriousness of the threat. He didn't have a whole lot of options, and he was short on time. "Fine. But here's my number." He wrote it below the note he had left about breakfast. "Message me on the hour, every hour, so I know you're still here. If she comes back, give me a call. Or have her call me. I'll be back this evening."

"And if she isn't back?"

Elliott paused. It made his heart sink thinking about it.

"I don't know." Elliott wished he had a better answer. But at this point, there was no way of knowing. He left the key on the counter.

Ripley led the way out of the apartment. Elliott hesitated, slowly passing through. The more doorways breached, the more confident he became to pass through others.

He didn't have much time to get to campus, but he didn't want to tether Ripley to a bench outside, and he definitely wasn't allowed to bring her inside to class with him.

He jog-walked to his apartment, Ripley taking a potty break, sensing absolutely no urgency in Elliott's schedule. They made their way into the building up the stairs and down the hallway to his unit.

Elliott raced into his bedroom and changed his clothes, opting for a button-down shirt and slacks, throwing on his rain jacket over it. He had no confirmation it would rain today, but the darkening clouds coming from the west hinted at it.

He crouched low in front of Ripley. "Sorry to leave you like this. I know the past few—" *Days? Hours??* It was a miracle. He knew it was Tuesday and had class. "You've been so patient. Hopefully things will be better soon." He petted behind her ears and leaned his cheek on the top of her head. She pawed and panted.

He grabbed his laptop bag, slinging it over his shoulder, and took one last look at Ripley. "Stay, girl." He backed through the doorway, a faint roll of thunder in the distance.

Chapter Twenty-One

Lacy stood across from Elliott's old apartment. It looked the same as she had remembered, four stories within a cluster of residences mostly housing college students. It wasn't a place she missed—loud music at odd hours, crowded streets, and drunken shouts nightly.

When she practically lived in it, she couldn't have imagined not liking the vibe. Whether welcome or not, aging didn't only change one's looks. It changed one's viewpoint.

Thankfully, the commute from downtown to Allston on the Green Line existed to get her here. This was Boston after all, though she may not have specifically written about the T.

Same with Elliott's apartment, but he had been in the forefront of her mind during most of the time writing the book. Would that mean he existed in this space?

She had about thirty minutes before she had to make the journey back in order to make the five o'clock broadcast. The promos had been awkward enough. They had to retake the first one six times, forgetting her lines and acting stiff in front of the camera, much to the displeasure of co-anchor Ross. How was she going to get through a half-hour live broadcast?

She set aside the worry and darted for the door to the building as a resident exited. He stopped mid-stride, holding the door open.

"Whoa, are you the news lady? Anna Summers, right? Live Action News 6."

"That's me."

"Cool. You look different in person." He stared at her a second longer. It was a genuine concern with what she was about to do. Did she look too much like herself to pull off being Anna, or too much like Anna to pull off being herself?

He turned his gaze to the building. "Uh oh. Is this one of your station's *Uncovered* stories about decaying buildings?"

Lacy smiled. "No, not today." *No time for chitchat.*

"Good. I've only been here a month, and I really don't want to have to move again."

"Just visiting a friend," she said hurriedly.

He gave a nod as she walked into the foyer. Just as she remembered, the mailboxes ahead, door to the stairs on the left. Elliott's apartment was on the second floor, and she raced up the stairs.

What did it mean that characters like that tenant existed in this place? Was she manifesting all of this in real time? Just how much control did she have over the story?

These were all things to bounce off of Elliott. And if she couldn't do that with real Elliott, then maybe she could with book world Elliott. She hadn't given a whole lot of thought about what she'd say. For one, she didn't know if he existed. For two, if she dwelled on it, she would've convinced herself not to show up in the first place.

Despite her misgivings, she knocked on the door to *211*. Nothing.

She knocked again. This time, footsteps grew louder.

The door swung open.

"Can I help you?" Elliott—a slightly younger version—opened the door. His hair was longer, scragglier, hanging down around his ears, tickling his shoulders. He wore a ragged The Four Eyes t-shirt and jeans that looked like they could walk off on their own without his body inside.

He was exactly as she remembered.

She smiled, cheeks turning pink. "Elliott?"

His eyes opened wide, eyebrows slanted. "Do I know you?" He leaned back from the doorway. "Wait, you're a reporter, aren't you?"

No, she hadn't thought this through.

She sucked in a breath. "Yes, but I'm also a friend of Lacy's."

"Oh. Well, she's not here."

So Lacy did exist here. What would happen if she met herself?

Elliott kept his eyes fixed on her. He knew something wasn't right.

"Would you mind if I had a glass of water?" She fanned herself with her hand.

"Um." Elliott scratched the back of his neck. "Sure." He opened the door wider, letting her inside.

The smell of bachelorhood hit her, the familiar aroma of old, cracked leather couch and whiskey spills on the coffee table. There was the shelf of *Star Trek* figurines. She didn't know all of the names, but enough to know the two in the unopened pristine boxes were Captains Kirk and Picard. His collection of Blu-ray sci-fi movies were stacked neatly by the television. She smiled when her eyes spanned the corner of the room, *The Lord of the Rings* chess set in its glass-cased glory.

"I think I have a bottle in the fridge." Elliott moved to the tight galley kitchen, with its laminate flooring, and oven whose door nearly hit the opposite cabinet, and white appliances. He opened the fridge, produced a bottle of water, and handed it over.

"Thanks."

"So how is it you know Lacy?"

Lacy took a sip of water. Not knowing whether the breakup happened already, she had to play it safe. "I've been looking into a story about local talent. Painters, musicians, writers."

"I see." He folded his arms across his chest. "Why not go to her apartment?"

Shoot. Good question. "She gave me this address some time ago, saying she spent a good part of her time here. She mentioned you're a writer? Figured I could interview you, too."

"I'm nowhere near the point that Lacy is at with her career."

"The story covers people in all stages." Lacy backed up a step, too aware of Elliott's staring, like he was figuring out her facial features. She pretended to take interest in his roommate Gavin's Pink Floyd poster. She'd never liked Gavin a whole lot, but his wannabe rock-star shenanigans inspired the career and backdrop in *Heartbeats of a Drum*.

"Well, Lacy doesn't come around here much. Not anymore, at least."

"Oh, I'm sorry."

His eyes narrowed and he bit his lip. "Yeah, me too." He stepped out of the kitchen, closer to her. "But I can understand. Her debut comes out soon. She's got a lot lined up over the next three months."

"Yes, but there should always be time for loved ones." The discomfort grew when she heard her own words, and she turned her back to him, perusing the Blu-ray collection.

He slowly followed her.

"Some would say it's better to step back, not clip her wings."

Lacy wanted to shut it down, erase his doubt. But she couldn't help feeling angry again. How did he get to choose what was best for her? She uncapped the bottle and chugged the rest of the water down.

"Can I get you another one?"

She shook her head and put the empty bottle on the coffee table. She shouldn't have come here. Her goal, stupid as it was, was to somehow see if he could help her get back to the real world. In what altered reality would that have worked out? And now she was risking being late for the broadcast, altering the roadmap to Lawrence's emotional confession.

"I need to—" A blue flyer on the table caught the words in her throat. A photo of a tall building with bird logo beneath it. The publishing internship, the one that he'd chosen to go to. Alone. A business card poked out underneath the flyer.

She knew the ecru background and gold embossed print. "When you said some say it's better to step back, did you mean him?" She held the card out to him.

Elliott tore it from her grasp. "That's nobody."

"That's Damien Lincoln, Lacy's publicist. What was he doing

here?" *Delivering that flyer, that's what.* Convincing Elliott to leave her. If only she'd seen his sliminess earlier and hadn't believed his lies and trusted him to guide her career. And to think she dated him, no matter how briefly. It made her shiver.

"You said it yourself, Lacy spent a lot of time here."

Her stomach turned with the onslaught of water mixed with the bombshell news. Her fall out with Elliott was because of Damien. She had to know if this history was real. The only way to do that was to go through this story to get back to real Boston.

"I'm going to miss the broadcast." She made for the door, the apartment suddenly feeling a thousand degrees. She needed a break from all of this. A time-out from moving between worlds, from thinking over what she had done to deserve this, and now from wondering if her perception of her relationship with Elliott had been distorted.

He followed, opening the door for her. "Sorry I wasn't of much help. When will that story be aired?"

She stepped out into the hallway. "What?"

"About the local artists?"

She shook her head. "Right. Yeah, um, keep an eye out for it in a week or two."

"Lacy." He reached for her wrist, the light touch sending goosebumps over her arm.

"What? How—"

"I'm not a fool. I know you, Lacy."

What now? Double down on being Anna? Fess up to the truth? *Air*. She needed air.

"You're different, but you're you. I knew it the moment you said my name."

"Elliott." She looked down at the floor. She needed to believe this was all fake. Most of all, she needed to get back to the station to get back home.

"Why the disguise? Why are you here? Did you find out about the internship? Did Damien talk to you?"

"I'm sorry." She turned away and ran distraught down the hallway to the stairwell.

"Lacy!" He trod after her. "Don't go."

That was enough to set her off running down the steps and out the building. She ran until she couldn't breathe anymore, until she was sure she didn't hear his footsteps behind her.

Chapter Twenty-Two

None of this is real.

Despite the number of times she told herself that in the subway, on the walk, in the elevator back to the newsroom, there was still a nagging feeling that book Elliott reflected a truth in real Elliott.

She had to pull herself together. There was only one broadcast left before the story's finale, and if she played her part right, she'd be back in real Boston shortly.

The newsroom was abuzz, people out of their cubicles and mingling like they finally discovered their squares weren't sealed off. She hurried to the recording studio, eyes adjusting to the dark. The countdown clock ticked down the minutes, just under nine left.

A frazzled Kimberly threw her arms up in the air. "Why are you making my job so difficult today?" She practically yanked Lacy over to the hair and makeup chair, teasing her tresses profusely, then powdering her face, calling it a touch-up when it felt like plastering on a mask.

"You know, that doesn't do a lot for my self-esteem, saying I'm difficult. You do realize I have to go on camera."

Kimberly rolled her eyes. "I don't mean that you need a lot of work. I meant that twice today you've shown up with little time left for me to do my job. Ross was little better, getting here five minutes ago. How you all look on camera reflects on me, too."

Lacy huffed. "You're right. Sorry. I had to take care of something." Although nothing had been 'taken care of' at all in her visit with Elliott.

"Here comes lover boy."

"What?" Lacy turned, Lawrence hurrying to her chair in a huff. Now wasn't the time to rehash their argument about their relationship going public. Except, as he neared…it wasn't Lawrence. "Oh my God."

A bald Elliott rushed to her, crouching down to speak with her. "What the heck took you so long to get here?" He leaned in further. "And you set it at Channel 6 and didn't name her April?"

"You look terrible." She flicked her gaze to his bare scalp, a sharp contrast to the long locks of book Elliott.

"You think this was a conscious decision?" His fingers circled his face. "Couldn't transform any part of me when I was a firefighter? No, instead I get Jim Cantore."

"Hey, Jim is a handsome man."

"What are you two talking about?" Kimberly shook her head. "It doesn't matter. You're on air in less than five."

"Great." Lacy rose out of her chair.

Kimberly backed her hands away. "I wasn't done."

"You're done enough." Lacy felt a little guilty to be so short with Kimberly, but she had too much to discuss with real Elliott to worry over how she treated fictitious characters. Although she did feel bad for leaving *other* Elliott the way she had.

She grabbed Elliott by the wrist and led him to the darker side of the room, behind the cameras and away from set.

"How did you get here? I saw you—Lawrence the weather guy—earlier, and he wasn't you."

"I didn't come here at the same time as you, if that's what you're getting at."

"Then—"

"I don't know." He shrugged. "I came back to your place after picking up bagels and your publicist was there."

"Miles? Why was he there?"

"He said you were supposed to call him a day or two ago and never did."

Shoot. She had ended their call in the parking lot after the book signing. Never quite had the chance or wherewithal to get back with him.

"I told him you weren't there, but he wouldn't leave."

"Did he see you disappear?" Good God, how was she going to explain that to him? She eyed the clock as if it had answers. Under five minutes to air.

"No. I left with Ripley, and he promised to stay until you returned." Elliott fell quiet, his stare turning down toward his shoes.

"Where did you say I was?" She waited, hand on her hip. She struggled to meet his eyes, Elliott dodging her stare. "Oh, no." She rubbed her face in her hands, the stretching of tension a minor relief given the circumstances.

"I know you're not wiping that makeup off!" Kimberly yelled.

"No!" Lacy put her hands down. It was going to take the orange goop Dad used on his hands after changing oil to get the makeup off her face. "Don't tell me you told him."

Elliott looked around the room as if he didn't understand what she was saying.

Lacy put her hand under his chin, aiming his face at hers. "You told him about this?"

Elliott slumped. "What was I supposed to do?"

"Make something up!"

"I'm sorry, but I was caught off guard."

She waved her hand to stop him. It wasn't right to point fingers at him when she was the one who dragged him into all of it. "Okay. What's done is done."

"Yeah, well tell Ripley that. I'm gone again, and the door to my apartment's probably open."

"I realize that's unfortunate, but there's something I have to tell you."

A man wearing a headset interrupted. "Anna, three minutes."

Lacy nodded him off. "It's kind of hard to believe."

"I'm pretty sure you can't surprise me at this point."

"Mmm." She giggled nervously. "The surprises don't seem to end."

Elliott sighed. "Just tell me."

"I went to see you, at your old apartment."

His face hadn't changed, as if the information had yet to reach his processing center.

"In this world," she said. "Like, book you."

He shook his head, eyes big. "You mean...you wrote me in this book? I'm a character?"

She closed her eyes, the details and reasons too illogical. "No, not really. I mean, I set it in Boston and wrote it around the time we broke up. I thought there was a chance you existed, and I was right."

"That is so weird!" He leaned in closer, excited. "What happened? I should go meet him. Wait—what would happen if I see him? Would we have to worry about a paradox?"

"Just stop." She grabbed his shoulders. "Listen, you said something that, well, I wouldn't have thought of as the writer of this story."

"What was it?" He must've seen the worry in her eyes. He grabbed her hands in his. "Tell me."

"You basically admitted that you loved me so much that you were willing to let me go. So that I could be my best. And then I found Damien Lincoln's business card alongside the publishing internship brochure."

His hands slipped away, and face turned pale.

"It's true, isn't it? It's not some dialogue I made up in my head, subconsciously."

Elliott still didn't say a word.

"All this time, I wondered what I'd done. If I had misread your love for me. But Damien got to you, didn't he?"

"I knew you'd be better without me, and he was right."

"That wasn't your call to make. So what, he suggested an alternative for you, to get out of my way?"

"He got me the internship through his connections."

"He paid you off, and you didn't have the backbone to stand up for yourself. To stand up for us." The words flung out of her mouth. Even she knew they stung, hitting something deep inside Elliott she wasn't supposed to access.

"Miss Summers, you need to be at the desk now."

Lacy nodded to the headset guy. "I'm coming."

"So that's it?" Elliott threw his hands up in the air. "We're not going to discuss this further?"

"We need to do this broadcast so we can get back. That's my priority." She turned away, headed for the desk.

"Fine." He shouted behind her, then jogged after her, stopping her in her tracks.

"What?"

He ran his hand through his hair, only to be reminded he didn't have any. "At least tell me who the love interest is. Who's your character supposed to be with?" He scanned the bodies in the room, landing lastly on her co-anchor, seated at the news desk ready to go on air. "It's that guy, isn't it?"

"Ross? No. He's working his way through a divorce." She didn't want to look at Elliott. "It's you."

"Book Elliott?"

"No." She wanted to smack him. She'd just told him she hadn't written book Elliott in the story. "You. Lawrence. The weather guy. And we're near the end of the book."

"The end? I don't know what I'm doing. What happens if—"

"I don't know. But I have to go." She walked around the desk and sat in the anchor chair next to Ross, a coworker mic-ing her up. She lost track of Elliott walking off to his end of the set and focused on the teleprompter.

A woman by the camera gave her the countdown signal to go live.

Ross spoke first, and after the initial shock of being live on camera, she read her script.

The first half of the broadcast was a blur, time flying by, taking turns speaking with Ross. She never realized how little the anchors spoke, the news stories by other reporters and commercial breaks taking up the majority of time.

She was cued again.

"Here to tell us the good news about a warm-up is Lawrence Ray." She cringed at his last name. She thought it clever at the time of writing, being somewhat related to the weather.

The feed cut to Elliott. He stared at the camera, rooted to the spot, speechless. The assistant rolled his hand in the air.

Elliott shook off the jitters. "It is good news, La—um, news lady. That's what I like to do, deliver good news, even if the receiver doesn't see it as good news."

He looked in the direction of the news desk.

What was he doing?!

"Yeah, we're going to be warming up here in Boston." He waved his hand in front of the green screen, circling downtown.

The assistant by the camera had his fist in the air, wiggling his thumb. He mimed the words. "Click the button!"

Elliott froze for a second, then realized what he was supposed to do. He hit the button on the clicker in his hand, the green-screen image changing.

"Yep, looks like with this warm-up, a storm will be rolling in, dropping an inch of rain—" He turned to the camera. "That's a pretty good amount of rain."

The assistant looked at him like she was watching a train wreck. A completely appropriate reaction.

"But you know what?" He pointed to the camera. "That rain may seem bad when it's happening. But good things come after it. That's how we have flowers, folks. So we can forgive that rain, right?" He looked at the desk again. "Sometimes what may seem like bad things have to happen in order for the good things to happen."

Lacy shook her head and folded her arms, his drift more than caught. “Sometimes a bad thing just leaves destruction in its wake.”

She hadn’t realized her mic was still on. The camera crew, even Ross, stared at her in disbelief.

Elliott took a few steps closer to her side of the set, completely ignoring the weather camera. “Sometimes a bad thing will suck you into its vortex, so it doesn’t have to be by itself. But you know what? Sometimes that person still forgives that vortex for sucking him into it. So maybe the vortex should stop complaining.”

“Are we supposed to get a tornado here?” Ross asked.

Lacy shot up from her chair. “Well, maybe you should run off like you did last time!”

Her blood seethed, heavy breathing matching Elliott’s. He turned his head to the cameras, and Lacy snapped back to what they were supposed to be doing. The crew stared at them, slack jawed.

The signal was given for commercial break, and everyone breathed a sigh of relief.

Except Lacy and Elliott.

Lacy shook her head. “Way to mess up the climax of the story.”

“What the hell was that?” A red-faced round man in a suit waved his arms in the air. The producer, Jerry. No wonder Kimberly didn’t want him out for her. “If you can’t get your emotions in check, then I’ll find someone who can actually deliver the weather.”

“Fine, I quit!” Elliott said. “I don’t care.”

“What?”

“You heard me. I quit.”

The man ran off, yelling at other people standing around.

Elliott took a few breaths, calming down. “It’s what you want, right? Me to run off?” He wiped his jaw.

“No!” She took a breath, calming the temper. “I wanted you to talk to me, not make the decision for me. But none of that matters when we’re stuck here. You messed up the story. How are we ever going to get back on track?” Her mind whirred, stretching plot points out into different branches.

"With the story, or us?" he asked. She didn't have the conviction to answer. "Maybe if you had told me what was supposed to happen."

"Lawrence altered his weather report to tell Anna how he felt, and she ran over to him, and they kissed on air." Maybe they could try again on the next broadcast. That would mean staying here longer. But not doing it could mean staying indefinitely. And there was the fact that Elliott just quit, which didn't improve matters. "But obviously—"

His hand reached around her back, pulling her into him. Her chest hit his as his lips met hers. She closed her eyes, and a warmth rose up in her. This wasn't happening. Not with Elliott. Before she could stop, tell him that this was all wrong...

Blackness.

Chapter Twenty-Three

Elliott regained his senses. They had separated somewhere between there and here. He swore he hadn't let go, tasting her lips and feeling the warmth of her body against his. It almost wasn't real.

"Where are we?" Lacy leaned on the wall, catching her balance.

"It's my apartment." He shut the door, surprised Ripley hadn't run in and tackled him. "Ripley?" Poor thing. Her human had vanished before her eyes. He peeked into the bedroom and bathroom.

"Should've guessed this was your place." Lacy stepped further into the living space, scanning the framed Outpost 31 and *X-Files* 'The Truth is Out There' posters. Having her inside his place was a little embarrassing. But exponentially better than the man, no, young adult cave he shared with Gavin back in Allston. These were his treasures, the movies and books and trinkets of imagined worlds that defined him.

She pointed to the corner at *The Lord of the Rings* chess set. "Hmm."

Someone knocked on the door. A bark on the other side.

"Ripley." He opened the door and petted Ripley. Her tail wagged fervently.

"She knew you were back." Mrs. Winters smiled, then glanced at Lacy. "Oh, I didn't know you were entertaining a lady friend." She walked right over to Lacy in the living room and stuck out a hand. "Hi there, I'm Ruth Winters. Elliott's neighbor across the hall."

"Hi." Lacy shook her hand. "I'm Lacy. A...friend of Elliott's."

"Well, aren't you just lovely. A nice upgrade from the last girlfriend..."

"Thank you, Mrs. Winters!" Elliott moved his way over to the ladies. "For keeping Ripley while I was away."

"Oh, no problem. I came back from a little grocery shopping, and Ripley was just sitting there in the doorway. A sad sight..." She shook her head.

"I apologize. There was...an emergency...with..." God, he was bad at coming up with excuses.

"My car." Lacy stepped forward. "He came down to help jump-start my car. And then he advised that I run it for a while, and we ended up going for a drive." She eyed him.

"Yes." He nodded slowly. "I'd forgotten that I left the door open."

She pointed at the two of them. "Something is going on here."

He really didn't want to have to tell another person the truth. It was bad enough sharing it with Miles.

She smiled. "A real love connection."

"Okay, Mrs. Winters." Elliott put his arm on her shoulder, guiding her to the door. "Thanks again for taking care of Ripley."

"You know I'm happy to watch her."

"I know." He waved as she walked across the hall. "Good night." He shut the door. "Welp, you met my neighbor." He sat on the couch, Ripley jumping up and laying her head on his lap.

"Oh, that reminds me," Lacy said. "I keep forgetting about Miles. I wonder if he's still waiting for me." She felt the pockets of her jeans for her phone.

"It's at your apartment."

"Shoot."

He stood to grab his phone off the kitchen counter, Ripley annoyed at the brief departure until he returned to the sofa. "Looks like he called me...a bajillion times. In his defense, I did ask him to."

She ran her hands through her hair, bangs clumping together.

Remnants of that hair and makeup lady's doing. "Why do you think we arrived here?"

The same question had crossed his mind. "This is where it happened to me. After you had vanished hours before, so I'm guessing it's wherever one of us stood when it last happened." It begged another question nagging him earlier. "Any idea how I got to where you were in fake Boston well after you had crossed over?"

She shook her head.

It was a lie. He didn't know how he knew. "What was happening at the time? Do you think it was because you met me—book me, over there? That triggered me to travel there?"

She bit her lip.

It was plausible. If there was anything he learned from sci-fi stories, it was not to encounter yourself when time traveling. The ripple effects could be disastrous. But Lacy didn't meet herself, she met him. And it wasn't exactly time traveling.

"You know something."

Lacy looked down at her shoes.

"Look, I'm not particularly keen to keep doing this, and the more we know about how it happens or when or any answers really, the better we can control it, or stop it all together."

Lacy sighed. "I transported into the story, and once I got my bearings and figured out what had to be done..."

"What happened?"

She sighed. "I wished you were there with me."

He stared at her. The words were something he would've loved to have heard a few hours ago. Not that he wanted to be implanted into another romance novel. She wanted to be with him.

"Although in retrospect..."

And the stinger.

She'd wanted him in an alternate universe. And once he arrived, his confirmation about the break-up circumstances had pushed them into, dare he think it, enemy territory. But she hadn't run out of his apartment. Not yet.

"Would that work for anyone?" he asked. "Wishing they were there?"

Her right eyebrow furled down, as if he asked her how many arms she had. "I don't know."

"Can you wish us back here? Is that how we came back?" *No.* It wasn't. It was the kiss. But that was the last thing he wanted to talk about. She had said his character was supposed to kiss her, and they were arguing, and something just...took over, and he did it. Thinking about it made his heart pound harder, and he turned away from her, as if she could hear it pounding against his sternum.

She moaned, and he turned back around. She winced, hands at her temples, and she leaned up against the kitchen counter.

"Are you okay?"

"Yeah." She said it through a tight jaw.

He shook his head. "Obviously you're not okay." He drew closer, and she put up a hand.

"Are you injured? Hit your head?" He worried it was a side effect of their travels. "Do you think all this transporting has altered your body? Like the risk of mutations in *Timeline*." Or *The Fly*. Good God, hopefully she didn't mix with molecules from other organisms.

"What? No." She pressed the bridge of her nose with one hand, the other still on her temple. "It's a headache. I think it's more the stress of going back and forth than anything to do with mutations."

"Have you been in pain all this time?"

"No. It happened the first time I returned, and the second...I was able to sleep after. I think it goes away when I'm a character because they weren't written to have headaches."

"They were written to be bald, though." The joke failed to lighten the mood. "Sorry. What can I get you?"

"Any ibuprofen? Take off the edge until I get back to my place."

What if she transports again? But he didn't want her to worry on top of being in pain. "Upper cabinet behind you."

She rummaged through the cabinet while he made for the sink, getting her a glass of water.

"Always keep some in stock because of my knee. Sometimes I get pain just from being on my feet for a good while. Not all the time. But certain things exacerbate it."

She took down an ibuprofen. "Hence why you didn't rescue the kitten from the crawl space."

"That's right. Almost forgot about Wolverine."

She tipped her head to the side, eyes squinting. "Hmm."

"What?"

"It's just that, I didn't feel a headache when I stepped into a character, but you felt your knee pain?"

He shrugged. "Did you specify that Aaron the firefighter had knee pain?"

"Not that I know of. To be honest, he mostly served to be another body to make the company size more realistic."

Elliott thought it over. "If Aaron's a blur on the page, maybe my body filled in the blanks. Your heroines are fully specified; mine was a placeholder."

Lacy stared at him, the pleasantness in her eyes turning south. She placed the glass on the coffee table and stood. "I should probably head back to my place."

"Lacy, about what happened back there." They had to address it. Her wanting him there meant something. And what she found out about him, about Damien Lincoln. And the kiss.

"I think it's best we leave it."

He stepped closer. "I did a terrible job explaining myself, and the stuff with Damien."

She stopped him with a hand, shaking her head. "Both versions of you explained all I needed to hear." She started toward the door.

Elliott followed her. "There's more to it than you think."

She drew in all the air from the room, body tense, and pivoted around. "You know, I felt bad, dragging you into this. Risking your life as a firefighter when you didn't ask for it. But six years ago, I didn't ask for what you did. Yet you took it upon yourself to control my life. So I don't feel bad anymore."

"Okay. I'm sure I deserve some of that." He wanted to reach out to her, connect with her. "I said I was sorry."

"No." She wagged her finger. "You didn't own it. You defended the choice."

"You went on a book tour, hit the *New York Times* bestseller list. Heck, you ended up dating Damien—" He stopped himself. "You know what, if I said sorry, I take it back. And if I didn't, good." His ears flared red now, blood roiling.

She scoffed, crisscrossing her arms over her chest. "I think it's best I face things myself from now on." She turned to the door, pulling it open, Ripley racing after her.

"Lacy, wait." He stepped after her, tripping over Ripley, catching cloth, warmth of her back, and—

Chapter Twenty-Four

It took all of Lacy's energy to blink. Her head felt woozy, mixed with a euphoria, a pleasure she'd never felt before. As if the cells of her body shook with delight. A cold spread over her fingers, up her hand, through her arms. But her chest felt warm, something wet was coating her. She felt her neck, the wetness along her fingertips. Her eyes focused.

Red.

A figure behind them. A man on top of her. A shimmery man with dark hair, pale skin. *Elliott?*

"Wha—?" Red covered his mouth. His sharp fangs.

"AAAAHHHH!" Her scream echoed in the room. Her voice gurgled, choking on the liquid.

Elliott yelled back, staring at the horror of her in front of him. "Oh my God! Oh my God, I'm so sorry!" He held her neck with his long, gnarled fingers. "There's so much blood!" He closed his eyes, looking away from her. "I'm gonna pass out! I'm gonna—"

Buckled in the seat. Heavy headphones cupped over her ears. She wore a slinky emerald dress and a gray suit jacket over her shoulders.

The floor and seat vibrated, moving as one, wavering in the midnight sky. Below, the city lights dotted along the grid of roads and up the high rises.

A helicopter.

She flung her hands to her neck. Fully intact. No blood.

She looked to her left, at the pilot. Elliott.

He wore similar headphones, and a stark white shirt under a dark gray suit. Armani if she remembered correctly.

"What's happening?" Elliott's voice sounded through her headphones.

"I don't know." She looked down, then closed her eyes, not knowing which was least likely to make her sick.

"Isn't this just the scene from *Fifty Shades*?" he asked.

She turned his way. "You read *Fifty Shades*?"

"No." He shrugged, looking out his left side window, then back to the front. "I...may have seen parts of the movie, in the background at a party or something."

"Mmhmm." She smirked.

He hummed, the notes unrecognizable, until he broke out into full song, hitting the refrain of Ellie Goulding's "Love Me Like You Do."

"This is why I'm better off alone." She said it half-serious but broke into a chuckle, until a new thought occurred. "Wait a second. Do you know how to fly a helicopter?"

She looked at him, and he looked at her, his hands on the controls.

"AAAAHHHHHH!"

Walking in a stone tunnel. No, a hallway. Long dress, lavender color. She stopped the patter of her uncomfortable shoes, no support in them whatsoever. Her sleeves extended beyond her hands, the neckline cut low over obscenely supported breasts.

Someone was running her way. A man in tights, ruffled shirt, and a floppy hat with a feather. She laughed at the sight of him, covering her mouth. It was funny and it wasn't.

"What the hell?" Elliott grabbed her elbow and guided her to the side of the hallway. She avoided standing too close to the lit torch jutting out. "Why do we keep switching?"

"How am I supposed to know?" she said. "It doesn't know which story to put us in. Like the curse is confused somehow. Do you think it could be weakening?"

Elliott's gaze hung lower.

She put a hand on one hip. "What are you looking at?"

He shrugged, shaking his head, the feather in his hat billowing. "Nothing. Just...your boobs look nice in that."

"Are you for real right now?"

"I am wearing the tightest things I've ever had around my legs. Cut me some slack. Literally." He yanked on the tights near his crotch.

"There they are!" A man with a terrible Shakespearean accent appeared at the end of the hallway, several men with him armed with swords.

"I think they mean us." Lacy grabbed his hand and pulled him in a run.

"After them!"

She ran with him, crisscrossing other passageways and rooms.

"Here." She led Elliott to a side chamber, their backs pressed up against the wall. A small table sat underneath an arrow slit, a few wooden kegs stashed to the side of the room. Footsteps sounded closer, then faded. "I think we lost them."

A raucous sounded outside. Elliott shot to the opening, Lacy stepping behind him. He backed away.

"What is it?" she asked.

Something swooped outside, blocking the light coming through. Brown, scaly something. It flapped its wings, a loud whooping as it curved around the front of the castle, spiky tail in tow. It opened its giant jaw, spraying amber fire with its screech.

Elliott gasped, pure delight across his face. "Yeeeeeeeesssssssss!" He turned to her. "Can we stay in this one? Please."

On a sidewalk. Sunshine, blue skies. Green grass. In a neighborhood of ranch-style homes.

Elliott stood in front of her. Jeans, t-shirt. She wore a tank top with shorts, feet in flip-flops.

She took a second to catch her breath. They weren't being chased, weren't flying blind in the sky, and no loss of blood.

Elliott patted himself down, as if he'd find a weapon, or maybe he wanted to make sure all of him made it through the ordeal. "I think... are we normal?"

"Well, we're not back in Boston." She looked around at the homes, a Honda Civic parked in one driveway, Chrysler Pacifica in another. "But we're at least in our time period."

"Jesus, Lacy." He sighed. "Did you write all of those books?"

She winced. "Since my books weren't selling in the numbers they used to, I thought I'd try a different subgenre. I started with short stories in different ones to get the feel for them."

"Is this one?" He landed his hands on his hips.

"I'm not positive, but I think we're good?" She shrugged. Good was relative. They were still stuck in this glitching of stories but could've died in the previous ones.

"Should we...talk about the vampire—"

"We will never talk about it." She turned around and shielded her eyes from the sun, squinting down the road. No buildings she recognized. What the heck? What story was this? "Maybe we should follow the road, see what we find."

"Uh, Lacy?"

She turned back around.

Thick, green tentacles waved in the air in place of Elliott's arms. "Want to explain this one?"

"Oh, no." She bit her lip. "I may have taken a stab at writing alien romance."

"That's great." He nodded. "Just great. Um, question. Did you read any alien romances before writing this one?" One of his tentacles smacked his face, leaving a trail of slimy ooze. "Pretty sure they don't boink like this." His eyes grew big. "Tell me they don't boink like this."

"Stop saying boink." She pressed her fingers on her forehead. "This is embarrassing." She never intended for these stories to see the light of day. Especially not in person, living through it.

Elliott opened his mouth, his tongue unravelling like a turquoise Fruit By The Foot. "Fur yuh? Or embawathing fuh me?"

Chapter Twenty-Five

Lacy's shoes squished slightly in the thick dirt cratered with divots. No, boots. Thick rubber boots atop her gray overalls. Standing next to a rusty blue pickup truck.

The smell of manure and chicken coop and Texas air meant only one possibility existed for this story.

Range of Attraction.

It had been her last release before *Thirty Love*. Unlike alien romance, she indeed read many novels in the subgenre, even as a teenager, and gave writing a full novel a go.

"Cowboys?" Elliott examined his jeans and checkered shirt, then lifted the cowboy hat off his head, rifling his hand through his hair. "Are these human ones or alien ones? Wait, let me guess. Werewolves?"

She shrugged it off, eyeing the barn in front of them. The smallest sliver of sun hung over the horizon, setting the sky shades of orange into deep purple above. "It was always my weakness." She would normally be ashamed to admit that, but at this point, it didn't matter.

"I guess I'll take a cowboy hat over being bald."

Lacy shook her head, the braid down her back swishing between her shoulders. Stuck again with him. *He's stuck with you, Lacy.* Damn her conscience. At least he wasn't the hero this time.

A man rushed out of the barn in only his sleeveless undershirt and jeans, sweat rolling off his muscles. "Doc, hurry!"

There he is. Jasper Donovan.

He waved them over to the barn.

"Book or unfinished short story?" Elliott asked.

"Book. A published one." She gripped the leather handle of a bag in one hand and handed him a gallon jug from the other.

He let out an oof, gripping the jug. "I can't believe I'm going to say this but thank God. I don't think Miles and I got to this one."

"What do you mean?"

"We studied up a bit on your books at your place. What's the gist?" Elliott stared her down. "More specifically, my role in it?"

"Now!" Jasper shouted from the barn.

"Come on." She broke into a jog as much as she could in the clunky boots, ankles giving way to the thicker dirt until she reached the more trodden path leading inside the barn. The tallest portion of the taupe building lay in the middle, the roof on either side offset and sloping downward. She walked through the double doors and down the aisle, cattle relaxed in their stalls, lazily chewing or lying in the straw.

"That wasn't an answer." Elliott puffed behind, catching up to her as she stopped in front of a stall.

An enormous white cow lay on her side, bits of straw and dirt sticking to her hide. Jasper knelt towards the rear, an older gentleman resting his elbows over the partition from the next stall.

"Doctor Vic." The older guy tipped his hat to Lacy.

"Mr. Donovan." Lacy nodded at him. What a difference knowing the details of the story. Barely any brain fog, at least, not with the names.

"Please, it's Clay. I thought we were over that already."

"Force of habit." She turned to Clay's son on the ground. "Jasper, how long?"

"Going on an hour."

"Presenting?"

"Head, for a while."

Elliott stood behind her, whispering. "Are you speaking in code?"

"Just, shush." She knew what had to be done. A small part of her thought there was a chance it differed from the novel, but of course it didn't. She'd need all the clarity of mind she could get without Elliott's buzzing in her ear.

She opened her bag and retrieved gloves that went up most of her arms. "We're gonna need that."

Elliott read the label off the gallon of obstetrical lubricant. "You're not actually serious?" His eyes went wide, horrified.

"Come on now," Clay said. "This is what, your fifth, sixth calving on Donovan Ranch?"

Elliott cracked an awkward smile, giving a light giggle that mimicked the Joker. "Right. Just...doesn't get any easier."

Lacy took a peek behind the cow and nodded. "I need her up on her feet."

Jasper nodded, turning his stare to Elliott. "Travis, a hand?" He moved to the front of the cow near the head.

Elliott looked at Lacy, confused.

Lacy stood up to meet him. "Get on the other side of her, help her stand. Once she's up, stand behind me. You pull me back if I need help."

"How will I know—"

She put up a gloved hand. "You'll know."

Elliott reluctantly walked around the cow, to her back.

"On three," Jasper instructed Elliott. "One..."

Elliott's hands hovered inches away from the cow's body. He shook his head vigorously.

"Two..."

Elliott panicked, planting his hands on the animal. He closed his eyes, turning his head, the disgust as intense as if he tried to unclog a toilet by hand.

"Three."

Jasper helped guide the cow's head up, pressuring her to use her front limbs. Elliott pushed as though rolling a thick tire in mud.

"Underneath, Elliott—Travis." Lacy bit her lip, the slip seemingly unnoticed by the two cowboys.

Elliott shifted his hands lower, palms up. Lacy rushed to his side, doing the same, lifting with all her strength. The cow struggled for two attempts, then successfully moved her hind limbs, lifting her backside up until she was on all fours.

"Okay." Lacy examined the backside, the calf's muzzle and bridge of the nose sticking out.

"Oh my God." Elliott bent over, holding his mouth. "It's coming out the butt."

"It's not the butt." Lacy shook her head. Even though she knew what was supposed to be done, didn't mean she'd be successful.

Thank God she hadn't needed to follow through with the brain surgery. The chances she got that wrong on paper and in practice were much higher.

The cow mooed and moaned, the poor thing wanting this to be over with.

Lacy nodded to Jasper. "Stay up there in case she tries to move. I have to get the calf's head back in, then try to get its legs out." She pointed to the gallon jug.

Elliott handed it to her, taking off the cap.

Lacy poured a copious amount on her gloves.

"You're just lubing it up," Elliott said. "Like this is completely normal. You plan on slipping in there, pushing it out?"

Lacy lost track of her own research and what piece of Doctor Victoria's knowledge guided her actions. She wrapped her hands around the calf's head, carefully applying pressure, maneuvering it back into the uterus. She felt for the forelegs, hands entrenched inside the mother cow.

"Oh my God." Elliott stepped back, one hand on his hip, the other over his mouth. "That's—" He dry heaved.

"I feel one leg..." Her head was damn near up against the cow's rear, but she didn't care. She couldn't let these people down, couldn't see this calf or mother die, even if none of this was real. It felt real, and that's what mattered. "And two."

She pulled, her gloved hand slipping on the hooves. "Damnit." She repositioned, pulling on the forelegs with one hand, the other guiding the head. The tips of all three peered out.

She looked over at Elliott. "Travis, come here."

Elliott shook his head, waving her off.

"Come on! She's having a contraction!" Lacy pulled, her arms squeezing tighter between the calf and mom. "Help me!"

Elliott ran behind her, wrapped his arms around her waist, and tugged.

Lacy tried with all her might not to let go of the calf. Knees, head, ears cleared, then the shoulders, and she felt herself slipping back. Elliott kept locked around her, and she fell back on top of him, the slick, wet calf falling on them.

It writhed and rolled in the straw.

Lacy huffed, catching her breath, her smile hurting her cheeks. She giggled with delight, Jasper clutching the calf to clean her up. He nodded at Lacy in thanks, and she nodded back.

"Get...off..."

"Oh." Lacy rolled off Elliott, helping him up.

"Amazing, right?" She clapped his shoulders with her wet gloves. "You did great."

He wiped the mix of lube, blood, and amniotic fluid off his arms, the straw sticking to it. "No—" He gagged. "Problem." He gagged again, hands on his knees, nothing coming up.

"Sorry. I just—I can't believe it worked!" She slipped off the long gloves, Clay taking them and the jug for disposal. She tidied and closed her equipment bag.

Elliott's face looked green. "I'm not sure if amazing is the right word. In fact, I'm not sure if any human should do what you just did."

She moved closer to him. "Oh, come on," she said low. "You would've done the same if it were Ripley, right?"

"I would take Ripley to the vet," he whispered. "You're a writer."

Lacy brushed the dirt off her hands. She desperately needed to wash up but didn't care. She had performed something she had only dreamed of doing. "Today I was a vet."

Her smile was impossible to wipe away. She caught eyes with Jasper, who smiled back as he cleaned off the calf.

"And tomorrow?" Elliott asked.

Her feelings teetered between anger and guilt. On the one hand, she struggled with knowing she was responsible for bringing him here and everywhere else they'd gone the past…two days? But she couldn't just forgive him for how he'd walked away from their relationship. She had meant her words—that she would take on this curse alone. But the curse had other plans.

Now more than ever she felt like she was being shown something. That the stories she fell into, at the moments she fell into them, were deliberately selected. It was a matter of fitting the pieces together.

Elliott regained his stomach for the moment. "I'm guessing Jasper over there is the love interest?"

Jasper aided the calf to her mother, wiping her down with wet towels. He was handsome, as were all the love interests she had written. Remarkably, too-good-to-be-true handsome, with rusty brown hair, strong, stubble-covered jaw, and crystal blue eyes.

"That would be correct."

"I see. And what's the scenario in which this one ends?"

Her weak smile turned downward. She had been so caught up in helping the birth of the calf that the thought of the story's timeline hadn't crossed her mind. "Shit."

"Shit? What did you forget again, or—"

"No, I didn't forget." Her heart beat somewhere near her pancreas, deep down in her gut.

"What's the matter?" Elliott touched her elbow. "What is it?"

"It's too early."

"What does that mean?" He looked around the barn. "The birth was too early?"

"No." She slid her elbow out of his touch. "The story. We arrived too early."

Elliott licked his lip, taking in a breath. "How far in the story are we?"

She swiped her forehead, forgetting her yucky, clammy hands were wiping the sweat. "Closer to the beginning than the end." She looked at him, this time not teetering. Just feeling awful. "About a quarter of the way through."

Elliott took off his cowboy hat and rubbed his hand through his hair. Whether he knew it or not, it looked natural, like he had grown up on a ranch. "Okay. We can do this, right? We can work something out."

"Doc Vic?" Jasper interrupted her internal panic. "Should we make plans for following up?"

Lacy looked at Elliott, then Jasper. "Yeah, sure. Give me a second with old Travis here."

Jasper nodded and stepped back.

"What do we do now?" Elliott asked.

"I guess take it one day at a time."

"One day at—we're talking days, not hours? How many days?"

"I don't know!"

Jasper looked over, and Lacy smiled before turning her back to him.

"We've gotten lucky so far with when we've landed in the plotline. Minus the short story horror we lived through. But not so much with this novel."

Elliott closed his eyes, his head hanging low.

"Let's make it through this first night, okay? Maybe we can come up with a way to expedite this, and we can go home and move on." Well, *he* could move on. This curse seemed to be a never-ending plague in her life.

"Lacy—"

"It's Doctor Victoria Brooks."

Elliott pressed his lips tight, letting out a huff.

"And you are Travis...actually I'm not sure if I gave you a last name."

"Great." He scratched his neck. "So what do we do now?"

She slapped his shoulder, half in pity, half delighted. "You're the ranch hand, Travis. You stay here for the night."

"Ranch hand?"

"Shouldn't be anything worse than what we did tonight." She patted his shoulder.

"Where will you stay?"

"I have my own place. In the meantime, you should probably get some sleep. Ranch hands get up early."

She turned around, traipsing to Jasper.

Elliott hurried behind her. "Just how early are we talking?"

"I hope you like sunrises. It's the coolest time of the day, before the Texas heat gets ya." She couldn't help but smile, a small punishment for deciding her future years ago without her input. "Sweet dreams."

Chapter Twenty-Six

Elliott's sleeping quarters were about a step above a barn stall. The small building between the barn and main house at least had a bed that kept the mattress a foot off the dirt floor. There was no heat or air conditioning, but what he gathered about Romancelandia, Texas—eventually he'd figure out the actual town name—was that the summer nights were a cool welcome from the day's heat.

As Lacy had warned. Or teased.

She definitely got satisfaction out of his predicament. The last thing he had meant to do was argue with her. They needed to get past his actions six years ago. Maybe he'd been a little over-optimistic in reuniting with her, hoping something was there between them. Not being the odd guy around women was never his strong suit.

He wrapped the thin blanket tighter around his body. It wasn't so much the rooster making noise as it was the hens, a constant clucking as the slightest touch of daylight made an appearance.

The splash of water rang in his ears before his body registered the frigid temperature. He threw off the drenched blanket and flung up. "Jesus Christ!"

"Yeah, pray that I don't fire you." Clay Donovan stood in the doorway of the sparse room, empty bucket in hand. "You're already half an hour behind." He threw the cowboy hat at Elliott, who caught it on his stomach.

A stomach that was growling from emptiness. Apparently, a growl loud enough for the both of them to hear.

"Don't you even think about breakfast until you're done cleaning all the stalls."

Okay. That's...a wake-up.

Elliott put the hat on over his damp hair and stepped out of the room, Clay moving aside as he walked past. He considered running for it, not only to get out of chores and locate dry clothes, but to find Lacy. What then? What good would finding Lacy do if he messed up the plotline?

As much as he didn't want to, he made his way to the barn. The double doors were already open. Jasper busied himself with the mom and calf further down the right row of stalls, paying no attention to Elliott.

He spotted the shovel along with the stacks of straw in the end stall. He'd seen enough *Yellowstone* to have an idea of how to clean out the stalls—shovel out the old poop and straw, put in fresh straw. Probably wouldn't admit that to Lacy.

It sounded easy enough, at first welcoming the cool water that soaked through his clothes. But then the fabric rubbed his ribs and under his arms, leading him to take off his shirt. Sweat dripped from his forehead around his eyes, down his neck and back. Before long, he didn't know if the animals smelled worse or if he did.

By the time he finished and made his way to the house, it was close to ten. He knocked on the frame of the screen door, the solid front door open behind it. A woman in a floral dress beneath an apron stood ten feet behind the door, wiping her hands in a towel.

"Well, are you coming in or not?" she asked.

Elliott stepped inside. "Sorry, Mrs. Donovan." He took a guess at her name. On the Donovan Ranch, the odds were in his favor.

"Have you forgotten how this works?" She chuckled. "For heaven's sake, it's Lottie. And I don't give two hoots that you were born in Oklahoma. I already told you I consider you a Texan. No knock necessary."

He followed her to the kitchen, a square room offset from the living area with oak cabinets and grouted tile countertops. A window sat over the sink, overlooking the northern boundary of the property.

He sat in one of the six chairs at the table, where his fried eggs and toast grew colder and harder by the minute. He didn't care. Cover anything with enough strawberry preserves, and it didn't matter how hard the substrate.

An old radio sat on the kitchen counter, the antenna sticking sharply to the north. It played country music—of course—and almost as many commercials as it did music. It rotated through ads of car dealerships, some annual Wild West event, and a local retailer that sounded like a small-town version of Tractor Supply. At least now he knew the name of the town. Hadford. Whether it existed in the real world, to be determined.

It was sometime through the third airing of a commercial about the rodeo this weekend that Jasper made an appearance. He hung his hat on the back of a chair at the table.

"Hey, Mama." He kissed Lottie on the cheek and sat next to Elliott. "Sorry I didn't get any while it was hot. Wanted to keep an eye on mom and baby."

Jasper's five o'clock shadow from yesterday had more than developed into 10 AM next-day shadow. His eyes nearly shimmered blue, his upper body lean and muscular. Had to have been at least an inch, maybe two, taller than Elliott. Was this the ideal man in Lacy's eyes? Is that how she came up with her heroes? He could've sworn the hero in *Heartbeats of a Drum* wasn't so in-your-face handsome.

"So, Jasper." Couldn't hurt to get to know the hero. How else would he guide this romance to happen faster? "You were out there all night?"

Jasper nodded. "I know you didn't grow up like I did, working the ranch. But the longer you're here, the more you've invested your time and energy, the more you're willing to do to keep it together."

No doubt there were men like this in reality, men who still worked the land and raised cattle. Though it was hard to believe they shared Jasper's looks. Hard to believe any man would.

The whole ranching thing seemed archaic, an ancient custom compared to where the rest of the world got along in terms of technology and types of jobs. But there was something to be said for Elliott's muscles aching, feeling like he accomplished something before breakfast—late breakfast—while working his body at the same time. He could see how people would become entrenched in it, even addicted to the work.

Jasper eyed Elliott as he spread jam on his fresh toast, care of Lottie. "Heard you got a late start."

Elliott looked down at his plate. "Yeah, I guess last night's excitement took it out of me a little more than expected."

Jasper slapped his thick hand on Elliott's shoulder. "A nice woman can do that to folks."

The toast caught in his throat, Elliott coughing, eyes watering.

"Heavens, you all right?" Lottie asked.

Elliott gave a thumbs up, downing some juice and catching his breath. Of all the ways to die in Lacy's stories, toast. "Where is she from, that vet?" Jasper asked, unmoved by Elliott's inability to eat.

"Doctor Victoria?" Lottie asked, back to her dishwashing at the sink. "She's a new one. Replaced Doctor Rhone after he retired. Poor thing. Has to be hard filling his shoes, especially here. People don't like change, you know."

Jasper stared across the kitchen to somewhere far off. "Oh, I think she's doing just fine holding her own." He launched out of his chair, bringing his plate to the sink and gulping down the rest of his juice out of the glass. "Word will spread about what she did last night. That'll get everyone comfortable."

Heat rose up Elliott's neck. He needed to know, but didn't know how to ask. He came out with it. "She live in town?"

Jasper's head tilted to the side, and he leaned up against the kitchen counter. He lightly elbowed Lottie. "I think Travis here has a thing for Doc Vic."

"What? No." Elliott shook his head, buying time. How could he get information without sounding suspicious?

The rodeo commercial began on the radio again. An idea formed, and Elliot sat up straighter. "On the contrary. I thought I caught a little gleam in *your* eye, Jasper."

Jasper looked down at his feet, Lottie giving him a delightful glance.

"Maybe you should invite her to the rodeo tonight," Elliott said. "Being from out of town and all. I bet she's never seen a rodeo."

"That's a great idea." Lottie elbowed Jasper back.

Jasper rubbed the back of his neck. "I mean, I guess, since we're going anyway."

"Yeah—wait, what? We are?"

"What is with you lately, Travis? As if you'd miss it." Jasper shook his head. "Someone give this man some coffee already."

"I'm telling you. If he calls me Mrs. Donovan one more time." She turned around and winked.

"You know, maybe it would be good to invite her," Jasper said. "Help her feel comfortable here. Meet some more people in town."

Mmmhmm, that's why. Elliott kept his grin to himself. He may not know where she was staying, but at least he'd see her at the rodeo tonight. The more he knew the plot of this story, the more he could do to move it along. Not that he wanted to see Jasper fall in love with Lacy. But it wasn't Lacy he'd fall for, right? It was Doctor Victoria. That was different. That was someone who wasn't everything Lacy was.

Lottie dried her hands in a tea towel, then took a sticky note off the bulletin board on the wall by the fridge. "Here. Give her a call."

"I think her number is still in my phone." Jasper took his cell phone out of his back pocket.

Of course it's still in your phone. Because you were falling for her last night. And this is what happens in romance novels.

Lottie stood next to Elliott, staring down at him.

He eyed her, wondering what he could possibly be doing wrong now.

She held out a hand.

"Oh." He grabbed his plate and silverware, handing it to her. Apparently, the late breakfast was over. Which meant he most certainly had more chores to do. Gathering eggs? Mending the fence?

There were general life skills that passed down the generations and had made their way to him. Changing a tire? Check. Keeping a budget? Theoretically, check. Mending a fence? Not on his radar. Maybe if he kept himself looking busy with the things he did know how to do, he'd get away with being an idiot for a day.

As if she read his mind, Lottie took a paper out of her pocket and placed it on the table in front of him. "Don't even think about leaving for that rodeo until you finish with that list. I don't want to see Clay have to keep his word about letting you go if you neglect your obligations."

"You know the rule," Jasper said. "Shoveling before covering."

Elliott blocked out the nonsense Jasper spewed, eyes blurred with the length of the list, continuing to the other side. "Yes, Mrs.—Lottie."

He had to make it to the rodeo so he and Lacy could find the quickest way back home. If he didn't break his back first.

Chapter Twenty-Seven

The good news about being the new livestock veterinarian in the area was that few locals put their trust in Doctor Victoria. That meant Lacy, after having a good, solid night's sleep, arrived to no appointments in the office formerly occupied by her successor, Doctor Rhone.

The bad news was that she knew what was to come. She had spelled out a few ailments with various animals in the book and eventually would be stuck treating them. Sure, she had success last night helping the birth of the calf, but that was nothing short of miraculous. Like when a mom lifts a car to save her kid. Only Lacy's adrenaline feat had been persistent optimism.

She still felt a bit of a high from it, and combined with the restful night, her booted steps had a spring to them. Despite the day's rising heat, Lacy delighted in exploring the Texas town of Hadford. The town she created. She'd taken care to fully imagine modern shops with the feel of an old western town, as if Disney's Main Street turned cowboy, complete with a drugstore, two banks, coffee shop, and hardware store.

She could practically draw the map from memory.

It was disheartening to have arrived in Hadford so early in the story, yet a part of her delighted in it. The only way authors in the real world saw their imagined worlds translated was by way of theme parks. And how many of those existed? Besides, this wasn't a theme park. It was really real. Well, as real as the curse let it be.

She had reveled in breakfast pastries from Honey Bunches Bakery, ate the famous brisket sandwich from No Slim Pickin's for lunch, and went shopping in the afternoon for her written rodeo outfit—a red dress with a tiny floral pattern, hitting her knees, with a denim jacket and boots. Her chestnut hair had dried and curled itself into long waves right out of the shower.

Ah, the magic of books.

Jasper had left a voice message on her cell phone inviting her to the rodeo. She texted him back that she'd be in the stands and would see him afterward. Jasper often competed in team roping locally with his dad. What she didn't know was whether or not Elliott would be there. She suspected he would, considering he knew nothing about the story's plot or anyone in it, and probably wanted to find her to get out of here.

Was it cruel to have left him last night at the ranch? Maybe. But she couldn't stay there, and it would've looked wrong for him to go with her—to the townsfolk and for the plot. She couldn't jeopardize the story's romance between her character and Jasper if they wanted a chance to return home. Besides, thinking of Elliott still elevated her blood pressure. Space and time away from each other would only do some good.

She drove her rusty indigo blue Chevy Silverado south of town. It took some getting used to, making wide turns, clearing the side mirrors when she went through the drive-through for a tonic, or coke, as they called all fizzy drinks. The outdoor arena was a short drive down a state road—as in less than a mile. Had something to do with her placing it in that general direction on her map, one she sketched loosely in one of her writing notebooks and not filling in the gap between it and the town. She laughed as the land turned to general brown dirt for the drive, a filler connecting the developed parts of her setting. A reminder that none of this was indeed reality.

She parked and bought her ticket at the entrance. The crowd

cheered in waves, the announcer loud over the speakers. Bleachers framed the longer sides of the oval arena, the shorter ends housing the gates and chutes for the contestants and their animals. Lights shone brightly in the stands, aiming down at the performers.

She found an empty space halfway up the bleachers, the metal still warm from the lowering sun and even slower lowering heat. As it was her first rodeo in attendance, it was surprisingly entertaining, with hardly any breaks between events, and each fascinating to watch. The team roping event kicked off with a set of brothers. Once the steer was released, the duo took off on their horses after it. The first brother roped the steer around the neck, but the second brother fumbled, only roping one of the two hind legs. Apparently not the desired outcome. The next team awaited in the box for their turn.

A woman with big fluffy blonde hair, in which Lacy mistook for cotton candy at first, homed in on her. She held food containers in one hand, the other blocking the light over her brow while scanning the stands. She smiled, stepping over people on the bleachers until she reached Lacy.

"There you are."

Lacy smiled politely.

"I don't know how the hubs can eat these things." She put down the stacked paper containers holding corn dogs next to her on the bleacher. "You're the new vet in town, am I right? Doc Vic?"

"That's me."

The woman rubbed her hands together, redistributing grease that had soaked through the paper, and stuck out a hand. "Margie Atwater."

Lacy shook her hand, this time smiling genuinely. Margie had been written as a larger-than-life side character, and now being face-to-face with her, she beyond lived up to the characterization.

"How's business been? Congrats on the calf last night, by the way."

The announcer revealed the team's score, and stated Jasper and Clay were up next.

"Oh, thanks. It's a little slow, but I'm just starting out."

A heavy-set man two bleachers down turned slightly, just enough to catch a glimpse of them.

"You'll help Doc Vic out, right Mr. Baird? I heard one in your herd may have eaten some wire. You'll be sure to give her a call on Monday, won't you, dear?"

He tapped two fingers down on the front rim of his hat before turning around.

"We'll get you sorted out right away. Only takes one or two people on your team, and word spreads faster than pink eye."

"I appreciate that." *Just not too soon.* Best she got out of here before then.

"God knows these folks need the help. They're just too darn stubborn to check their egos at the door. Especially for a lady."

It had seemed like something a woman vet would go through in a tight-knit small town, but now that Lacy was living through it, were people really like that in the real world? Had society not gotten past that, regardless of where they were in the country? Was this why her books hadn't been doing well? Stereotypical characters, cliché plot devices.

The announcer pulled her attention to the event.

"Ladies and gentlemen, a big hand for Clay Donovan and his son Jasper Donovan."

Lacy clapped, sitting up taller to better view the far-left side of the arena. The steer released, and Jasper sped out of the box, ringing the rope around the head and one horn. He veered to the left, Clay going after the hind legs, roping them with what looked like no effort at all. Father and son took up the slack, facing each other, stopping the clock.

Margie jumped up, clapping and hollering. Lacy let out a supportive yell. Jasper found her in the stands, shooting her a grin.

"Flawless, those two." Margie sat back down. "Mm. That Clay Donovan is just as handsome as he was back in high school."

Lacy chuckled.

"Don't get me wrong. I love my husband, but that family has the good looks gene."

"They're pretty easy on the eyes," Lacy said.

"It looks like that Jasper may have his eyes on you." Margie's eyes turned sly. "I saw him giving you that Hollywood smile."

"Oh, I don't—"

Margie's elbow flapped against Lacy's arm. "Lookie here. He's making his way over."

Jasper walked behind the gated area and climbed the bleachers.

She leaned in. "I'll leave you two alone." She picked up her corn dogs and checked the stand. "Hey, Kenny!" She waved at a man in the distance and worked her way across the bleachers.

Jasper sat himself next to Lacy. He took off his hat and loosened his hair. "Glad you could make it."

"Yeah. Glad I had the chance to watch you and your dad in action. Impressive."

"Nah." He shrugged it off. "Been roping since I was a kid. Do something that long, it's second nature."

Lacy nodded. Perhaps it applied to her writing. It was so second nature that she hadn't reassessed whether she needed to change it up. Throw a wrench in her writing formula. There were certainly aspects to work on, especially after living through them.

If she ever made it back from this. And going home meant having Elliott by her side.

"Hey, how did Mom and calf do this afternoon?"

"Mom and baby are doing well."

"Did you leave Travis to watch over them tonight, or—"

"No, they'll be all right. Besides, Travis is in the chute. I think he pulled second or third in the order."

"What do you mean?" *In the chute*. The only people in the chute were those competing.

"Bull riding. It's his thing. He's trying to work his way up and out of here."

Lacy stood, the smell of popcorn and corn dog adding to the churning of her stomach.

"Where you going?"

"I'll be right back." She put out a hand to stop him from

following her, then fumbled over the crowd through the bleachers, making her way to the chutes. The journey took an impossibly long time.

She stood at the edge of the bleachers, overlooking the gate and chutes. A team of people hovered over a man in a cowboy hat and blue tartan Western shirt below, readying him for the event. He sat on a giant beast of a brown bull that grunted and huffed at its confinement in the chute.

"Elliott!" She said it through her teeth. She waved her arms in the air. "Travis!"

Elliott turned and saw her above him.

"What the hell are you doing?"

"Giving you what you want."

She shook her head in confusion.

"You're all mad at me. Figured you'd like to see me suffer. Earn your forgiveness."

"Get off that thing right now."

"I don't really have a choice here, do I? Trust me, I tried talking my way out of it. Jasper gave me this whole pep talk on how I shouldn't give up on my dream. My dream, apparently, is to die tonight."

"You can't do this. Just let go as soon as you're let out. Then run as fast as you can to the wall."

"Isn't letting go how these guys get hurt? Besides, is that what happens in the story?"

Shoot. "Fine," she said. "If we're going by the book, then you need to cover."

He looked at her blankly.

"Eight seconds. And then let go, got it?"

The team of rodeo staff surrounded Elliott, asking if he was ready.

"*Let's hear it for our next rider! Travis Mulder Scully Picard, the Third!*" The announcer went over Travis's stats, and the traits of the bull, named Mitch. A joke proceeded about its rhyming nickname.

There was nothing she could say to make the situation better.

"Waiting on the signal!" a staff person shouted.

Elliott turned back to Lacy. "What's the signal?"

"A nod."

"Wish me luck." He nodded.

"One hand up!"

He raised his hand in the air. The gate opened and Mitch flew out, bucking back and forth, front legs, hind legs.

Lacy couldn't watch, eyes closed, expecting the crowd's 'Ohh' in disappointment. But one second passed. Two seconds. Three seconds.

Someone tapped her shoulder, and she opened her eyes. Jasper pointed at Elliott.

Elliott sat on the bull, grip tight, free arm flailing about.

The noise of the crowd grew as the clock ticked off the seconds. The announcer grew louder and more enthusiastic with each second.

"Is he gonna do it?" she asked.

"That's eight!" Jasper yelled.

Lacy jumped up and cheered.

The crowd's applause deadened into confusion, then exploded in a cacophony of surprise.

"What's he doing?" Jasper looked at the clock, then back at Elliott.

The man kept his grip, as if letting go meant his certain demise. "He doesn't want to let go," Lacy said.

"You covered!" Jasper yelled out.

"Let go!" Lacy added.

Two men ran out into the arena, approaching the bull yet keeping their distance.

"Let go, Travis!" Jasper shook his head. "I've never seen him do this."

Me neither. A drastic understatement. But Lacy couldn't keep her eyes off him. "Elliott!"

Something in Elliott snapped, and his attention whipped to Lacy. As he turned, his grip loosened, and the bull bucked, flipping Elliott backwards, landing him face down in the dirt.

The two men corralled the bull back into the gate, out of the arena. Elliott lay on the ground, face down, not moving.

"Shit." Lacy jumped the rail, lowered into an empty chute, and climbed over the gate. She ran to the center of the arena and fell next to Elliott.

"Elliott."

He lifted his head, face full of dirt sticking to sweat. "Am I dead?"

"Not yet." Lacy sighed, helping him get up.

He put an arm over her shoulder, picking up his hat that had flung off easier than he had.

They limped across the arena as the crowd hollered and clapped. Two EMTs took him aside on the other side of the gate. One checked his pupils and had him follow a finger.

"Is he okay?" Lacy said.

"He's awake, standing, talking," Jasper said. "All good signs."

She nervously awaited until the EMTs said a few words to him, Elliott nodding in agreement. Her anxiety melted as he walked over, a faint smile on his face.

"That was the most idiotic thing I've ever seen anyone do," she said. "But I'm glad you're okay."

He gave a thumbs up, too weak to come up with a quip.

"God damn, Travis!" Jasper helped him up to the bleachers, then gave him a bear hug. "That was crazy. I mean, you won, but that was crazy."

Elliott nodded, eyes not half open. "What did I win?"

"I'll have Dad pick up your belt and check. But more importantly, drinks on me!"

Elliott raised his hand for Jasper to lead the way.

Jasper took over supporting Elliott. "What do you say?" Jasper eyed her. "Come with us for a drink? A bite to eat?"

"Are you sure that's wise?" she asked Elliott.

"They said nothing crazy. I don't think a drink would hurt."

A bar was the last place she wanted to be, but she needed to keep an eye on Elliott, just in case he was hurt worse than they thought. "Okay. I'll come."

Jasper exchanged words with his dad, then they carried on their journey to the parking lot. Elliott began to come back to life by the time they reached Jasper's truck.

"I'll meet you two there," Lacy said.

"Sure. Just follow us," Jasper said. "Oh, one question though."

"Yeah?"

"Who's Elliott?"

Lacy swallowed hard.

Chapter Twenty-Eight

It took some convincing at Grits & Grain, the local microbrewery, to get Jasper to drop the Elliott inquisition.

"Funny enough, Travis has a cousin back East—Elliott—that I knew, and it's almost creepy how similar they look," Lacy had said. "I accidentally got confused back there."

"You'd be amazed how often it happens at family reunions," Elliott had chimed in.

Luckily, after the first drinks were down, Jasper let it go and didn't seem to care about Travis at all.

The three of them sat at a high table, the crowd growing as the night sky darkened. Every now and then someone would come up to congratulate Jasper for the night's win, and upon Jasper pointing out Travis, they'd proceed to tell Elliott how his ride would live in infamy. With his increasingly reddened face, Elliott didn't care much to relive the experience.

Jasper placed his hand on Lacy's knee. "Another round of drinks?"

She put her hand on top, lacing her fingers between his. If they wanted to get home, they needed to move this along. Could she somehow expedite it, make it so that they didn't have to live through the entire three hundred pages? She looked directly at his eyes, trying her best to give a smoldering look.

"I don't know about you guys," Elliott spoke up. "But I'd really like to order food."

Her focus snapped back to Elliott, who patted his stomach.

"Yeah." She grabbed one of the menus laying on the table. "Should probably eat something before any more drinks." She looked at the menu, black scribble-scrabble inside. Lacy used the giant pages to block Jasper's view of her while she tried to get Elliott's attention.

Elliott eyed her over his menu.

She tipped her head towards the bar.

Leave us, she mouthed.

Elliott raised his menu again, and a waitress approached the table. "Are we wanting refills here?"

"Sure." Jasper set down his menu. "Another round, but we'd also like some food."

"No problem. What can I get ya?"

Lacy pulled out a detail she'd nearly forgotten. "Jasper, split some nachos with me?" Victoria and Jasper had shared nachos in the book, just in a later scene.

"Sure."

"Nachos sound good," Elliott said.

Lacy stared at him, biting her lip. He wasn't getting her drift, and she needed him to, fast.

"I guess nachos for the table." Jasper smiled at the waitress, handing her his menu. "And some wings."

"Not too spicy," Lacy added, gripping Jasper's hand a little tighter beneath the table.

Jasper nudged her arm. "I'll be back in a minute." He rose out of his high stool. "If she comes back, can you tell her to bring a glass of water, too?"

Lacy nodded, her fingers lingering on his fleeting hand until he slipped completely away, headed for the restroom.

She kicked Elliott's shin under the table.

"Hey!"

She leaned over the table, mouth clenched. "What are you doing?"

"I'm drinking, hopefully eating soon. I'm starving."

"You know what I mean."

He mirrored her, leaning in too. "Just what do you mean?"

"Whatever the gender-switched equivalent of a cockblocker is, you're being one."

"Oh, I'm sorry. I didn't realize I was being a twat-swatter."

Lacy shook her head. "Got the first part right."

Elliott scoffed.

She shut her mouth in a huff. She glanced at the hallway to the restrooms. No Jasper yet. "Look, I can't get him to fall in love with me if you keep interfering."

"Well, maybe I don't want him to." Elliott's chest heaved up and down with his heavy breathing.

"What do you have against Jasper? You didn't like Derrick the firefighter either. Is there any hero you can tolerate?"

"No. Because I don't want anyone else falling for you."

Lacy dropped back. Her words, her air, all knocked out.

He didn't know what he was saying. The beer got to him. Or the fall. Or the teleporting thing he said, with mutations.

"Elliott..." She shook her head. "I don't know..."

It went against everything that was supposed to happen. What needed to happen to get home. Jasper needed to love Doctor Vic. Yet her heart tripped up at Elliott's words. Her confused emotions whirled in a pain above her eyebrows and in her temples.

She got down from the stool. "I need some air."

"Lacy—"

"Please." She signed for him to stop. "Just tell Jasper something came up."

She pushed through the crowded bar, outside into the open air. Her instinct was to take the truck on a drive, but she'd had too much to drink for that. She walked along the main street, past the hardware store, a bank, Honey Bunches Bakery. She needed to get away from this place, from everything happening to her. It was a recurring nightmare, the same pattern but with new people in a new setting.

She slowed as she left the shops behind her, the town thinning out to streets of houses. She turned toward the water tower with *Welcome to Hadford* painted on it, and a monarch butterfly perched on a blue bonnet below the words. She'd never climbed a water tower before. It was something teenagers did in movies. But when else would she be walking the streets of a Texas town with nothing else to do?

She reached the base of the tower and climbed the ladder. *Don't look down. Not yet.* She sat on the walkway that wrapped around the lower bulbous part of the tower, legs dangling freely.

As much as she wanted to escape, this was a part of her. This town, these people, they originated with her. She made this happen. Whether she had hoped to live in a vet's shoes or wanted to give readers what she thought they wanted in a sexy doctor or military romance. They were all pieces of her.

The ladder clanged with the sound of boots hitting metal. There was nowhere to hide up here, and she didn't care. She wasn't moving for anyone.

"Not sure Jasper bought you were called in for a farm animal emergency."

She let out half a chuckle. "Definitely won't when he sees my truck's still in the parking lot."

Elliott sat next to her, hanging his legs over the side. "Do you know how hard it is to climb a ladder wearing one of these?" He took off his cowboy hat, the stray strands of hair happy to stand up again.

"Surprised you found me up here."

"Honestly, I came up here to try to find you down there. Couldn't let you roam around in the dark."

She sighed, slipping her hands under her legs, the metal cool on her palms.

"You know, if you're going to be stuck in a fictitious world for an unknown amount of time, there are worse places." He faced the night sky. "*It's wondrous, with treasures to satiate desires both subtle and gross; but it's not for the timid.*"

"Hmm. James Fenimore Cooper?"

"Q."

"Ah. That was my second guess."

He chuckled.

"I know now that I've missed the mark, in several ways, with my books lately. But if I got anything right in *Range of Attraction*, hopefully it's this." The lights of the town did little to mute the brilliant night sky, more stars than she'd ever seen blanketing the darkness. A tall butte sat to the north, modeled after the real Cerro Castellan. No other town could be seen, because she hadn't envisioned anything beyond, other than the Wild West town on the other side of the butte. "Somehow it's more amazing than what I envisioned."

"Maybe it's an amalgamation."

Lacy looked at Elliott, eyebrow furled.

"You know, a melding together of how you and your readers pictured it."

She looked out past the town. "Maybe." She closed her eyes, taking in the cooler breeze at this height. "Why didn't you tell me?" She turned back to him. "That Damien came to you about the internship? If I had known, I would've dropped him right then."

"I knew you'd figure out the kind of person he was eventually. You were always good at reading people."

"If that were true, I would've known you didn't love me like I thought you did."

Elliott shook his head. "That's the thing. I did love you, Lacy. I loved you so—" His voice choked up. "I came back for you."

"You what?"

He pressed his lips together, staring off at the stars for ages.

She gave him the time. They sure as heck had enough of it.

"A few days after I moved. I was miserable up there. I couldn't focus, didn't want to eat. Didn't even want to show up for work. I knew I had screwed up, and I got on a train back to Boston, showed up at your place and..." His face carried the weight of disappointment. "Damien pulled up, and you came out. He put his arm around you and kissed your cheek. And I knew. It wasn't just that he had played me. It's that I had let myself down."

"Just thinking about that creep makes me shiver. I wasn't with him that soon. It took weeks of charming and weaseling into my life for me to start dating him. It wouldn't surprise me at all if he saw you and played it up."

Elliott scoffed. "God, I was so stupid."

"I think when it comes to being duped by Damien Lincoln, we can both cut ourselves some slack there."

"Deal."

It felt good to lay it all out, but they still hadn't hit the core of her frustration with him. "Why didn't you call? We'd spent two years of our lives together, and it felt like I lost my best friend overnight."

"I am so sorry, Lacy. I'd like to blame it on work or you moving on with your life." He shrugged. "But you know me. I never stick my neck out if I can avoid conflict. I'm not the risk-taker. Hell, after all this time, I don't think I've changed one bit. I'd still be the guy waiting at the car on the roadside."

"Are you kidding me?" She spread her arms out in the air. "In the short time you've been back in my life, you fought a fire, broadcasted a weather report on live TV, and now you're a rancher in Hadford, Texas. You flippin' rode a bull, Elliott. Not a mechanical one. A live one. In front of an arena of spectators."

He laughed it off. "Well, I can't say I *chose* all of those things."

"But you did have a choice. And you did them, even though they made you uncomfortable. And I would be an idiot to not realize you did them for me." She looked down at her feet, the distance to the ground below dizzying. "I'm the one who should apologize. You were right. I'm the vortex that swept you up in my mess."

"Now you must be the one who's kidding." He grinned before working his way to stand, keeping hold of his hat. "Look at this. When else would I ever see something this amazing? It's yours. From you, Lacy. Take that in. I get to see a part of you that others could only imagine. That's pretty damn cool."

"Okay, Mr. Brightside. Or should I say, Mr. Mulder Scully Picard the Third?"

"Hey, you didn't give me a last name. Soo yes, I took the liberty."

She laughed. "Hadford will never forget that name."

"No," he laughed with her, "I don't think they will."

He held out a hand, and she accepted, the pulling helping her to her feet.

They stood facing each other, the night sky dark, carrying the traces of voices from below. A coyote howled, a reminder of the clichéd utopia they were living in.

"What are we gonna do, Elliott?" She was tired of it all. Tired of flirting, tired of playing someone else, tired of living through these scenarios.

He stuffed his hands into his tight denim pockets. "I think the first thing we do is get down from this tower."

"Okay. Then?"

"Then we walk back through town. Head back into Grits and Gravel—"

She chuckled. "Grits & Grain."

"Whatever it's called. I see now why it's hard to remember details."

"It's a lot. So we go back there..."

"Yes," he said. "And we see Jasper."

It's not what she wanted to hear, but the romance with Jasper needed to happen. Couldn't it wait until tomorrow? What was another day? But thinking about more time here, away from the book tour, away from Miles and her obligations. Elliott away from his new job. From Ripley.

Elliott grinned again, as if this were all a joke. "And then we lie through our teeth."

"Do you think he bought the whole Elliott's cousins with Travis bit?"

"I wouldn't."

They cleared the walkway and climbed down the ladder. Lacy's legs shook more than on the climb up. Elliott helped her with the landing, hands on her hips. He took a second to meet her eyes.

A memory flashed of him during the broadcast, reaching out to her, his lips, their bodies close...

"We'll get through this," he said. "Like how we get through writing."

She nodded, dissolving the thoughts that made her heart race. Her focus needed to be on Jasper.

She couldn't let the big picture overwhelm her, like writing an entire book in one sitting. That's not how books were made.

Elliott was right. They'd survive this the way they knew how. "One page at a time."

Chapter Twenty-Nine

The walk back to Grits & Grain Brewery lasted an eternity. Lacy tried coming up with excuses to tell Jasper for her abrupt departure and return, but it was too hard to focus. Elliott stayed as silent as she did, walking alongside her like they were marching in a somber funeral procession.

He stopped her in front of the entrance. "You got this. If anyone can finish a story, it's you."

She took in a deep breath and let it out. "One page."

"One page." He smiled.

She entered the bar, Elliott behind her. The music was louder than when she had left, seats filled, standing room at the bar nonexistent. She could walk right back out, put a pause on all of this. But nothing would have changed to get them closer to home.

She weaved through the tables, Jasper seated in the same spot, chatting with a crowd gathered round the table. He turned for a second and did a double take, eyes widening when recognizing her. "I thought you were—"

"Plans changed. Come with me." She didn't care to shout over the music to chat, especially not in front of these strangers. Lacy grabbed him by the arm, leading him away from the high-top table onto the small rectangle of a dance floor. A growing mass of people danced in sync to the country song.

"I have no idea how to do this." She'd reviewed the fundamentals of square dancing for the book, wanting to blend them into a modern dance. But she had interjected the bare minimum steps, and those had cleared out of her memory before the book hit shelves.

"I've got you." Jasper stood beside her, shimmying into order with the rest of the dancers.

She followed his lead, tapping a heel, kicking back a foot, rotating to face another way. As she relaxed, she started to enjoy it. The song hit its bridge, and the dancers changed up.

"What's going on?"

"Here." Jasper stood by her, his right hip to her left, arm behind her back. They joined hands across the front of their bodies and moved with the rhythm.

Lacy giggled, missing steps.

"It's all right. Just have fun with it."

She looked at Jasper, this man who couldn't have been drawn more physically attractive, letting loose on the dance floor, teaching her with patience while making mistakes himself, glowing amidst his friends and neighbors. He gave her hope that not every character she created was one-dimensional. That he had a layer or two of reality behind him.

The final twangs of the guitar rounded out the end of the song. The dancers stopped, clapping with delight.

"That was fun," Lacy said.

"Glad you enjoyed it." Jasper faced her, body inching closer. His eyes looked deeply into hers, hands reaching out to touch her. The next song started, a slower ballad. Some people went back to their tables while others joined the dance floor.

His hand slid around her waist. "Shall we?"

"Jasper, you owe me a dance." A petite woman with pretty hazel eyes nudged him, long curly hair flowing under a white cowgirl hat. She folded her arms.

"Rachel." Jasper looked achingly at Lacy. "I'm sorry. Lost a bet."

"No, you go ahead." Although they'd made minor progress, she couldn't deny the relief, even if short-lived.

Jasper tipped his hat to Rachel before holding her hand and swaying to the music.

Lacy shuffled through the dancers, heading back to the table. She rounded a couple and bumped into someone. "Sorry."

"I'm not." Elliott wrapped one hand behind her back, the other clasping to her hand. "Couldn't leave you hanging." He guided her towards the outer border of the dance crowd.

She fought the urge to stop him. Jasper was dancing with someone else. Why not dance with Elliott for a song? "You know, you're starting to pass as a cowboy."

He smiled, the reaction weakening her guard.

A sense of connection washed over her, an appreciation he was here. Not in having somebody to commiserate with. But having *him*, his humor and quirky perspective and unique charisma. There was comfort being in his arms.

"You didn't look so bad yourself, that last dance."

She shook her head, chuckling. "Watching me, now?"

"It's hard not to." He pulled her closer, his cheek almost touching hers. He smelled of leather and hay and hops. Things she wouldn't have assigned to a hero, wouldn't have known were intoxicating.

Her head told her to back away. Her heart...

"It's funny," she said, swallowing the emotions. "I invented that dance. Yet I was still bad at it."

"You're good at this one." His feet slowed past the rhythm of the song, her steps matching his lead.

She fought the urge to lay her head on his shoulder. But it was all she could think about.

She turned her attention away from Elliott, seeking Jasper through the dancers. He turned in time to catch her staring at him and flashed a smile. Rachel looked at Lacy, then at Jasper, jealousy in her eyes.

"She doesn't seem too happy." Elliott caught the exchange.

"Nope." Lacy chuckled.

He turned back to her. "You look happy."

Lacy's mouth opened, surprised. Whether it was the shock of his forwardness, or the fact that he identified her feelings before she did, she wasn't sure.

But she faced him, no more than a book's width away, his hand burning through her skin on her back. Her heart racing, blood thumping through her neck.

Feet still. Bodies still.

He leaned in slowly. He couldn't reach her fast enough.

He kissed her, soft and gentle.

Heartbreaking.

Warmth tingled through her body, her shoulders, chest, knees. He kept a hold of her lower back. She broke their intertwined hands, resting her hand on his chest, feeling his quickening pulse through her fingertips. He reached up for her, cradling the back of her head.

She ached for more, wanting to relish in the warmth forever, wanting to feel him closer, taste him, touch him.

A shadow arose from her left, and she broke their blissful kiss, stepping back from Elliott.

Just in time to see Jasper's swinging fist.

Chapter Thirty

I can't believe this is happening.

Elliott had thought it many times over the course of the last... twenty-four? Forty-eight hours? It didn't matter. He was here, in this fictitious world, but this was real.

This kiss.

Yes, it was their second kiss, but this one...she had kissed him back, melting into his hands, his touch. Her sweet lips tasted of heaven.

Until knuckles hit cheekbone.

Lacy uttered a scream, Jasper wedging between them, throwing Elliott another blow, this one in the stomach. Elliott doubled over, struggling for air. His stomach tensed and tightened, the wind not coming back into his lungs.

Lacy yelled something, the shorter girl Jasper had danced with saying something back to her.

He couldn't spare precious seconds trying to figure it out.

Jasper rushed at him, a tackle position Elliott didn't know how to avoid. The man's head dug into his torso, arms around his waist, carrying him off into the circle of bystanders who parted for them.

It happened in flashes. Elliott's back smacked the floor. Someone grabbed his hand, helping him up. Jasper came at him again.

But this time he tripped, landing on his hands and knees.

Lacy reached Elliott. "Are you okay?"

"I have no idea."

She looked back at Jasper, who got back up on his feet. "Let's get out of here."

Elliott nodded. Sounded like a wonderful idea.

"Victoria!" Jasper grabbed her elbow.

Lacy pivoted around. "What has gotten into you?"

"I saw him kiss you."

She looked at him with furious eyes. This was the hero of the story. Elliott could see Lacy's churning gears, the mental battle she carried.

"Go home, Jasper." She clung to Elliott's arm.

"You're not leaving with him, are you?"

She reached out, touching Jasper's heaving chest, stopping him from getting closer. "He's too stubborn to actually get medical attention. But as a vet, I can at least patch him up."

"I'm good," Elliott said, despite blood rolling down his face. Not that he wanted her to leave him. Definitely didn't want her to leave with Jasper.

Lacy leaned in close. "No, you're not."

Jasper rested his hands on his hips, anger still seething in his eyes. The shorter woman said something to him, and others in the crowd quieted him down, assimilating him back in their revelry of drinking and dancing.

"Come on." Lacy grabbed his wrist, pulling him towards the door, leading him outside.

The cool night air made him more aware of his injuries, the wetness of blood and sweat trickling over his skin. His body had been through the gamut today, and Jasper had capped it off with mind-numbing pain.

"Left my hat in there. It's bad luck."

"We're past that point."

He stumble-followed her to her truck, the rusty pickup parked between two decked-out trucks. Everything was bigger in Texas, even the fake one. "I think one of these is Optimus Prime." He held his stomach, the chuckling not so pleasant.

"Might want to lay off the jokes."

"Never."

Elliott shimmied between the two trucks to the passenger side. "Is it really that bad?" He bent down to check himself in the side mirror, but his back ached and abs hurt as if he'd slept on jagged rocks.

"Here, follow my finger." He did as he was told, apparently to her satisfaction. "Any nausea?"

"No." Only the shame of taking a beating.

Lacy walked around to the driver's side and got in. She popped the door handle and pushed the door open for him. "Get in."

"Yes, ma'am." He crawled up into the seat like a wounded soldier off the battlefield. His cheek stopped bleeding, a soreness pulsating through his face more so than blood seeping from it.

She drove through town to a small, gated two-story apartment complex. It looked more like a motel, a u-shape of rooms around a swimming pool. "Can you manage the stairs?"

He nodded. "Legs are fine. The one area he didn't go for." Once he said it, his right knee throbbed, not wanting to be left out of his woes.

They climbed the two flights, Elliott stopping at the top to catch his breath, a side muscle threatening to cramp. He made the rest of the journey to the third door down.

Lacy held the door open for him, revealing a one-bedroom apartment with wall-to-wall tile floor, minus the throw rug in the living room. There was an old TV stand with a small flatscreen set, a couch, and a few potted plants by the sliding doors overlooking a barbecue place next door. She ordered him to sit on the couch.

After the grueling labor of the morning, the pounding taken on the bull, and the brawl in the bar, the soft cushion of the couch was nirvana. "I'm afraid I might not get up from here." He closed his eyes, leaning his head back. He could easily fall asleep like this, even though he knew he'd pay for it in the morning if he didn't tend to his wounds.

"Here." Lacy had a bag of ice wrapped in a towel and planted it on his right knee. "I know you said they were fine, but your knees took a beating from that bull ride. Ice each one for a few minutes, especially your bad one. I'll be right back."

She disappeared into the bathroom, then came out with washcloths and a first aid kit. She surfed through the items in the kit. "Here we go. Don't ask me why these things show up in a kit, yet menus have no food items listed." She sighed. "I guess I'll take what I can get."

"Your menu didn't say anything?"

"Just black chicken scratch. Are you saying yours did?"

"I mean, I was genuinely hungry. Maybe my imagination made it happen?"

"Who knows. I feel like the longer I'm in this, the more confused I am with it all." She wiped his face with a wet cloth, then cleaned the cut on his cheek. The rubbing alcohol stung, but he winced away the pain. It wasn't lost on him that he was the one on Lacy's couch, not Jasper. He would take a hundred punches if it meant he could be with her.

"I'm sorry," he said.

"For what?"

"I know you didn't want me to get in the way of you and Jasper. For the story."

She shook her head. "It's not your fault. He was doing his thing, and I..." She bit her lip.

That kiss. The blissful magic he had felt before the hurt.

"I probably should've stopped him from dancing with Rachel. But I didn't."

Thank goodness she hadn't. He switched the ice pack to his left knee.

"You were amazing, by the way."

He raised an eyebrow. "Were you in the same bar as me or..."

She shook off the joke. "I guess what I mean is, you didn't act like him. Quick to throw punches. Enraged with testosterone."

"I have a feeling that's meant as a compliment. 'Cause, you know, I do have *some* testosterone."

"Oh, I'm aware. I think it took some of that and who knows what else to do what you did at the rodeo."

"Oh, that? Psht. All you gotta do is be terrified to let go."

She laughed, the kind that simultaneously tore his heart apart and delighted him. She took a deep breath and sighed, her hair falling forward on her face before she tucked it behind her ear. Did she have any clue how gorgeous she was?

"You did worry me, though, at the end."

The event played over in his head, bringing up the question that had been nagging him ever since. "Is that how the scene played out in the book?"

"You mean Travis riding the bull?"

"Yeah. Did he hold on for that long?"

She shook her head. "From what I remember, I focused on describing Jasper's event. I think I had mentioned it later, kind of in passing, that Travis added a medal to his wall. I'd forgotten Travis was into that until they announced you."

"Hm."

"What is it?"

He sat up and lifted his knee onto the couch, keeping his body turned toward her. "I know you've been trying to get to the part of each story where the hero and heroine realize they're in love."

She nodded. "That seems to be the part that sends us back."

"I can't help but think that no matter how much we do play the part, we end up changing the story, at least a little bit, right?"

She leaned to her left, elbow high on the back cushion of the couch. "I've thought about that, too."

"You have?"

"I mean, think about what happened last time. When I was the news anchor, I visited the real you, or...the real you in the world of the book. That never happened in the book."

"And this right now." He laid his hand on her knee. "I highly doubt Doc Vic took Travis the ranch hand-slash-bull-rider to her apartment. Where she wooed him."

She scoffed. "Oh, is that what this is?"

He shrugged playfully. "It's understandable. Travis is pretty irresistible."

She chuckled. "So what are you trying to say? That we can alter the story as we please? I know we want to speed things up, but what if the changes we make change the outcome of the story? It's something I worry about with practically every move."

"That's the part I don't know." He had thought about it even before this trip but didn't take the time to really process the what ifs. "Honestly, I was too worried during the last one to find out."

She lifted an eyebrow.

"You know, the weatherman, news reporter story? You told me my character was supposed to kiss you..."

"Oh." She tipped her head back. A sly smile still reading on her face. "That's why you kissed me then. Because it was in line with the story."

No, I kissed you because I couldn't stand not kissing you anymore. "It did send us back," he managed.

"It did." Her nodding ended slowly, her gaze shifting lower, to her hands, then the floor. "It's funny, though." She looked at him straight on, brown eyes piercing him. "I didn't say anything about Travis kissing Victoria, back at the bar."

The beating in his chest escalated, overpowering the soreness and aches of the day. He'd laid out his truth about the breakup on that water tower. She'd understood. And she forgave. Something he didn't know would be possible. Had only hoped. If there was any lesson in his past behavior, it was to not let this damn woman go ever again.

He put power behind his voice. "That's because it wasn't Travis kissing Doc."

She leaned in closer, the rising and falling of her chest quickening. "It wasn't?"

He shook his head slowly. "No." The restraint he held for her, her beautiful face in front of him, those soft lips so close to his. "Lacy..."

"Elliott." Her silky voice beckoned him. Dared him.

He couldn't hold back anymore. He didn't care about the bruises and aches. The grit and grime of the rodeo. The beer and sweat of the bar. He didn't want her flirting or wooing anyone else. Not Jasper, not the weatherman, not the firefighter. He wanted her to himself. Every piece of her.

He was the man sitting next to her, the one she took home with her tonight.

She chose him.

He kissed her, tasting her lips, her neck. Felt her smooth, warm skin. As he unbuttoned her dress, he looked into her eyes. He wanted her to know, to show her in every way he could, that he chose her right back.

Chapter Thirty-One

Elliott cracked an eye open, the other feeling quite comfortable being closed, buried in the pillow.

Lacy sat on the side of the bed. He admired the curves of her back, her hips, until she covered them with her dress. The memory of last night flooded through him. He had slept with Lacy Travers. And it wasn't some drunken, how-did-that-happen sex. It was tender, the kind he hadn't had since dating her the first time, and better than he'd ever remembered.

He wanted to wrap her in his arms, eat breakfast in bed, not care if they were stuck here forever.

Lacy turned for a peek at him. "Hey, sorry to wake you."

"It's okay." He reached out for her, but she stood as his fingers grazed her back.

"I've gotta get you back to the ranch."

He turned fully on his back before sitting himself up, leaning against the headrest. His ribs hurt like hell, his face feeling like it went through a washing machine with a brick. "You want me to go back there? After the way Jasper acted last night? After staying all night, here with you, with what happened..."

He tried to read her, but she closed her eyes, hands on hips. "I don't—" her palm embraced her forehead, as if the thought were hurtful. "I can't keep doing this, Elliott."

Did she mean living through the story? Or did she mean being here, the morning after their amazing night? Did the whole thing mean nothing to her?

She sat back down on the edge of the bed. "Over and over, the same thing. Flirting with the hero, playing into the part, letting him love me and express it."

Was that because she wanted to be with him? How else could he get through to her that he was here for her, to make sure she was okay, to help stop this thing that doesn't seem to want to end?

"So I have an idea." Her eyebrows perked up.

He shifted in the bed, sitting taller. "Okay."

"Thinking about last night..."

So...she did remember last night. Good.

"How we were saying we've changed parts of the story before. But still managed our way back to reality."

Not the train of thought he'd hoped for.

"I think we should try to push Rachel and Jasper together."

"The girl he danced with?"

She nodded. "She definitely had eyes for him last night."

"Okay." Sounded better than the alternative. "But what about getting back home?"

She held up her hands. "Hear me out. What if it isn't me he has to love—just that he has to love someone?"

"You mean, make Rachel the focus of the story? She's the heroine?"

"Yes! Exactly!" She stood, pacing the bedroom floor, an energy moving through her. "It happens all the time in romances. The hero thinks he's found the perfect woman. All the while, the real heroine is in the background, spending time with him, slowly building that connection until it hits him in the face—that he's in love with her."

"And not you."

She nodded. "Not Doctor Victoria." She beamed with delight at the idea.

The smile was impossible to hold back, Lacy's enthusiasm infectious. He'd be all for redirecting Jasper's affection to someone else, foregoing having to see Lacy on the receiving end, yet again.

"Okay." He swung his legs over the side of the bed, his body screaming with creaky aches and swollen bruises.

"You think it's a dumb idea."

"No, not that." He stood, grabbing his shirt and pulling it over his head. "It's just—what if the purpose of the curse is for your character to be the heroine? You've been the heroine in every one of these, right?"

She bit her lip, sitting back down on the bed in disappointment.

He wanted to point out the obvious. *He* could be the hero. Well, not him, really. Travis could be the happily-ever-after for Doc Vic. He'd played the hero before in the news station story, why not this one? But if the curse would accept Travis as the hero, wouldn't they have transported back last night?

"I have to try, in the hopes that I'm right."

He didn't want to completely demolish her idea. "All right." Now he was the one pacing the bedroom. "Let's say it'll work that way, Jasper falling for Rachel instead. How can the two of us being here help that along?"

"We go on a double date."

Maybe it wasn't such a bad idea. Although he couldn't see Jasper agreeing to that, considering Jasper couldn't stand to see Elliott with Lacy last night.

"Me and Jasper, you and Rachel," she said. "Let Jasper think he's going on a date with me, Rachel goes out with you. We'll get them talking. Jasper will see how Doc Vic is the wrong person for him."

Not the pairing he'd pictured. "How are we going to do that? Be mean to our dates?" Bar fights, cow births, bull riding—it sucked, but he did it because he was here with Lacy, and he'd do just about anything to keep it that way. *Just about*. "I'm not going to tank her night to make a point, even if she is a fictional character."

"We'll drive the conversation somehow. Just please, say you'll do it." Her pleading eyes softened. "I'm asking this time. Your decision, not the universe forcing you."

He appreciated the sentiment. But how could he turn down more time with her? "Okay. Double date."

"Good." She checked the time on the wall clock. "Shoot, if I don't get you back to the ranch soon you're going to be punished for it."

He looked out the window, the sliver of sun now a half circle. "I think we're past that point already."

"Come on." She grabbed the truck keys and waited for him at the front door of the apartment.

Her abruptness added to his barrage of bruises. He slipped on his pants and boots, then looked for his hat for a second until he remembered he'd left it at the bar. This wasn't how he'd imagined the morning going.

He followed Lacy down to the truck, Lacy's brisk footsteps treading on the awkward silence between them. The longer they ignored talking about last night, the more likely they'd never talk about it. It threatened to be something that happened in their past, like their first time dating. To have been reunited with her only for it to be taken away again...

He got in and buckled up, Lacy starting up the engine and flicking on the radio. It was set to the same station that had played inside Lottie Donovan's kitchen, running the same commercials about Wild West Fest and the feed store.

She pulled out of the apartment parking lot, driving onto the main road through Hadford, leaving Grits & Grain Brewery in the rearview mirror. It wasn't going to take but a few minutes to arrive at The Donovan Ranch. Now was Elliott's chance.

"About last night." He looked at her, wanting to make a connection. Her gaze remained laser-focused ahead on the road. "It's not something I had planned—not that I hadn't thought about it at all, because I have—not in a disrespectful way." *Doing great, Elliott.*

"Can we just focus on the plan for tonight, instead of complicating things?" She turned to him, briefly, gaze meeting his for a split second before they returned to the road.

He smiled weakly, hoping for a reassurance. A touch of her hand. But she wasn't giving it to him. It sent a tightness through his chest.

"Fine." He rested his elbow on the door, biting his thumb.

She pulled onto the dirt road leading up to the house on the ranch. She turned to him, opening her mouth, looking like she was about to explain herself. Say something that would mitigate the hurt Elliott felt, not related to his recovering face and body.

But Jasper came down the front porch stairs, approaching the truck.

Lacy locked eyes with Elliott for a second. Eyes full of pity or sorrow. Or was it remorse? "I'll take care of him."

Elliott exited the truck. He wanted to yell. Pull her aside, shake her out of this morning-after emotionless coma.

But he wasn't about to argue with her or with Jasper. He stuck by the barn door, close enough to hear how she'd take care of it.

"You're bringing him back here?" Jasper asked.

"I could've reported you to the police last night. You know that, right?"

Jasper nodded and wiped his nose with the back of his hand. He traced an arc in the dirt with the tip of his boot.

"I know I'm not from here," she said. "But where I'm from, if one person wants to get to know another person, they do stuff together. A movie. A meal. A drink." She shook her head. "Not a fight."

Jasper looked to the ground, cowboy hat blocking his face. "I'm sorry."

"What was that?" Lacy folded her arms.

Jasper looked up. "I apologize." He looked over at Elliott, who ducked back. "I saw the two of you kiss and lost it."

"We danced, Jasper. You know, like how you danced with Rachel? I didn't come in, busting her up in the middle of the song, did I?"

"No." His chest slumped. "What else do you want me to say?"

"I want you to make it up to me, Jasper." She rested her hands on her hips. The hips Elliott had admired from the comfort of the bed this morning.

"Tell me. I'll do whatever it takes."

Lacy turned away. Was that a smirk on her face? "Did you know Travis was interested in Rachel?"

Jasper shook his head. "I had no idea."

"Yeah, so, he was pretty bummed seeing you two dancing. I felt sorry for him, so I asked him to dance. He agreed, hoping to catch her attention, and I played along with it. It was just a small kiss. It didn't mean anything."

The words were lead in his stomach. Was she fooling Jasper, or fooling herself?

"If you want to make it up to me, and to Travis, then maybe you can make an arrangement for the two of them?" She looked over at the barn, then back to Jasper. "I think he deserves it, after your little brawl."

Little? The bruised ribs and black and blue cheek on Elliott's face begged to differ.

"No, you're right. I'll give her a call." He reached for Lacy's hand. "I want to make things right."

"Okay." She squeezed his hand. "It's set then. Dinner, tonight. Travis and Rachel. Me and you."

Jasper's lips curled into a smile. "Really?"

"Unless you want to disappoint me two evenings in a row."

"No, ma'am." He tapped the brim of his hat with a finger.

Lacy replied with a smile, then headed back to the truck. She took one last look over at Elliott before getting inside and driving off.

The last thing he wanted to do was go on a fake double date with Jasper and Rachel, especially if last night had meant nothing to Lacy.

Jasper looked his way, and Elliott turned into the barn. There wasn't a good place to hide to avoid the confrontation. He walked down the middle aisle, almost reaching the mama cow before Jasper stopped him.

"Travis."

Elliott turned around, staying in his spot.

Jasper tipped his head, beckoning him over.

Great. Elliott walked back, meeting him just inside the barn doors.

He readied to dodge, just in case Jasper hadn't gotten it all out of his system last night.

"Two things. First, sorry about last night. Things got a little out of hand."

More like out of fist. Elliott simply nodded.

"I know it hasn't been incredibly long, but you and I've got a history, and I don't want to ruin that."

"I appreciate that."

"Doctor Vic told me about your thing for Rachel. Come out with us tonight? Dinner on me."

What would happen if he said no? Elliott sighed. "You sure?"

Jasper chuckled. "I don't ask twice."

"Fair enough."

Jasper made for the corner of the barn.

"What was the second thing?" Elliott asked.

Jasper turned around and handed him his cowboy hat. "This'll be the only time I touch this thing. Don't want to be cursed."

"Wouldn't want that, for sure." *If he only knew*. Elliott placed it on his head. "Thanks."

Jasper grabbed the shovel leaning up against the wall, aiming the handle at Elliott. "Now get to it."

Elliott stood corrected. The double-date dinner tonight was the second to last thing he wanted to do.

Chapter Thirty-Two

Lacy had messed up.

The last thing she wanted was to complicate things with Elliott.

She hadn't planned on sleeping with him. She had brought him back to her place to fix him up. Lord knows he had it rough yesterday. But then he'd been charming and funny. He was in that tartan Western shirt, and his hair was a mess and God, kissing him melted her to mush.

She craved his mouth just thinking about him.

No! Stop it.

Things were weird now because she had thrown out all inhibitions. She could barely look him in the eye, embarrassed and awkward and sorry. He'd been her first true, deepest love, years ago. She thought she'd moved on, but that connection, the fire and heat between them, had only grown. But she had no idea what the newer, older Elliott was like, day-to-day, in the normal world. There had only been this chaotic one. How could that be the basis for rekindling a relationship?

Not to mention the plot of *Range of Attraction* was all out of whack. After last night, she didn't want to deal with building a fake relationship with Jasper. She came up with the best solution she could muster.

She suggested the double date occur at the Annual Wild West Fest, since that was at least featured in the story. The day had finally fallen into evening. She was thankful for it, given that she canceled the one appointment at the vet clinic and holed up in her apartment until the sun set. That part was not in the book either.

According to her world-building, the Annual Wild West Fest was in its sixty-fifth year of running. The town wanted a way to attract tourists and their dollars away from the big Texas cities. So they bought a strip of land on the other side of the butte and built the equivalent of a Hollywood set in the style of an old west town. The dirt road stretched by a haberdashery, saloon, jail, post office, bank, market. Open year-round, it provided locals steady employment, but once a year, the town put on its biggest display of cheesy rituals—swearing in of the new sheriff, bank robbery, high-noon duel, the evening cabaret.

She tried not to think of how unusual it was for most of the townsfolk of Hadford to have appropriate costumes for the occasion, especially Doctor Victoria. But there hung the dress in her apartment closet, a lilac number that scrunched in at the waist with too many buttons in the front, with gloves and hat to go with it.

It also wasn't the easiest getup to put on but describing that made for boring reading. Readers wanted to picture the dress in all its magic, not the insanely complicated operation of putting on the dress.

She was right in thinking that book magic would do its thing because when she stepped into the bathroom, her hair was pinned off the face, hat intact on the top of her head. The bunched undergarments and layers of dress straightened themselves out, the outfit fitting as neatly on her as the white gloves.

Her cell phone went off, a text message from Jasper that he was waiting outside. She threw the cell phone in her handbag, a little number that hung off her wrist, and she locked up behind her.

She greeted Jasper with a smile.

"Ma'am." He wore a charcoal gray frock coat, black vest, and silk puff tie over a white collared shirt. Quite the formal wear. He opened the passenger door for her as she got in. His cowboy hat sat on the console between the front seats.

Jasper came around to his side and got in. "You look great." She buckled up. "You gonna be hot in all that?"

"Not gonna be. Already am." He turned up the air conditioning, and they drove off out of town, heading north around the butte.

She took off the gloves, the heat hitting her hard.

"It's fun to dress up, but I don't know how people back then functioned."

She chuckled.

"There are plenty of tourists who don't dress up. It's just one of those things we locals like to do. Enhances the ambiance."

It sounded funny, coming from Jasper.

"I do think some people take it a little too seriously. Like they're channeling their ancestors or something."

"Oh? You wouldn't happen to be one of those people, would you?" She leaned over, glimpsing his black boots at the pedals, silver tips shiny.

"Now there's no harm in looking good. Except for the whole overheating issue."

"You really don't have to keep all of that on for my part." *Damnit.* Hopefully he didn't take it as innuendo. That was the last thing she intended. Sweat formed at her temples and under her arms. Maybe this was all a bad idea. Maybe she should just kiss Jasper now, see if he realizes his love for Victoria sooner than he did in the book. Then again, if that was all it took for her heroes to fall in love, she really did do her readers an injustice.

"I do want to apologize, again, for last night. I'm not usually like that." He pressed his lips together, looked out the driver's side window, then back at the road. "It was wrong of me, and I told Travis that, too. He said he had a little too much to drink, got a little reckless. It happens."

"That's what he said?"

"Yeah." Jasper turned the radio on, but the commercials made him turn the volume almost all the way down. "Are you saying that wasn't the case?"

Lacy shook her head. "That sounds about right." Was Elliott drunk last night? He hadn't slurred his words, and it was a downright miracle he could stand, let alone walk after the day he had. And do everything else he had done last night...

What is the matter with you, Lacy!

"You okay?" Jasper asked.

"Hmm?" She was gnawing on her thumbnail and put her hand down. "Just get a little nervous on dates."

He reached over and grabbed her hand, hopefully not sensing its scorching temperature.

Elliott couldn't have been drunk. He had spoken with her on the water tower, sober as anything. It was simply a lie he told Jasper to smooth things over and make tonight happen.

Why care anyway? If sleeping together wasn't a reflection of feelings for him, then it shouldn't matter.

They arrived at the *Welcome to Deadstone* gateway sign. The amalgamation of Tombstone and Deadwood she'd devised amused her enough to stop the swirling thoughts. Parking attendants guided traffic through the rows of vehicles, and Jasper slipped into the next available spot.

She stepped out of the truck, into the dry heat.

One page at a time. It was how she'd get out of here. And how she'd sort things out with Elliott.

In fitting with the theme, Jasper offered up his elbow, and Lacy held onto it as they walked through the old west town. There were enough people in costume to get a feel for the time period, and as Jasper had said, enough in modern clothing to scream tourist trap.

All Lacy wanted to do was get to Deadstone Saloon and have a bite to eat. She hadn't eaten most of the day, her stomach in knots over worrying about her plan. But as they neared the saloon, the first bit of excitement today struck her.

She'd get to see Elliott again.

She'd left him on a terrible note this morning. If she just had a chance to explain her behavior. That last night was good. Amazing, in fact. Overshadowed by the stress of being here.

The saloon sat halfway down the town strip. They stepped through the chest-level swinging doors, more there for the aesthetic than an actual entrance. A set of regular double doors were located a few feet beyond those, sealing in the climate control customers needed in the Texas heat.

Inside, the room overflowed with noise. A piano player pounded out lighthearted tunes. A group of rowdy tourists downed shots at the bar. Women dressed in low-cut dresses flirted and laughed with customers, giving them peeks of skin through slits at the leg, black gloves to their elbows.

Circular tables filled the room, waitstaff busily taking care of diners, weaving between tables. Thankfully Elliott and Rachel sat at a table furthest away from the bar, away from the early evening drunks. Elliott stood halfway up out of his chair, waving them over. He wore a brown waistcoat, the sleeves of his cream shirt rolled up his forearms, with dark trousers. He wasn't supposed to look that devastatingly sexy.

"We took the liberty of ordering appetizers for the table. Although I'm not sure potato skins were a thing back then." Elliott's hand slipped into Rachel's. "We also ordered a round of whiskey. Apparently, that's what they're known for, luckily for me." He briefly crossed glances with Lacy.

"Sounds good." Lacy eyed the physical contact before turning to the newly arrived waiter, who brought four glasses of whiskey, neat.

Lacy took a hefty gulp. Even though whiskey tended to warm her, the relaxing effect was well worth it.

Elliott whispered something to Rachel, who giggled with delight.

"You're so funny." She slapped him playfully on the arm.

Lacy glared at Elliott. Did he not remember the goal here?

"So, Rachel," Lacy said. "Are you from Hadford?"

"Lived here all my life. Jasper and I actually went to school together. Same graduating class."

"Is that right?" It came out sounding too eager. "I'm sure you've got stories about this one." Lacy wagged her thumb at Jasper.

"Nah. No crazy stories about me." Jasper waved down a waitress and asked for beer, his whiskey untouched.

"Actually, I wouldn't know if he had any," Rachel said. "I wasn't exactly in that friend circle, or much of any." She shrugged. "I wasn't high on party invite lists."

Lacy's shoulders dropped, feeling sorry for Rachel, despite her fictitious existence.

"They didn't know what they were missing." Elliott put his arm over her shoulder.

Lacy eyed him again. "And Travis? Seems like you two have gotten to know each other in a very short period of time."

Elliott put his free hand on his chest. "Me? I've had a crush on Rachel for a while now. I told you that, remember? Last night?"

Her heart sank.

This was no innocent Elliott attempt at flirting with Rachel. He was terrible at flirting. But he was trying. Hard.

This was a message. One that Lacy received loud and clear.

She had hurt him with how she handled things this morning. And yes, it was fine for him to be upset because she wasn't exactly a good person for how she handled it. But not only was he playing with another woman's feelings, he was sabotaging their plan to get back home.

She turned to Jasper. "Will you excuse me for a minute? I'm going to hit the restroom." She faced Elliott and Rachel, smiling. "May take a minute with all the costume pieces." She stared at Elliott, looking for signs he registered what she meant. When no such signs appeared, she kicked his shin.

He grunted. "Enough with the kicks," he let out through a clenched jaw.

"I'll be right back." She touched Jasper's shoulder before heading to the back of the saloon, around a wall to the restroom corridor. She waited in the short hallway for an eternity.

Finally, Elliott came around the corner. "This place is crazy—an alternate reality, in which the entire town is role playing a past reality. This is *Inception*-level bonkers."

She pushed him on the chest, surprising herself. She hadn't meant to make it physical. "What the heck are you doing?"

The joy wiped off his face. "Double dating, remember? That's what you wanted."

"Don't get smart with me. You know I meant for the two of them to be set up. She's obviously more interested in *you* than Jasper."

"Is that what you're angry about? Or are you jealous?"

"Are you kidding me right now?"

Elliott stepped closer, and Lacy backed away, the wall stopping her. He put a hand on the wall, leaning towards her, the hypnotic aroma of whiskey and spice and desire knee-weakening. It sent her straight back to tasting his lips, running her hand through his hair, touching his flesh. Her breath quickened.

"Look at me, Lacy. I can't keep—" He bit his bottom lip. "Tell me last night meant something. Because it meant something to me."

"Elliott." *Stop looking at me that way.* Her legs were about to give out along with her restraint.

"How is it that you can sleep with me, then—"

"What the hell!

"Oh shit." Elliott backed away from her in a hurry, Jasper stepping in between them.

Lacy put a hand on his back. "Jasper."

He wriggled off her touch, facing Elliott. "You slept with her?"

Elliott's hands hung in the air, up in defense. "I...can explain?"

Lacy held onto Jasper's arms, worried he'd deliver Elliott another blow.

"That's it. You, me. Outside." He stepped closer to Elliott, getting in his face. "The old-fashion way." He backed off and walked back into the heart of the saloon. "A duel!" Jasper shouted at the bar. The entire patronage repeated it after him, applauding and cheering.

"A duel?" Elliott shook his head. "Is this for real?"

Lacy closed her eyes. *Shoot.* "I did write one with Jasper in it. To be fair, it didn't have Travis. This is...off script."

"Aren't those reserved for like, cheating at cards, or stealing a man's horse?"

She shrugged, at a loss for what to do. How to solve this. "What do you want me to say?"

"How about everything you're not." Elliott stormed off. The crowd grabbed at him, pushing him towards the front of the saloon, out the door.

A man in costume shoved his pistol into Elliott's hand. Elliott examined the gun as if seeing one for the first time.

"They're not real!" Lacy's voice didn't carry over the crowd. She ran towards the doors, squishing between people, but couldn't reach Elliott before he slipped outside.

Rachel grabbed Lacy's hand. "What happened back there?"

Lacy shook her head. "Long story."

The two of them made it outside. Jasper stood off to the right, in the middle of the road. Another man checked his holster and firearm, theatrics for the crowd that grew by the second. People lined the porches up and down the faux-kerosene-lamped street, parents holding children up to see an old west's wildly, historically inaccurate—for the sake of the plot, she had justified—duel.

Another man helped Elliott in the same way to the left, Elliott keeping an eye on Jasper. The man whispered something to him, Elliott's face grimacing.

"This is crazy," Elliott said.

The man ignored him and put the gun in the newly appointed holster. He then turned to the crowd, raising his arms to hush them. The chatter and excitement died down, the only sound that of the wind and a held baby blowing raspberries.

Jasper wiggled his fingers near his gun.

Lacy half-expected Elliott to mirror him.

But he didn't. He stood there, staring at Lacy.

The kicked-up dirt settled to the ground. Someone whispered behind Lacy, asking what they were waiting for.

Elliott turned his focus to Jasper. He raised his hands in the air.

"What's he doing?" someone whispered.

Elliott lowered to the ground. Down on his knees.

"Oh no," Lacy said.

"What?" Rachel asked.

Lacy brushed her way through the tight crowd until she stood in front of the bystanders. *His poor knee.*

"Get up!" Jasper yelled.

"I'm not doing this," Elliott replied.

"Everyone is watching. Fight like a man. Defend yourself."

Elliott's gaze turned to Lacy. They locked eyes. He was breathing hard, no doubt in pain. In front of all these people.

"Get up," she said.

He was fixed on her. "No."

He pressed his lips together, letting out a wince. His focus veered back to Jasper. "I'm in love with her."

"What?" Jasper asked.

Lacy shook her head. She couldn't have heard it right, either.

"For real?" Jasper squinted in the sunlight.

"Yes. I've loved her for a long time." He turned to her. "I was an idiot back then. I didn't call you after seeing you with Damien because I thought I couldn't compete. I mean, who am I? I'm terrible at finishing just about anything, especially novels. My fear of losing my hair borders on unhealthy. I value my Montgomery Scott articulated action figure almost as much as my dog."

"Sounds to me like he's still an idiot," said a crowd member dressed for the gold rush.

"Shh." His bandit partner elbowed him.

"I'm not going to miss my chance again," Elliott continued. "I love you. The kind of love that makes me do things I never thought I'd do. I'd fight fires, report the weather in a hurricane, and ride ten bulls if it meant I could spend another day with you. In any reality. The kind that, no matter how much you try to shake me, I'm not letting go."

Tears welled in Lacy's eyes. What has she done? This wasn't supposed to happen. She should've never gotten him involved in this. He deserved better. So much better.

"Wait a second," the gold rusher said. "Isn't that Travis Mulder Scully Picard?"

"Yeah, you're right," the bandit said. "Saw him last night on that ride, and no, he won't let go."

Murmurs grew through the crowd, and within seconds a chant began.

"Don't let go! Don't let go!"

Rachel nudged Lacy. "What are you still doing here? Go get him."

Lacy's legs moved like a rusty machine, a zombie, the pressure of the crowd pushing her to Elliott, her eyes too watery to see clearly.

She stopped in front of him, Elliott still on his knees, looking right at her.

"You don't love me." She shook her head. "Not the me I am now. You can't love this."

He planted one foot in front of him, and she couldn't help but assist him off his other painful knee. "Tell me, how'd we come back from fake Boston? It wasn't because Lawrence loved Anna and kissed her. It was because I love you. No matter where we are, or where we go next."

It was everything she'd wanted to hear years ago. She fought for the right words. "Elliott—"

Elliott's glance shot to behind her, pulling her out of their confessional bubble.

Jasper approached, placing his gun in his holster. "I can respect that."

The shock on Elliott's face mimicked hers. "You can?"

Jasper took off his hat and looked at Lacy, eyes slightly squinting.

Elliott looked at Lacy. "He smizing at you right now?"

"I respect that." Jasper nodded. "Because that's how I feel about her, too."

"Excuse me?" Elliott squinted, perplexed. "You've known her two, three days?"

Jasper grabbed Lacy's hand. "Victoria..."

"You've got to be kidding me." Elliott threw his hands in the air.

"I know it doesn't make sense but love never does."

"What a line."

Lacy put up a hand to shush Elliott. That's why he'd said those things—to get Jasper to confess sooner. He couldn't brush off Rachel, so he executed the same plan they'd tried in the firefighter story.

"I have fallen for you, Doc Vic." Jasper reeled her in, lips moving to hers.

"Hey!" Elliott shoved him, and Lacy grabbed Elliott's wrist tightly.

It was all she could do before the twilight vanished.

Chapter Thirty-Three

Elliott stood in the doorway of his apartment, Lacy's hand still clasped to his wrist. She let go, as if she had touched lava.

Ripley's barking echoed faintly from behind the door across the hall. It was the only noise that broke through the gaping silence between them.

"Say something," Elliott said. "Tell me what you're thinking."

"I'm thinking, thank God we're back." She covered her mouth and chin. "Your ruse worked."

"Ruse?" It took him a second to understand. Was she implying he did all that, said those things, just to make Jasper jealous? "You can't be serious."

"I should go." She stepped for the door. "I'd better call Miles, after all his worrying—"

He stepped in front of her, blocking the doorway. "I meant what I said." His chest hurt, head pounding. "I love you."

"You can't." She shook her head. "You were mocking Jasper for knowing Vic for a few days, and you're doing the same with me."

"I've known you for more than two days, Lacy. We have history. And yeah, there was a time when our paths didn't cross. A long time. But the heart, the soul of it, is still there. Don't tell me you don't feel it."

She held her stomach, her voice weak. "The sooner I leave, the better."

"Please don't walk away from this. I was foolish to let you go once. I won't do it again."

"You deserve better, Elliott. To find someone worthy of your affection. Someone who won't drag you through this nightmare."

"So now you're making the decision for me? Like I did back then for you." He shrugged. "Is this some sort of punishment? Haven't we learned anything? That it was wrong then, just like it's wrong now."

"This is no way to live, let alone have a relationship. I can't do this to you."

He placed his hands firmly on his hips. "It's not entirely your fault I'm here."

She crinkled her eyebrows in confusion. "What are you saying?"

"The book signing. I was there to see you, despite being terrified."

"But, why?"

"Because after all this time...What I had told you that night on the water tower? I hoped, for years, for the chance to tell you. That's why I don't regret any of this."

He stepped toward her and wiped away the tear dripping down her cheek. "All it took was seeing you at that table." He nodded, holding back his own tears. "I'd never stopped loving you, Lacy."

The door behind him opened, Ripley bolting across the hallway, nearly tackling him.

"Hey, girl." He choked back the vulnerability, greeting Ripley with pets. "I'm back. I know." He knelt and closed his eyes, letting her give kisses on his face.

"Car trouble with that lady friend of yours again?" Mrs. Winters stood in the doorway, her black turtleneck unfortunately highlighting Ripley's shedding fur.

"Thanks for your help again." Elliott looked around the room. No Lacy. *Oh no.* Could she have transported again? So soon?

"Hope I didn't intrude," Mrs. Winters said. "I saw her headed to the stairs just as I was walking over."

Elliott ran to the doorway, past Mrs. Winters, down the hall to the stairs. But she was gone. Not to another novel. Not to a short story.

To anywhere other than here.

Chapter Thirty-Four

Lacy pushed the carriage down the aisle, eighties music droning on as she passed two thousand boxes of cereal.

It had been a week since she'd run out of Elliott's apartment. The same amount of time since she had last transported. She still felt skittish in every doorway, wondering if it was bound to happen again. But she was willing to go alone if it had. That was the only way to carry on existing. Alone.

So she continued with life. Sort of.

The first task was explaining to Miles what had happened, confirming what Elliott had told him. He hadn't been thrilled about the time he spent waiting for her in her apartment but had started his dive on the mysterious curse woman. He'd scoured the camera footage from the bookstore—he'd told Lacy not to ask about his connections—but she hadn't used a credit card. However, he got a plate read from the parking lot footage, only to find it didn't exist in the system.

"They said it wasn't a vanity plate but was too far down the line in its letters and numbers, like it was printed out of turn," he'd said. "But that's not the craziest part. It said two-hundred-seventy-five years of independence at the bottom."

He'd given up after that, too spooked, but did have to inform her two more venues had canceled book tour appearances. It was then she put the entire tour on hiatus. There was no telling if she'd transport again, and if she did miss a book signing, then she'd disappoint the few fans she had left. But that wasn't the only reason.

She had lost her way with her writing. Because she'd lost her way with her life. What she didn't know was which one affected the other more—her writing influencing her life, or life influencing her writing. In any case, she needed to stop using sales numbers as a gauge for her happiness.

But where to start? It was hard for her to plan for anything with the risk of vanishing. So for the first time in years, she didn't plan her next fifty steps. She simply stayed inside, mindlessly watched television, and ordered take out until she was sick of the same three places.

And now she went grocery shopping. An excuse to get out of the apartment. To have one small goal and achieve it.

It also helped her avoid the fact she hadn't contacted Elliott.

He had knocked on her door, two separate times. Pleading to talk. The second time he brought Ripley, and Lacy almost caved.

Then the calls, and the final text message.

Say the word, and I'll let go.

It made her physically ill, her stomach knotting and head aching. Why couldn't he see that with her, he was cursed for life. That no one would love the mess that was Lacy Travers.

She selected a box of cereal off the endcap, checking out the nutritional information, as if she would process it or care what it said. She swerved around the end of one aisle into the next. Her carriage bumped into another.

"Sorry," Lacy said, mindlessly.

"Are you?" The woman said it eerily, giving Lacy spooky flutters in her gut. Something with the disheveled gray hair, the draping clothes, looked familiar.

"Do I know you?" Her eyes clocked the cat pin above her chest. Her caffeineless fog dissipated, the realization horrifying. "It's you."

The woman tried to swerve her carriage away, but Lacy blocked it with her own.

"You're that woman from the bookstore. You did this to me, with your curse."

The woman turned around, leaving her carriage, and ran down the aisle.

"Hey!" Lacy chased after her, cereal box tucked in her arm like a football.

The woman bolted out of the store.

Lacy paused at the sliding double doors, closing her eyes stepping over the threshold. She opened them, still in this world. The woman ran across the parking lot, and Lacy took after her.

"Hey!" The security guard waved behind Lacy.

A car honked, the driver waving his hands at Lacy for trying to cross.

She held up her free hand. "Sorry." She continued to run, losing sight of the woman. She stopped running, spinning in one spot, scanning the lot.

There. Fumbling for her keys.

"Found you."

"Get back here with that!" The guard stopped short of a car, its screeching wheels coming to a halt.

Lacy made it to the woman before she could get in her vehicle, blocking the driver's side door. "Is it broken?"

The woman looked around, but no one was paying attention to them. Other than the guard running their way.

"Tell me." Lacy didn't know whether to scream or cry. "Every curse has a way to be broken." Elliott had told her so, and the very thought of him, for the millionth time, pained her heart.

The woman softened. "You started it. You can stop it."

"So it's not over?"

"You haven't gotten it yet, have you?" The woman slipped past Lacy, unlocking the car door. "You don't want this."

The security guard huffed, bent over, resting his hands on his legs.

"Ma'am. You need to come back inside with that." He grabbed Lacy's elbow, guiding away from the car.

"Wait." But the woman had already started her car and moved out of the space. "No, no!"

"Ma'am."

Lacy turned back to the security guard.

"Let's go back inside and sort that out."

"There's no sorting necessary. You can have your box of candied Wheatie-o's, whatever the hell this is." She wriggled her arm out of his reach and handed him the box. He kept a pace behind her as they approached the sliding doors.

The doors whooshed open, and Lacy stepped through.

Chapter Thirty-Five

"We want Gavin! We want Gavin!"

Lacy opened her eyes, a black stage before her, guitars and microphones in their positions waiting to be touched. She stood in the wing, forward enough to see part of the audience outside—women atop men's shoulders, clapping to the rhythm of the chant—but far back enough to not be seen by most of the crowd. She wore a black tee and jeans, her Converse sneakers sticking slightly to the perpetual thin layer of spilled drinks on the floor.

A bulky guy in a too-tight t-shirt approached her. "He's asking for you." She followed him without saying a word. It had been days since she'd transported to a story. Why now?

The curse lady. *She* made this happen, just like the rest. And this one, the location, the part of the story, this was deliberate. Lacy could sense it in her bones.

The bouncer led Lacy past a group of young men, arms crossed, staring her down without as much as a hello. She stopped at a dark room, the bouncer leaving and shutting the door behind her. It was small, no more than twelve feet by twelve feet. A table sat along the wall, water bottles, soda cans, bags of chips and pretzels, fruit tray. A man sat before her, head down, near jet-black hair parted along the side, the longer ends swooping down over one side of his face, a few strays at the crown refusing to lay down. His wrists were covered in wide bands, and he wore black pants and a black t-shirt.

"I can't go out there." His dark eyebrows brought out the green in his eyes. There was an ordinariness to him, nothing about one feature that struck her, but it made for an overall handsomeness. There was something about him that attracted her to him.

The door muffled the crowd's cheers, a chant that made sense now. They were waiting for him to come on stage. Those men were the rest of the band. And he was Gavin Torres, in *Heartbeats of a Drum*.

Her first published book. The one that started it all for her.

"Night after night. Playing the same damn songs. And what for? For people to sing along for two hours, clap their hands? We're not changing the world for the better. We're not even changing music."

The words echoed a discussion about writing she'd had long ago, when she'd doubted pursuing publication. When it seemed like everything worked against her, and she'd lost hope. A conversation she'd had with Elliott, at their go-to bar, Mac's Tavern. Funny how she hadn't realized she'd felt that lost hope recently, putting out book after book. Not connecting with fans. Heck, not connecting with it herself. Imposter syndrome, self-deprecation, yes. Wondering what it was all for...

"You do it to bring them joy. Even if it's for two hours out of their lives, they're allowed to forget everything else."

"When do I get to forget, huh? Is that what I'm supposed to do, forget about Reed?"

She covered her mouth. She'd forgotten the tragedy in this story. Gavin and his brother Reed were two of the five members in Black Onyx, and while on the biggest tour of their careers, their bus was in an accident involving a collapsed bridge. Four of them made it out. His brother didn't.

She shook her head and knelt before him, hands gentle on his knees. "You know what?" She shook her head. "You don't have to do this, Gavin. You never gave yourself time to grieve."

He brushed off her hands and stood, pacing the room. "I can't just leave all those fans out there and leave the guys to do this on their own."

"I'm sure the guys can handle it. We'll postpone. The fans know what happened."

"Nobody knows what happened!" He screamed it, letting out cries. Tears.

"Gavin." She wanted to hold him. She'd known him, some ten years ago, starting his story. And it felt like she knew him now. His hurt was so raw, it filled the room. She reached for his shoulders.

He swiped her hands away. "It was my fault he died."

"What?"

"We had a fight, earlier that day, and he wanted to talk it through." He said it through his sobs. "I wouldn't give him the time of day. I was too stubborn to listen. He went back to his bunk, and then it happened."

Shit. How could this have gone out of her memory? The back half of the bus was crushed on impact. The four survivors had been seated in the front half.

"If I had just—"

"Shh." She held his face until he gave in and buried it in her shoulder. "It wasn't your fault."

"Please, don't tell me that." He backed away.

She shook her head, half in agony for him and half frustrated. "I don't know what you want from me."

He grabbed her hands, holding them close to him. "I don't need words. I don't need pity. What I need, what I want, is you. Right here, in the room. Just be."

She bit her lip, squeezing his hands. It flooded back to her, the storyline, the heart she had thrown into it. It was the most quoted line from fans. *Just be.*

It struck her. His handsomeness in the ordinary, the something special. She had thought she modeled him after Gavin, the rocker roommate. But standing in front of her, behind the rockstar hair and clothes, the essence of this man was the one who had convinced her in real life to keep going with writing. The one who showed her how love truly felt.

And she understood.

The room faded away, Gavin dissipated into blurry pieces, and her stomach dropped until her feet landed.

Chapter Thirty-Six

Never had Lacy imagined that the end of the curse would place her in a jail cell. She'd been more focused on why it happened, what would end it. If it would ever end.

Two cops along with the security guard had been waiting at the storefront upon her return. They arrested her for shoplifting, trying to explain away her sudden vanishing and reappearance.

So now she sat on a bench in a cell with an older woman who smelled of booze in the corner, and another woman clinging to the vertical bars whispering gibberish. All Lacy had was time to think.

Living in *Heartbeats of a Drum*, even for just a snippet, had been enough to know what it meant. None of her books had been as successful as that first, because she'd forgotten what real love felt like.

She'd been in love with Elliott while writing it, and that love had poured into the pages. The break-up had left her feeling like she'd been wrong about love. He had left her in the dust, for his own gain—so she thought at the time. Since then, she'd been fantasizing about a hero swooping in; a firefighter to save her, a neurosurgeon willing to drop his dreams, a jealous cowboy with unwavering loyalty.

But really, it looked like a man pushing a pregnant cow up off the floor, despite his disgust over the blood and lube and bodily fluids. Swooping her up on the dance floor so she wouldn't be alone even though his body had been thrashed to high heaven. Keeping her company in the bathroom to make her feel safe and cooking her stir-fry while she slept, no matter the crazy story she had told him.

And what had she done? She'd been as bad as her created heroines who didn't risk anything, never gave of themselves. Women who never showed vulnerability. Perfection happened *to* them.

But *Heartbeats* was messy. Complicated. Raw, emotional, and real. Heroes couldn't be heroes all the time. And heroines didn't always know what to do, didn't have all the answers. Knowing they had each other, through thick and thin, that was the beauty of their relationship.

It was the beauty of her and Elliott. A messy past. A messy present.

When it came time to make her phone call, she didn't hesitate.

Chapter Thirty-Seven

"Here you go." James handed Elliott a beer. It felt chilly on his already cold fingers, sitting out on the back patio of the house on Templebrook Avenue.

"Just keep 'em coming." Elliott took a swig from the bottle.

"That bad?" James sat next to him. It had taken effort to come over, and Elliott was glad that Jules was out taking Sasha to gymnastics. He didn't have the fortitude to listen to her optimism. It had been tough enough to show up to class and lecture for an hour at a time. When he first returned to his ten o'clock class and the students inquired about the lady who had knocked on the door, he fought back the impulse to kick them out of class.

"I told her I loved her. In about every way a person could."

James winced. "Sorry, man."

Elliott picked at the label on the glass bottle. "You know, part of me thought I wasn't good enough for her. I kept dating these women who treated me like shit because I didn't deserve better. I never thought I deserved better than Lacy."

"It wasn't all bad, was it?"

It was awful and scary and dirty and painful. He couldn't explain what really happened to James. He wouldn't understand what it was like, let alone believe him. Punches, blood, birthing goo, rodeo dirt. Alien arms. He chuckled, shaking his head.

"There." His brother pointed, still holding a beer bottle. "That look."

"What look?"

"That one you made. Something you remembered. A good part."

It had all been good parts. Every damn minute.

A pounding on the gate. "Hello? Elliott?"

James looked back at the side gate. "Expecting someone?"

Elliott unlocked the gate. It took a second for him to place the thin face and dark hair, a suit less tidy than the last time he saw him. "Miles?"

"Who's this?" James asked.

Miles extended a hand for a shake. "Miles Astair."

"He's Lacy's publicist."

"You mean the one—"

"Not *that* one," Elliott said. "What are you doing here?"

Miles glanced at James, then back to Elliott. "Can we talk somewhere...more private?"

Elliott shook his head. "Just out with it." He really didn't have the patience anymore. "This is my brother, James. He can hear whatever it is."

Miles inhaled, lips pursed. "All right. I've posted bail for Lacy, and she's requested that you pick her up."

"What?"

"Whoa. Maybe you were right," James said. "She has changed."

Elliott shushed James, showing the palm of his hand. "What was she arrested for?" There had to have been some sort of mistake. Or maybe she had transported to a story, and something went wrong coming back, and she found herself in a jail cell.

Miles again glanced at James, who looked more like a bodyguard next to Miles's narrow frame. "Apparently, shoplifting at a grocery store. She carried a box of cereal out of the store without paying for it. Then fled the scene."

"That's ridiculous," Elliott said.

"That she did it, or was arrested for a stupid box of cereal?" James asked.

"What—but—" Too many questions, too many synapses firing at once. He closed his eyes for a second. "Okay. She was arrested and called you."

Miles nodded.

"If she wanted me there, why didn't she call me?"

"She said you wouldn't answer."

He stared at the sky, rocking his head back and forth. "That's probably true." All his attempts at communication had gone unanswered. There was only so much snubbing a man could take. "So why didn't *you* call me?"

"She said you wouldn't answer that, either."

He bit his bottom lip. Again, accurate.

"Anyway, are you really going to leave her waiting longer at the jailhouse? Not exactly the safest area."

"She's literally surrounded by police, is she not?" James shook his head, pointing his thumb at Miles as if saying, *This guy*.

Elliott did have a teeny tiny piece of him reveling in the situation. That maybe a little extra jail time wouldn't hurt, like she was in time out to think about what she'd done. But the overwhelming piece of him felt bad for her. And then felt bad he had felt an ounce of satisfaction at her expense.

Miles waited with his hands on his hips. "Oh, and another thing. She confronted the bookstore lady in the parking lot, before the arrest."

Elliott's eyes widened. "Bookstore lady. As in..."

Miles nodded.

As if the information Miles had found out about her wasn't scary enough, no doubt she sought out Lacy again.

Miles nodded to the gate. "I can drive."

Chapter Thirty-Eight

"Lacy Travers."

Lacy's stomach somersaulted at the sound of her name. This was it. Not only was she getting out, but it was her chance to fix things with Elliott.

Lacy exited the holding cell and followed the officer down the hallway. She received her belongings, which amounted to her purse she'd left in the grocery carriage, and walked toward the entrance. She'd gone through what she'd say to Elliott, mulling over whether to first thank him for coming to get her despite her behavior, or profusely apologizing for her behavior.

She ran her fingers through her knotted hair, cursing having left the apartment in a frumpy shirt and frumpier sweater. It didn't matter. Drapes would do if it meant Elliott gave her another shot to right her wrongs.

Her nervous optimism was shattered at the sight of Miles waiting on the steps, hands in the pockets of his slacks.

He forced a smile. "Do you think going public with this will hurt or help your career?"

Lacy broke down, whimpers and tears, snot and all.

"Oh, honey." Miles stretched his arms out.

She buried her face in his shoulder.

"I was just joking. Your career will be fine. You'll see."

"It's not that." The words muffled through the sobs.

Miles patted her back. "I know."

"He wants nothing to do with me."

"That's...that's probably not true."

She backed off of him, wiping her eyes and nose. "You saw him?"

"I went to his apartment first, like you said. Then the university, and finally his brother's place. I should start charging you for mileage."

His attempt at making her laugh meant well, but didn't work. "He wouldn't come. Did he say anything at all?"

Miles took in a deep breath, slipping his hands back in his pockets. "I'm paraphrasing here, but, after I told him where you were and the circumstances, and asked him to come, he said he wishes it didn't take you getting arrested, needing him for something, to contact him."

"He hates me." Her sobbing crescendoed again.

"I don't know about that." He patted her shoulder. "I took it as him caring so much about you, he doesn't just want to be your get-out-of-jail friend."

She sniffled. "Really?"

Miles shrugged. "Possibly."

She sighed, the relief of releasing her pent-up feelings washing over her. "I'm sorry. I don't mean to dump all of this on you." Her thoughts flashed to Elliott's office. "*I'm used to being dumped on...I don't have a fetish or anything.*" She chuckled. It broke into a giggle that broke into a full, hearty laugh. She couldn't stop, holding her stomach from the tightening.

"Are you okay?" Miles looked at her like she was every bit as crazy as she acted.

She shook her head. "No, I'm not." She wiped her tears, this time from the laughing.

"How about we get you home?"

"You've done enough, Miles. Thank you. For tracking down Elliott, bailing me out."

"What are publicists for?" He smirked. "What are you going to do?"

"In the long run? I don't know. For now?" She took in the buildings, traffic moving along the street, the noises of horns and squeaky brakes and pedestrians chatting. She was back home, in present-day Boston. Where she'd wanted to be. Sure, there were problems here, too. An impending judgment, a faulty career, a tattered relationship. But a plan started to form to address at least one problem. A crazy one, but maybe that was required given her new normal. "I think I'll walk."

Chapter Thirty-Nine

Elliott clicked to the next slide in his presentation. Judging by the couple of students staring out of the windows, he was losing their attention.

A student raised a hand, and Elliott pointed at him. "Go ahead."

"Are you saying that romance is not a component of fantasy?"

"I'm saying that it's not a requirement in the fantasy genre, no."

One student half-stood out of his seat, leaning toward the window.

"But so many have romance," the first student said. "*The Last Unicorn*, *A Wrinkle in Time*. Find an adult fantasy that doesn't at least have a romance subplot."

Elliott wagged a finger. "Ah, but were they crucial to the plot?"

"What would *Lord of the Rings* be without Aragorn and Arwen?"

Several more students stood, rushing to the windows.

"What's going on?" Elliott asked. A thumping echoed through the room. Rhythmic. Music. A screechy voice.

The rest of the class rushed to the windows, lifting the shades that had been lowered halfway.

Elliott stood on tiptoes, peeking glances at the square outside.

He knew that rhythm. The bass. That melody. The first lines of The Proclaimers' "I'm Gonna Be."

A terrible voice rang out with the original music beneath it.

"Isn't that the chick from before?" one student said.

"I think so!" shouted another.

They parted for him, Elliott nearing the window. He squinted at the bright outside. Two large speakers, their extension cords across the lawn, sat on either side of a woman holding a microphone. Singing.

Lacy.

"She's terrible."

Another student covered her ears. "Make her stop."

A crowd formed around Lacy, most getting out their phones, videoing her.

A student opened the window, the music ringing louder. "Campus security is coming."

Sure enough, two officers on bikes were pedaling over.

"Oh shit," Elliott said. The last thing Lacy needed was another encounter with law enforcement. "Wave her in!"

The students waved at her. Lacy waved back, throwing down the microphone upon seeing the officers coming her way, the music continuing. She ran to the building.

"She's coming!"

Elliott froze. What was she doing? What was *he* going to do? "Okay, class dismissed. All of you out."

"For real?"

"Want us to distract security?"

"Yes...In fact, no homework if you get them to back off."

The students filed out in excitement, shooting ideas off one another to accomplish the goal.

The singing continued, growing louder.

Elliott stepped to the door, Lacy appearing in the doorway.

She lay on the floor, splayed out.

Elliott stepped toward her, looking down. "What are you doing?"

"Sticking my neck out."

"Come on." Elliott reached out a hand. "That can't be very comfortable."

She shook her head. "Not until you promise to hear what I have to say."

Elliott nodded, and she accepted his hand. Her hair had returned to normal, no curls or blonde streaks visible. His breath caught at the sight of her The Four Eyes t-shirt, the same one he'd owned ages ago. The growing footsteps down the hall snapped him back, and he gestured for her to stand along the wall, away from the window in the door.

He watched a young woman walk by. "Just another student."

He turned to Lacy, her face flushed pink from her trip up the stairs.

She spoke over her quick breaths. "My stories—my idea of perfect love is a failure—no, that's not right. I swear I practiced this."

"What are you trying to say?" He grabbed her hands to calm her down. "Not from practice."

She gave a nod. "What I'm trying to say is, you're not those heroes I wrote. You're frustrating and really bad at being a firefighter, and you're grossed out by cows, and I would never trust your report of the weather, and I love every bit of you."

She walked back to the classroom door. "You've shown me, time and again, how you feel. Now I'm showing you."

"Lacy."

She opened the door. "Hold this."

He held the door open, and she stepped through the doorway. "I love you." She moved back and forth, in and out of the classroom and hallway. "I love you."

"Don't—no, come on."

She ran up the wide steps to the storage closet, pushing down on the handle. "Shoot, it's locked." She turned around, staring at his face staring up at her. "I had imagined there would be more doorways to do this with."

"Stop, Lacy." Elliott shook his head.

She slowly made her way back down the broad stairs, face turning redder by the step. She stopped at the last one.

"I'm glad I was cursed. It wasn't for those men to fall in love with me. It was to be reminded of what love really is. And in doing that, the curse is broken."

"How can you be sure?"

"Even if it isn't, I don't care. I found something more important to me than anything. And if I have to keep going into a story, fine. As long as I can come back here, to you. I—"

"Would you just shut up for a second?"

The breath fell out of her. "What?" Her eyes were set on him, mouth agape.

He walked over to her, her height only slightly higher than his. "You're a mess."

She nodded, her gaze turning to her feet. "I know."

He touched her cheek, her gaze piercing his. "And I love you for it." He grinned and all doubt, all worries about the past, the curse, the future, melted away.

He caressed her face and pulled her close.

Her eyes welled with tears as he kissed her.

The closing of his eyes was the only reason the world went dark.

Epilogue

And so it was, three months later, after sorting through their stuff, donating and selling off duplicates of silverware and glasses, buying new bedsheets and bath towels, they moved in together.

Lacy parked Brego—coined by Elliott after sadly parting with Artax—in a spot two blocks from the apartment building. She carried a suitcase full of clothes, the rest in garment boxes with the movers.

Miles stood at the front steps of the building, a five-story complex one block away from Back Bay Fens, arms crossed around a stack of papers.

"I think helping your client move is a whole new level of assistance," Lacy said.

"I knew you'd be here, as per your shared schedule." He handed her the stack of papers as she settled the rollaway bag next to her.

She leafed through the first pages, red pen scribbles in the margins. "Are you telling me you not only printed and read my manuscript, but you have comments?"

"A suggestion here and there. But mostly I highlighted parts that made me laugh, and parts that...you know."

"That what?" She pretended confusion, wanting him to say it.

A shoulder lifted, his eyes to the sky. "Made me...feel feelings."

"Did you cry, Miles?"

"Just go on, before I take the pages back."

She walked up the stairs, holding her key fob at the scanner to open the front door. She looked back at Miles, then the luggage. "You mind?"

He scoffed, then picked up the suitcase.

She held the door for him. "Top floor."

"You're kidding."

"Nope. But..." She stopped, pressing the button for the elevator.

"Oh, thank God."

They rose to the fifth floor and walked two doors down to her new place. The door was already open.

Elliott peeled off the layers of packing paper from his Montgomery Scott figurine—Lacy had learned to recognize most of them—placing it on the kitchen counter for the time being. Lacy wrapped an arm behind his back, and he turned, showering her with kisses until she stopped him.

He looked in her eyes, and she directed him toward Miles. "Oh." He parted from her. "Hey, Miles."

"Elliott. I didn't realize you two rented out a studio apartment."

Lacy smiled at Elliott, then turned back to Miles. "Open concept. Fewer doors."

Miles shook his head. "Well, despite your aversion to doors, I'm happy to see you two like this. Anything that helps with Lacy's career, I'm in."

"You mean with *our* careers." Lacy covered her heart. "And you're such a supportive friend."

"I'm gonna go, before one of you does vanish in front of me. If you only knew the constant fear of losing your top clients."

"How do you think we feel?" Lacy joked, grabbing a hold of Elliott again, him wrapping his arms around her.

"Ugh. Let me know what they say about a release date once you have one."

"Of course," Lacy said.

Miles walked out without another glance, leaving a silence that settled between them.

Elliott leaned in, kissed her forehead, then pulled away.

"Didn't trust the movers with those?" She pointed to the unpacked figurines, Captain Kirk standing pristine in his box next to Scotty.

"Two things I wouldn't trust anyone else to take care of. You, and these guys."

"What about Ripley?"

At the sound of her name, she looked up from her lazed-about spot on the floor, already claiming a nook.

"And Ripley. Of course. Although"—he held up a finger in the air — "I can't believe none of the main characters in the stories we were transported to have a dog."

"An egregious error on my part." She walked over to Ripley, crouching down and petting her. "That's why our new one has a heroic, loyal, loving pooch, inspired by the best. That's right."

Elliott checked the time on his phone. "Should we grab some lunch before my afternoon lecture?"

"Sure." She grabbed Ripley's leash and attached it to her collar. "You pick."

"I was thinking lasagna?"

"Ooh. I haven't had that since the fire station."

"Been craving it, with a little kick to the sauce." He closed his eyes, savoring the memory. "You sure you don't know how to make it?"

"Sorry. That was Rory's department."

Elliott grabbed the keys, and Lacy waited for him with Ripley in the hallway.

"You know, I try not to dwell too much on those events."

"I know." He locked up, and they walked to the elevator.

"It could've been worse, getting stuck in my historical romance, for instance."

"Yeah, I'm not sure how I'd manage in the eighteen hundreds."

She chuckled. "It's almost a shame I hadn't written other stories. All this time I could've been in a Why Choose."

Elliott chuckled. "Yeah."

The elevator doors opened, and Lacy led Ripley in, Elliott following.

"Wait, what exactly is a Why Choose?" Elliott asked as the doors closed.

Lacy giggled. "Maybe next time."

Almost a year and a half had passed since Lacy's last foray into signing books. But this time, she hadn't much time to take in the *Valentine's is for Books* sign or the red glittery hearts adorning the front windows, with Elliott at her side in Books & Bean.

The long line kept her busy, which also meant *Quantum Love* resonated with people. Who wouldn't love a story about romance, teleportation, and the most patient, loyal dog a couple could have?

Elliott handed her the open book, his signature on the title page. He had a few sayings he rotated through, like *Follow your heart*, or if it was an aspiring writer, *One page at a time!* This one read *When you find her, never let go*.

She smiled at Elliott, who chatted with the next fan, a mom holding a toddler at her hip.

"I told him how Lance and Zoey's story has given me hope." The young man in front of Lacy wore a black t-shirt with *Trekkie* in white letters.

"I'm glad to hear that." She signed her name under Elliott's and handed it to the fan. "You never know what can happen. Thanks so much for coming out today."

"Hey guys!" Sasha waved, James and Jules standing behind her.

"You know you could've skipped the line," Elliott said.

"That's okay," Jules said. "We've had a blast meeting people in line, haven't we, Sheryl?" She looked at the woman waiting behind her, who gave a brief smile.

Elliott and Lacy signed the book, and Sasha cherished it in her hands. "I can't believe my uncle is an author."

"Make that two of us," Elliott said. "Though I wasn't warned about the hand cramps." Elliott shook out his hand.

"Didn't think you'd have a problem with that grip of yours, Mr. Mulder Scully Picard." Lacy nudged him.

He chuckled, then leaned to her ear. "I want to kiss you right now."

Nearly a year and half with Elliott, and he still gave her goosebumps.

A figure cast a shadow over them, a woman, standing at the table, the line flanking behind her. A few wisps of hair fell loosely from her otherwise neat bun, matching her gray sweater, a colorful pin of a bluebonnet attached near the chest.

"I love your pin," Lacy said.

"Thank you," the woman said. "My husband got it for me for our twentieth anniversary. Reminds us of a special place."

Lacy turned to Elliott. "Maybe I should start wearing pins, what do you think?" He reached for a fresh copy off the stack.

"That won't be necessary." The woman pulled out her own copy and placed it on the table, the silhouette of Zoey holding hands with Lance in a doorway full of stars on the cover. A gorgeous sapphire ring adorned the woman's hand with a matching wedding band.

Without a word, Lacy opened it to the title page. She signed her name below it, then handed it to Elliott, who stared slack-jawed.

"What is it?" Lacy whispered.

His eyes fixated on the ring, his hand moving to his pants' pocket. He shook his head. "Um, nothing."

Elliott signed the book and handed it back to the woman. He wrapped his arm under Lacy's, reaching for her hand. He stared at the woman.

"Congratulations," she said.

"Oh, thank you," Lacy said. "We're really happy with how the book turned out."

She leaned over the table, lowering her voice to a whisper. "I meant breaking it." The woman winked and turned around, disappearing into the line of fans.

Lacy squeezed Elliott's hand tight.

He met her grin with his own, laughter spilling between them.

It was one of countless moments they'd share that afternoon, that year, and in all the years waiting ahead.

Thank you for reading! Did you enjoy? Please add your review because nothing helps an author more and encourages readers to take a chance on a book than a review.

And don't miss more from Mary Shotwell with the *Waverly Lake* series, starting with WAVERLY LAKE, available now. Turn the page for a sneak peek!

Also be sure to sign up for the City Owl Press newsletter to receive notice of all book releases!

Sneak Peek of Waverly Lake

FRIDAY, JULY 24

Somewhere among the bustle of the morning pedestrians lining the sidewalks of Manhattan, Kara Carter strolled with a bounce in her step. Her energy could be blamed on the high-octane caffeinated coffee she guarded with her bony elbows, or the three packets of sugar she had poured in it. Perhaps it was the fact that the horns honking, sirens blaring, and neighbors shouting through the pane of her one-bedroom apartment window had become soothing for her, lulling her to sleep in an ironic security blanket. But anyone who knew Kara, or at least knew Kara as she was in New York City, knew that today was an important day.

She had awakened nowhere near refreshed, the anticipation too much to allow rest through the night. The meeting had been marked on her calendar for a week, after her return from photographing elephants in Namibia for an ivory trade piece. There was no hint to the meeting's topic, but she knew what it was about. She could feel it in her gut. Her photographs helped win *International Ecologic* the reputed Carroll Award for Excellence in Environmental Reporting. It was time for her to call the shots—literally. The stories she wanted to cover. The art she wanted to capture and create.

Her phone buzzed in her purse pocket, the one kept closest to her chest for such an occasion.

"Hey, babe." Marcus Goodwin's soothing deep voice greeted her. "I just wanted to talk to you before you arrived and say happy anniversary."

"Happy anniversary to you. To us," she said. Two years. They had met at the magazine—she the junior-level photographer, he the new assistant executive editor. They had kept their dating low-key. Society said it was tricky dating a colleague, but they were the exception.

"I didn't want to make a scene at work."

"I know." She stopped at a crosswalk, the crowd growing in all directions. "You hate PDA, especially at work."

It was effortless with Marcus. Work together yet separately, dinner together, weekend together. Repeat. Sure, it was routine, but it was reliable. Two years of reliability.

They had technically celebrated their anniversary last night. Marcus had insisted on taking her to Maître D', the newest eatery in the Village, but he couldn't get a reservation for Friday night, so they settled for Thursday.

"You're radiant," he had said, lifting his glass of champagne. The candlelight and instrumental music added to the surreal movie feel of it all. "No matter what tomorrow brings, know I love you and believe in you."

He had done it. Two years in the making, and he had gotten on one knee and opened the box, adding, "Enough to want you as my wife."

Just thinking about last night, rolling the diamond around her finger, nearly brought back tears of joy. She couldn't have planned it better. College, internship, job, dating, marriage. And now—crossing fingers—promotion. It was all working out.

"I'll see you in a few, fiancée?"

The word tickled her ears. "Yes, Mr. Goodwin. Crossing over to the building now." She slid the phone into her purse.

"Good morning, Miss Kara," said Barkley, the doorman to the First American Bank building in Midtown. His beyond six-foot stature dwarfed her five-and-a-half-foot frame. He glanced at his watch and smirked. "Is it possible you're here early this morning?"

"You'd better believe it. Today is my day."

"Well, you go and grab it then, Miss Kara."

His morning pep always put a smile on her face. She headed to the elevator, a gaggle of men in suits already waiting for the doors to open.

She rode the elevator up to the eleventh floor. The elevator opened as Suzie walked by the front doors of *International Ecologic*, the green leaf logo etched on the glass.

"Morning, Kara." Suzie, one of the office assistants and, quite frankly, one of her best friends in town outside of Marcus, held the office door open, eyeing the elevator.

"Morning."

"That was quite the crowd in the elevator with you."

Kara shook her head. "They say New York has a shortage of men, but I have yet to see it in the corporate world."

"Amen to that. Maybe I should move to corporate." Suzie chuckled, a high-pitched genuine laugh. "Care to join me?"

"No, thank you. You know I'm taken." Kara briefly flashed the ring on her hand. They had agreed not to make it a big deal in the office today. But what was the harm in telling Suzie?

"Are you kidding me?" She hugged Kara. "Here I thought I'd try to introduce a little fun in your life, and you've gone and nailed that coffin."

Kara gave her *the* look—the one she gave whenever Suzie took a backhanded stab at Marcus. *That* was the harm in telling Suzie. Ever since his arrival, she had put up her guard and wanted Kara to do the same. To Suzie, Marcus was either a liar or, in fact, as boring as he seemed.

Kara embraced his sense of order. What was wrong with structure, with knowing what to expect? Heck, her first love, Danny Bennett, had given her a taste of unpredictability and unreliability and all the other negative "uns." He had toyed with her heart, and she learned her lesson. No more Danny Bennetts.

Marcus walked into her office as Kara organized the top layer of her desk. He always made sure his shirts were crisp and ties perfectly knotted. Kara especially liked his choice for her special day—a perfectly fitted charcoal suit with a splash of blush on his tie. It brought a flash of color to his fair complexion. And made her feel underdressed in her navy pants and white high-collared shirt. "Why would I need to cross over to corporate to find a man when I have the perfect one right here?"

Kara rested her head on his shoulder and kept her eyes locked on Suzie.

"Ugh. You guys are depressing."

"Kara, come on now." Marcus slipped away, straightening his jacket.

"It's just Suzie. Lighten up. We're all friends." She rolled her eyes. "See you in the meeting, Suzie?" Surely, Suzie would be there at least to record the meeting's minutes.

"I wouldn't miss it. Considering it's my job and all." She walked off down the hall.

Kara patted Marcus's arm, thin yet solid under his firm-fitting suit jacket. "Come on. We have to get going."

He scratched his neck beneath the shirt collar. "Well, just remember. Whatever happens in there, I'm here for you."

Kara raised her right eyebrow. The rogue eyebrow had a mind of its own when she was confused. No *Good luck*? No *I'm proud of you*? What did *I'm here for you* mean?

"You coming, Kara?" Jamie, the newest addition to the administrative team, stopped in her doorway.

"Yep. Be right there," Kara said.

"See you later then?" Marcus said.

"Later? Are you not coming?"

"Afraid not." He adjusted his perfect tie.

"But I thought—"

"Hey." He placed his hands over hers. "You'll be fine. You're a great photographer. Have some confidence in yourself. Okay?"

Kara nodded. "Okay."

"Good," he said. "Now get."

She grabbed a notebook and pen. Marcus held his arm out for Kara to leave the room first. She turned out of the office and walked down the hallway, smoothing down the flyaways back into her sleek ponytail. The only privacy the conference room afforded was one of sound, with a glass wall separating the room from the general office space. The long table was occupied by five coworkers.

Kara checked her watch. Even though she had arrived at the building early, she made it to the meeting room at nine o'clock on the dot.

"You're all here." Editor-in-chief Rick Simon clapped his hands upon entering. "Let's get this going. I don't want to waste your time."

Rick's bluntness was also reliable—and very much appreciated.

"Many of you already know of the success stories *International Ecologic* has had in the past few weeks," he said. "Mainly, the Carroll Award for Excellence, for which we would be remiss to not acknowledge Kara Carter, who is with us here today." He gestured to the distant end of the table at Kara. She nodded in recognition. Suzie clapped and the others joined, reluctantly, based on their lack of enthusiasm behind it.

"That achievement is the good news," he said. Kara's heart sank. What was happening?

"Unfortunately, the bad news is, well, bad."

Her mouth turned dry, and she swallowed hard. Her hands grew sweaty.

"Subscriptions have declined the last six quarters, this last quarter being the worst. It's been my opinion, as well as that of our sister company, that it's time to go completely digital."

Kara sighed, releasing the tension built up in her body. Going digital wasn't bad news at all. In fact, she had been awaiting the transition for over a year. It was long overdue to keep up with the times, let alone the competition. She didn't need to see the numbers to know the sales of physical copies weren't worth the print costs.

"It may take some time, but we believe the magazine will endure the transition and eventually rebuild its fan base. We have already procured a new generation of readers in the online environment with the little we've done with it so far. All around, we will become more efficient and cost-effective."

"Sounds good to me," Meredith, a junior writer, said.

"Yeah..." Rick stared at the table. "It is good. Unfortunately, in our efforts to streamline, we will have to make some cuts. That means employees."

"How many are we talking here?" Calvin, an art designer, squirmed in his seat.

Rick held up his hand. "We've looked it over, many times. Crunched the numbers. We tried to find alternatives. But we're going to have to let six of you go."

"Six!" Meredith shook her head. "When will this happen? Does everyone else know?"

Kara looked at her coworkers. All five of them. Suzie met her gaze, a look of dread on her face. Kara cleared her throat and found the strength to speak. "You've already decided, haven't you? It's the six of us."

Her colleagues looked each other over, back and forth, like tourists crossing Seventh Avenue for the first time.

"I'm terribly sorry," Rick said. "I wish there was a better way. Of course, once we get our footing back, you may be able to reapply for your positions when announced."

"Reapply?" Calvin said. "I've worked here for six years."

And Kara the last four. But not as long as at least two other photographers.

Marcus stood outside the room, leaning on Vince's desk and chatting. Kara locked eyes with him briefly before he turned away.

"I'm sorry we couldn't do more," Rick said. "We've organized a severance package for each of you. I know it's not much, but I'd be happy to serve as a reference for your next endeavor."

His assistant, Giles handed out sealed manila envelopes. Poor Suzie had to sit there with her competition, who was keeping his job.

No one bothered to open their packets. The newly unemployed huffed out of the room, the air sucked out of their lungs and joy sapped from their faces. Kara took a breath, stood tall, and approached Marcus at Vince's desk.

"You knew about this, didn't you?" She slapped his arm with the envelope. It was painful to believe it, but it was obviously true. "You knew and you didn't tell me."

"Kara—"

"How could you not tell me?"

He couldn't manage to look her in the eyes, opting for the floor.

She sighed and put her fist on her waist. "Everything I've built here. It's over." She turned away and stormed off to her desk. Or her former desk.

"Kara! Come on." Marcus trailed behind her. "What do you want me to say?"

Giles interrupted, delivering an empty box on her desk. It sat there, awaiting the contents of her life, her goals, her dreams in its four cardboard walls.

"Nothing." Kara stacked her papers and camera equipment into the box. "Say nothing, Marcus."

"What are you going to do? Where are you going to go?"

She paused to look him in the eyes. "I don't know."

"You can find something else. I'll help you. We can look together."

She picked up the weighted box, struggling to keep her fingers underneath to support it. "Together? You should've thought about together when you decided not to tell me I was going to lose my job."

"Come on, Kara. It's our two-year anniversary. Let's talk about this tonight and we can celebrate our engagement. You know how you overreact. Don't make a decision in the heat of emotions."

"I don't—I can't even look at you right now. You made a very bad decision by not telling me. But as much as I hate to say it, you're right. I don't want to make a bad decision in reaction to it." This certainly was a curveball. Her gut told her to leave him in the dust, but her head forced her to weigh two years of history. Not to mention they were planning to marry sometime in the near future.

"I think I'm going to need time to process this and plan what's next. Time to think. Which is what I have an absurd abundance of now."

She brushed past Marcus and refused to look back. "Please open," she mumbled, pushing the elevator button. "Please, please, please." If Marcus was coming after her, she didn't want to argue. Not now, after her livelihood had been pulled out from under her.

The elevator doors separated, welcoming her into their cold, steel arms. As the elevator descended, her emotions rose. She fought back the tears. It wasn't worth it. "Just a job," she whispered.

She arrived on the ground floor and rushed out.

"Got the good news already?" Barkley said from behind the reception desk.

She walked by, unable to say a word. She exited the First American Bank building onto Seventh Avenue, the brake screeches and vehicle rumblings hitting her at the same time as the smell of dirt and meat vendors and sweat. Half an hour ago, she was an award-winning photographer with a promising career and a fiancé, and everything had flipped upside down. She made the journey to her apartment building but didn't quite make it up the stairs before she let the tears roll freely.

Don't stop now. Keep reading with your copy of WAVERLY LAKE.

Don't miss more from Mary Shotwell with the *Waverly Lake* series, starting with WAVERLY LAKE, available now.

And visit her website for more about her books and the latest in publication news: www.maryshotwell.com

---

Kara Carter has her future set—the right photography job, the perfect reliable boyfriend, and her own apartment in New York, until one morning changes it all. She has no choice but to move back home to Waverly Lake, North Carolina, a town she had sworn off for ten years.

It's one thing to return as a failure, it's another to find her neighbor is the one and only Danny Bennett, the boy who broke her heart senior year of high school.

As Kara helps with the family's furniture business—and steers clear of Danny—she is pressured into teaming up with her dad for the Annual Waverly Lake Regatta. But when her dad's accident results in forfeiting his sailing team slot, no one in Waverly Lake can forgive her past—except Danny.

Danny Bennett, now a single father of seven-year-old daughter Hannah, can't help but be drawn to Kara. When he offers to help Kara race in the regatta, little does he know how the woman who stole his heart long ago will change the way he sees family, love, and parenting a child with autism.

Can these high school sweethearts sail through the pain of the past?

All reviews are **welcome** and **appreciated**. Please consider leaving one on your favorite social media and book buying sites.

Escape Your World. Get Lost in Ours! City Owl Press at www.cityowlpress.com.

Acknowledgments

Writing *The Romance Loop* was nothing short of a blast. I had a wild time poking fun of the tropes we find so endearing in romance, while paying homage to the genres I grew up reading. I had hoped others found it as fun as I did, and luckily my editor, Tee Tate, once again understood the heart of my manuscript. Thank you, Tee, along with Jenny, Tina, and Yelena from City Owl Press.

Many thanks to my agent Dani Sanchez at SBR Media, who took a chance on me and fought for this story to get in the right hands. To the number of agents who read earlier versions, thank you so much for taking the time to provide feedback in a time where such is seldom given.

I am so thankful for Jihun Park for the cover art! Many ideas were thrown around and explored, and he really executed what was in my brain wonderfully.

As always, gratitude to my family. I couldn't write as much as I do were it not for my supportive husband, Matt. Thank you, Luke, for being a goofball, Evan for being a goober, and Avery for making me feel like a rockstar.

Finally, I want to thank authors who opened doors to other worlds for me at a time when I needed to escape, whether that be to shires, past or future centuries, space, or the bottom of the ocean. We still need these stories, desperately, just as we need the hope of a happily ever after we reliably find in romance.

About the Author

Mary Shotwell is the author of small-town love stories with happily-ever-afters for all seasons. Her debut romance novel *Christmas Catch* (Carina Press, 2018) was a Golden Leaf Finalist and earned a starred review from *Library Journal*. She loves incorporating her science and nature background into her fiction. When adulting, she's a wife to husband Matt and mother to three children. She currently resides in Tennessee.

Visit her website for more about her books and the latest in publication news.

www.maryshotwell.com

instagram.com/authormaryshotwell
facebook.com/AuthorMaryShotwell
tiktok.com/@authormaryshotwell

About the Publisher

City Owl Press is a cutting edge indie publishing company, bringing the world of romance and speculative fiction to discerning readers.

Escape Your World. Get Lost in Ours!

www.cityowlpress.com

facebook.com/CityOwlPress
x.com/cityowlpress
instagram.com/cityowlbooks
pinterest.com/cityowlpress
tiktok.com/@cityowlpress

www.ingramcontent.com/pod-product-compliance
Lightning Source LLC
LaVergne TN
LVHW010610100826
845148LV00014B/2908

* 9 7 8 1 6 4 8 9 8 5 6 2 1 *